PLAGUED

A NOVEL

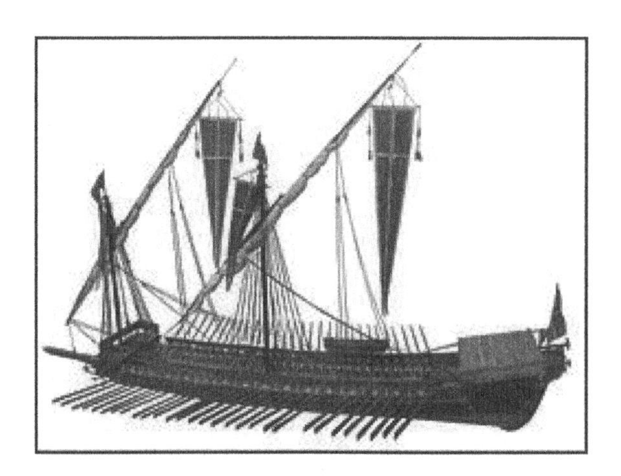

PLAGUED

A NOVEL

Book I of The Michael of Rhodes Series

by

Mary Donnarumma Sharnick

www.fireshippress.com

PLAGUED by Mary Donnarumma Sharnick

ISBN-13: 978-1-61179-319-2 (Paperback)
ISBN -978-1-61179-320-8 (e-book)

BISAC Subject Headings:

FIC014000FICTION / Historical
FIC002000FICTION / Action & Adventure
FIC019000FICTION / Literary

Cover work by Christine Horner

Address all correspondence to:
Fireship Press, LLC
P. O. Box 68412
Tucson, AZ 85737
Or visit our website at:
www.fireshippress.com

Dear Doris –
What a pleasure to meet you!
As ever, Mary

Dedication

FOR MY FATHER
Carmen F. Donnarumma
who gave me history

July 26, 1922-March 18, 2013

Acknowledgements

This novel, the first of an anticipated Michael of Rhodes Series, would not have been conceived without The Book of Michael of Rhodes: A Fifteenth-Century Maritime Manuscript in three volumes, edited by Pamela O. Long, David McGee, and Alan M. Stahl (The MIT Press: Cambridge, Massachusetts, 2009). I am particularly indebted to Alan M. Stahl, PhD, of Princeton University, who so graciously afforded me his generous, ongoing assistance. While I have incorporated a number of documented names, terms, dates, and locales from the manuscript, the plot of PLAGUED is my own invention and the characters imaginary rather than historical.

The Boundaries of Eros: Sex Crimes and Sexuality in Renaissance Venice, authored by Guido Ruggiero, PhD (Oxford University Press:New York, 1985), enhanced my understanding of the machinations involved in the historical Clario Contarini's crimes.

Michael Rocke's Forbidden Friendships: Homosexuality and Male Culture in Renaissance Florence (Oxford University Press:New York, 1998) delineated differences between Florentine and Venetian points of view regarding man-boy sexual relations during the time period in which this novel takes place.

The detailed galley models and the always generous assistance from the staff members at Venice's Museo Storico Navale, a short walk from the Arsenale, increased my knowledge of and appreciation for Venice's global maritime presence which was, for a period of time during the early fifteenth-century, called the Stato da Mar, and was without peer.

My continued gratitude to the gracious and talented captain and crew at Fireship Press—Michael James, Midori Snyder, Sophia Lotter, Christine Horner, Chris Paige, and all who assist you. Together you are a writer's dream team.

To those who continue to support my research, I am entirely grateful: The Beatrice Fox Auerbach Foundation, Wesleyan University Writers' Conference, Chase Collegiate School.

To the writing students who accompanied me and my husband to Venice in June, 2013, the heartfelt thanks and continuing love of a surrogate zia. Your enthusiasm for travel and our shared company, your willingness to encounter the new and undiscovered, your fresh eyes amid storied sites and buildings, and your delightful "putti-ness," made the early summer days of 2013 among the most delightful ever spent at home or abroad.

You are: Conor Bronsdon, Lauren Crowe, Alexia Dvarskas, Hayden Hall, Alex Kenworthy, Justin Kenworthy, Daniel O'Neill, Jeffery Zoldy.

To the hospitable folks at Auburn University, for allowing me to share my imagined Venice with you, my thanks. Chantel Acevedo, for your family's warm welcome, and Jay Lamar, for the memorable Southern hospitality at your family's farm.

To all the constituencies at Chase Collegiate School, thank you for your enthusiastic and patient support. Administrators Joseph Hadam and Kyle Kahuda, I appreciate your unequivocal "yes" to every opportunity. Colleagues each and every one, for your daily care and generous friendship. Helen Drake, for loving Venice, too. Carol DiFolco Riebe, without whom no fax would ever arrive at its intended destination. To the parents and families, for your trust. And always, to my students.

To Safwat Salama, for our years of friendship and delicious meals. To the peerless staff at Pensione Accademia. You each and all comprise my family in Venice.

Rachel Basch, Carol Snyder, Jeanne Archambault, Francine Knight, Daniel and Joyce D'Alessio, Phil and Barbara Benevento, Pamela and Michael Hull, Suzanne Noel and Jim Wigren, Patricia and John Philip, Sharon and Dan Wilson, Leslie Hadam, Barbara Ruggiero and David Whitehouse, Terry and Chris Dannen, Elaine Muldowney, Ruth and Frank Steponaitis, Linda and Dan Sloan, the Shove family, the Bradley Family, the Paolino family, the

Chiusano and Cutrofello families, Liza and John Fixx, Bruce and Becky Baker, Martha Kellogg, Diana Smith, Andy Fee, Julia Pistell, Anita Bologna, Kristen Baclawski, Mark Albini, Zach Grappone, fellow Fireship authors.

To Veronica and Robert Sharnick, my continued thanks for your unwavering support.

Maureen and Fran, Teresa and Ed, Ellen and Mike, Alessandra, Egon, Caroline, Colin, Emily, Ethan, George, Erin, and cousins on both sides of the Atlantic, for always believing the next book is being written.

My mother, Louise Giordano Donnarumma, our love and admiration for showing us how to go on after Dad.

Wayne Sharnick, as long as we both shall live.

Note to Readers

Michael of Rhodes was a flesh-and-blood historical figure who has left scholars and students of history a stunning maritime record of his tenure with the Venetian fleet. He drafted his manuscript between 1434 and 1436. He died in 1445.

What immediately interested me upon learning of him was that, between 1401 and 1434, a period of thirty-three years during which Michael was engaged in the service of Venice, no personal record of his experiences exists.

That gap of time called for a novel, or a series of them!

And so I began to envision a Michael of Rhodes that his own manuscript does not reveal. I began to imagine the Michael of Rhodes who, at age sixteen, left his home for adventure. I began to feel as if I knew this boy who yearned to replace the small world he inhabited with a larger one he dreamed about and craved.

As a plan for a fictional series developed, I knew Michael would encounter both the Myth of Venice (the idealized party line of the Republic, as it were) and the Reality of Venice (the daily struggles, large and small, of specific, fallible individuals in a singular time and place).

In addition, The Death, or Plague, from 1347 through 1401 pretty well decimated Venice's sea-faring population, among others. And for the only time in its history, Venice recruited foreigners, among them Michael of Rhodes, to help man its fleet.

Around the same time, reaching a zenith with an unusually large number of convictions and subsequent burnings by 1406, a culture of sex abuse involving young boys (puers) and older, though not yet legal youths (adolescens), abounded, both on the galleys and in Venice proper.

How might Michael have experienced the world if the three realities collided? What would his coming-of-age have entailed? And how did he emerge from his trials the intelligent, articulate, highly-regarded seaman, mathematician, leader, man of faith, and diarist that his own words reveal?

If a historian's task is to link documented facts in a logical fashion resulting in a contextualized point of view, the novelist's job is to explore how her protagonist might have felt as a person living in that context.

I hope I have succeeded in the fictional pages that follow.

"In the name of God, I, Michael of Rhodes, shall write below about the time I came to Venice. It was on June 5, 1401.... And first, I signed on in Manfredonia as an oarsman with the nobleman Pietro Loredan..."

From THE BOOK OF MICHAEL OF RHODES

"St. Sebastian, your faith is great, intercede for me, Michael, a miserable sinner, to Lord Jesus Christ, and may I deserve to be freed from plague, epidemic, and illness by your prayers. Pray for me, St. Sebastian, as you deem worthy to carry out the promises of Christ."

From THE BOOK OF MICHAEL OF RHODES

"...a time of calamity comes to all alike. Man no more knows his own time than fish taken in the fatal net, or birds trapped in the snare; like these the children of men are caught when the evil time falls suddenly upon them."

THE BOOK OF ECCLESIASTES

"Our body is not made of iron. Our strength is not that of stone. Live and hope in the Lord, and let your service be according to reason."

SAINT CLARE OF ASSISI

PROLOGUE

8 April 1401—ISLE OF RHODES

"Push," Michael exhaled, bracing his right leg on the rock wall that separated his family's low stone cottage from the lemon grove. Grasping the Venetian galley oar he had bought with a purse of coins from three months' labor picking lemons and hauling fish with his father, he leaned his tall sturdy body forward, pushing back along the pebbled ground a line of four yard-length bags of dirt and gravel.

He moved backward along the wall to repeat the exercise, then hopped over the stones to do the same with four more bags on the other side. Right-handed by nature, he doubled his efforts whenever a left-bodied thrust was needed so that he might strengthen his less-able limbs. The oar weighed one hundred and thirty-two pounds. With each subsequent thrust, it felt even heavier. Over the course of two years and hundreds of practices, the muscles of his left arm and leg had strengthened. Now when he wound his goatskin belt around each tanned limb to measure it, the left arm and leg were just short of equal with the right.

Even his mother had noticed, pinching his biceps with her work-roughened fingers and teasing him, "So you are a strong man now. Good, the better to help your father."

"Push," he panted, his neck and back drenched after the eighth exertion. He felt his broad chest tighten. His body told him to rest. His heart beat drum-like, and his veins bulged, small, blue-green hills on the of backs of his hands. Michael would become one of the great sea power's oarsmen despite his mother Alda's vociferous opposition. He had not worked so diligently to remain at home. He had a plan.

"But you are Greek, and the son of a fisherman. Rhodes of the Colossus, not Venice, is in your blood."

Her voice rose to shrillness as she walked from the chickens to his side. Her quick, irregular pace matched her disconcerted disposition. She clicked her teeth together, biting her words.

Michael retorted, "The Colossus fell centuries ago. The Rhodes of the past is no more. We are just one more port among hundreds of ports, each one a tasty morsel for hungry Venice. Venice is where greatness lives, so Uncle Elios and the dockmaster tell me. And even Papa agrees with them. Even Papa admits that."

He spoke matter-of-factly and reached for his mother's hand. But she pulled away, crossing her arms against her drooping breasts. She glanced beyond her earnest, black-haired, muscular son toward the rocky cove where her husband fished every morning. Where, in fact, he was fishing now, without Michael. Shielding her heavy-lidded eyes from the sun's piercing glare, she sighed an exhalation that did not yet indicate resignation. Then, turning her eyes back, she remonstrated, "You must stay here and help your father. He is getting too old to manage the fishing alone. His back cracks when he lifts the nets. He slips on the rocks. He cannot see beyond the length of his arms."

A pang of guilt cut through Michael's certainty. But he pushed it away. He would not be deterred. If he did not leave now, when opportunity presented itself, he would certainly find himself marooned for life, destined only for years of common toil and nondescript burial in an unmarked grave, his deeds remembered solely by his intimates, if indeed a wife and children were to be his.

His mother continued, "The Venetians want you and the others only because their own men have died from The Death, like your brother"—at this she made the Sign of the Cross on her forehead. "Otherwise, you would be worthless to them. Your father says they are nothing but thieves."

Her voice was bitter and she scowled.

Michael knew she was partly right. Never before had a doge sought foreigners to join his own citizen-sailors on the galleys. But The Death, unrelenting for the last half-century, if the elders' calculations were true, had felled so many native Venetian rowers that a swarm of trained recruiters now sailed the Adriatic and beyond into the Aegean seeking strong young men like Michael to man their massive fleet. He was ready for them. In fact, yesterday afternoon he had met one called Zen, youngest son of the famed Carlo Zeno, naval hero of Venice's war against the Genoese. At least Alda had been away when the recruiter, directed by the wharf's custom house controller, came by to watch him practice. Two coves away on her weekly visit to the Widow Kari while the two spoke, Alda did not yet know how imminent her son's departure was.

Looking into his mother's eyes, Michael saw that she pleaded rather than berated. He knew she meant, "Don't go. I have no other sons."

He loved her, he conceded to himself, but he could not bear the thought of living and dying with nothing in between but the boring drudgery she and his father accepted as their lot. As all their neighbors did as well, it seemed to him. And though Michael's brother would never return, Petros's death at least was a storied one. Michael wanted a story too, even if he himself died before its telling. If he did not go now, when he was young and strong, he would never leave. And when he was aged and withered, full of regret, he would be angry at himself for not having tried. Of that he was certain. Every night since Petros had set out, Michael had dreamed of his own departure, too.

Petros, Michael's only brother, a sailor nine years his senior, was already one year destroyed by The Death. His body had been found, along with the bodies of the rest of the crew, on Rhodes's largest merchant ship, which had gone missing, despite no reports of storms or pirates. Another ship, passing through the same waters near Salonika, had been drawn to The Helios by the tornado of gulls circling above it. When the captain, a black-toothed curmudgeon named Chron, sent a party to investigate, only four of the five sailors returned. The fifth, Ari, leapt to a watery death only moments after observing the carnage.

"All dead, and Ari right after he saw!" the youngest, Tarsis, had cried. "Even the rats were dead, and the gulls flew about with remnants of the human corpses—fingers, entrails, tongues—in their beaks. Burst bodies everywhere, black blood oozed and dried, eyes not quite rotted, still wide open."

Known to all as Ari the Swimmer, so swiftly did he move through the waves, the suicide had already lost his wife and two daughters to The Death before he set sail. He was "a decent sort," according to Uncle Elios, who had baptized Ari's children.

The retired captain never failed to repeat to Michael how the grieving fellow had thrown himself into the sea, "but not for a swim." Chron routinely chuckled at the irony. Ari had not, at least according to Tarsis, the old man related time after time, uttered a last word as he leapt. Chron always smirked at this juncture to imply suicide a cowardly act. Then, he always made certain to announce, "I ordered my men to shoot flaming arrows at the ship of doom. What else was there to do?" And the marksmen's fiery missiles turned The Helios into a burning sacrifice. Alda did not intend to endure again such loss with her second and last son.

Chron had been recently relegated to the Rhodes counting house due to his advanced age and a rheumatism that prevented him from lifting much more than a rucksack. The old seaman retold the story to Michael every Friday afternoon when the two met to survey the ships that had docked at the largest piers. The facts repeated themselves like a haunting ghost tale in Michael's head. It seemed as if the failing captain had lost all his other sea chronicles to this one, so completely had it taken hold of his memory and speech.

"It is his last chapter," Michael's Uncle Elios, the village priest and Alda's older brother, had said. "Chron's days at sea are over. Now he merely counts and recounts—not only the harbor's profits, but, more to the point, the dwindling turns of the tide left in his own life."

Michael had forced himself not to picture his brother in death after Chron's fourth or fifth telling. Rather, he closed his eyes and instead recalled Petros's laughing face and burly hug when he lunged at Michael in false rage. "Michalli", he had called him in the old Greek way. "Michalli, I am going to capture you!"

His brother's voice had been hearty, rich, and full as a thick lamb stew on a damp winter's day. Michael longed for that voice daily, weary of his father's extended, dark silences and his mother's raw, strident scoldings. His parents had changed after their first-born's death. Rarely did a smile light Alda's face. Theodore's brow bore creases from his frowning.

With Petros gone and her daughter Mina five years married and a half day's walk away from the port, Alda would be childless once Michael sailed. Mina did not visit often, as she needed to tend to her own four children—her only daughter had been born blind—and a husband prone to too much wine. As for Michael's father, Theodore—Theodore the Humble, his neighbors and fellow fishermen called him—he had gone mute and brooding since his first son's death. Occasionally, when Alda fried squid and flavored it with lemon juice, or baked bread sprinkled with garlic-laced olive oil and rosemary, he grabbed her by the shoulders and kissed her mouth hard. But since his Petros's demise, Michael had never once heard his father speak his mother's name or seen him lie down with her on the straw-covered bedstead and shoo him laughingly outside. Instead he slept in the stone shed, a battered row boat for his berth, his dead son's fishing cap his only bedmate. His laughs had turned to mutterings and increasingly frequent growls.

Michael stopped a moment to wipe his broad, calloused hand across his dripping brow. Despite his love for her, his mother was only a woman nonetheless, so how could she possibly understand? Didn't she see that destruction happened everywhere, that she could lose him close to home just as easily as she could were he at sea? No doubt, she would die at their cottage. The humble, one-room dwelling was, after all, where she was meant to be, the enclosed yard the extent of her female dominion. But his father might have ventured farther. He could have striven in a larger world, gone off to explore for himself. No, Michael would not be content with his father's life ("such as it is," he spoke to himself), just beyond the garden and the shed. It was too small, a speck in the great cosmos, a tiny boat in just one sea. A life in which manhood diminished, perhaps disappeared entirely from the sheer monotony of the daily dropping and lifting of scanty nets.

Pulling from that sea just enough to eat, and sometimes not even. After a successful morning's haul, perhaps humble Theodore and his fellows, Hercules and Kristos, could afford to buy a jug of wine at the dock hostel where sailors from the large ships gathered. There, sitting silent in the dark, smoke-filled canteen with no stories of their own to tell, they listened to the assortment of men from the galleys proclaim their real, even if magnified, adventures. "Braggarts," Theodore called them. "Without homes. Creatures from a malignant world." Their world, malignant or not, was what Michael wanted—the world of many seas, exotic journeys, rousing skirmishes, and a few momentous battles from which to learn what kind of man he could be. Perhaps even a hero. He had to get to the Venetian fleet, if just to try. The feared and consequently respected fleet of the Republic every man called la Dominante, the Dominant One. A fleet that smacked of legend, like the ancient myths his uncle had taught him from the moment he would listen.

Having stacked the filled sacks into four two-bag piles, Michael returned to the rock wall to retrieve the oar. He carried it to the shed, hoisted it with both arms evenly spaced, and, bending down from the knees so as not to strain his back, lowered it and laid it flat across them. He ran his fingers along the oar's twenty-six-feet of tawny smoothness, then closed his eyes to remember yet again his first sighting of a Venetian war galley, its rowers three to a bench, pushing and pulling in unison, calling out the thrust and return in what to him sounded like a melody. That had been eleven years ago.

He had just turned five, old enough to keep up with his father's pace to the short dock in the cove his mother could see from the doorway, old enough to accompany Theodore to the pre-dawn dropping of the nets. Sitting in the rowboat within sight of the big harbor and chewing on a crusty piece of the previous night's bread that his mother had handed him before crossing her arms against her chest to say good-bye, he watched the ripples in the water against the coming dawn. Then, just as the sun rose, he heard what had sounded like a chorus singing. He turned to look. That was when he knew.

It was not so much the looming brown galley itself, but more the synchrony of the rowers that mesmerized him. Their cohesive movements, matched with their booming voices that became one voice, urged him to abandon home, even though he could not yet reach the door latch to let himself out or in. Even then, he yearned to join this crew of men. With them he would be able to become a part of something bigger than himself, than his parents, than the island of Rhodes. The seas and the lands that sprang up from them belonged to the rowers, he believed. They would become his, as well, he decided then and there. He had dropped the bread crust, forgetting sustenance for a moment, hungering instead for adventure.

"Michael!" He was called to the present by his mother's voice, which rang from inside the cottage. "I made you mussel stew tonight."

He wiped his brow, hungry. He must tell her, must tell his father when the three of them sat together at the table ("Bless Our Lord for this day's food") that in one month's time he would board a grain boat to Manfredonia, where, Zen had assured him, signed contract in hand, he could finally join the Venetian fleet.

PART ONE

GALLEY

"He listens well who takes notes."
Dante Alighieri

Chapter 1

3 May 1401—LEAVE-TAKING

"Tomorrow!" Alda exclaimed.

She had just turned from the fire and laid the steaming cauldron of fish soup on the rough-hewn table. Theodore and Father Elios sat next to each other on one bench. Michael, adjacent to them on a stool, posed upright and stiff, watching and waiting as Alda, still standing, placed her worn hands on her crooked hips. She glowered, red-faced and fuming. Her gray-flecked strands of hair frizzed from beneath her head scarf.

"Well?" She addressed her husband.

Theodore, the sleeves of his tunic crusted with the sea's salt, did not meet his wife's gaze, but instead looked from the soup to his son and back to the soup again.

"I am not hungry," he said. Pushing his brother-in-law off the bench so he could stand, he looked at Michael, muttered, "Good riddance, then," and walked out of the cottage. They heard the shed door slam. Then it was quiet. Only Michael's breathing quickened at his father's rebuff.

"You are a fine son," Alda muttered, staring Michael down as she dished the supper out to her brother. Elios was already ripping the bread and placed one piece by the bowl for each of the three left at the table.

Michael remained still. He had delayed his news to his parents for as long as he could. Then he had invited his uncle, thinking the priest's presence would be a calming one.

"Let us pray," Elios said, as if nothing out of the ordinary had occurred, and he reached out his hand for his nephew's and his sister's.

Alda sat down, albeit noisily. Her stool banged against the table and she adjusted and readjusted herself upon it as the three joined hands and her brother intoned his thanks for the food. After the communal "Amen," no one spoke. Elios slurped with abandon as he ate. Alda watched the filmy broth as if it told a secret. Michael, wooden spoon in his right hand, held it in abeyance. Then, when his uncle finally used his chunk of bread to wipe his own bowl clean, Michael laid the spoon down, leaving his own meal untouched.

While Alda collected the bowls and spoons, dumping her and Michael's uneaten portions back into the iron cauldron so the liquid splashed onto the dirt floor, Michael and Elios went outside to escape her agitated clattering and to wait.

"So, now we practice patience for your mother," the priest said. "She will not want you to leave with her disapproval. You will see."

Michael picked a sprig of rosemary from the herb garden to the right of the cottage door. He held it to his nostrils and inhaled. At sea, he knew, he would be miles and months away from the plentitude of garden and grove. He would thirst for fresh water, cower from the scorch of the sun, release his sure-to-be unruly bowels into the unsteady bucket beneath his bancho—one of the seat's triad of rowers married, as it were, to one another's frailties and to the resolute will of the Venetian Republic. Retching in distress, whether from tumultuous waves or beans gone rancid, he would wonder, Zen had warned him yesterday, why he had ever left his home.

"I won't," he'd countered, and Zen had laughed, his well-formed body—though not a rower's—able to wield Michael's equipment with force and precision, as he demonstrated, first removing his recruiter's maroon tunic, then lifting the oar with both hands and holding it mid-air until the count of two hundred. He is a show-off, Michael had told himself.

"We all do," Zen had said. "I did, my very first voyage as carpenter's apprentice on my father's galley." And he pointed to his chest to show Michael the jagged scar where the ship's surgeon had carved out of him a fist-sized tumor ("It grew after a rower, crazed with pellagra, swung at me with a hammer."). Michael stared at the scar, which crossed Zen's chest in a diagonal stripe. "The doctor sewed my chest up with fishing line, poured the first mate's liquor over the wound, then sent me back to my father's cabin. No one, especially not my captain father"—Zen's face contorted in a grimace, as if his mouth could not stand the taste of his progenitor's name—"looked to my cries," Zen said. "They were part of a day's sail. Nothing less. Nothing more." He had scratched his nose then. "Be sure you understand, Michael, no one will notice your cries either. No matter the reason."

He rubbed his broad hands over the scar, stopping them where his heart beat beneath. It was as if his mind had separated from his body, given his suddenly vacant expression. Then, as if jolted back into Michael's presence, he dropped his hands from his chest. His warning spoken, he smiled again and continued, "But now I have no such trouble. I do the swinging if need be." He punched the air, his fists hard circles of bone encased in practiced flesh. "Besides, if my recruits do well and show promise, hefty bonuses await me in San Marco. Ducats and, finalmente"—he let the syllables of the word hover in the air so that they mimicked the waiting itself—"my own galley to command."

He grinned at Michael as he spoke of his potentially aggrandized future.

"So make me a rich, honorable man, Michael," he laughed, coming close and pretending fisticuffs. Then, clipping Michael's face in a brisk farewell, he shouted as he went. "If you think you are strong enough, meet me by the pier at dawn two days from now. I will have your place assured and you will see if your efforts here have made you ready."

"Michael," Alda called now from the cottage, so that her son was startled from his pleasing reverie.

She opened the door and Michael watched her take a seat on the first bench he had known, the lopsided stone one he had sat on so often as a child, waiting for her to pick the tomatoes or flick black beetles out of the zucchini flowers. He did not sit with her, but instead walked ten paces to the wall and the lemon grove. Pressing his palms onto the wall, he flung his legs over it so that he landed among the lemons. Stooping down, then, he picked up one of the fruit, bit into it, and squeezed the juice into his mouth, holding his head back to savor the acid tartness.

When he was done, he threw the gnawed lemon rind farther back into the grove. Alda stood up and looked at him.

"How can you stand the taste without honey?" she asked, a homely enough way to break the silence between them.

Michael shrugged. Then, taking his time, he made his way back over the wall and into the yard. With Uncle Elios in the lead, the three paced along the low stone wall. Initially, they walked single file, Elios first, Alda in the middle, and Michael behind them both. But as the sun disappeared in a blaze of red, their perambulations slowed, and Michael sidled against his mother. He reached for her right arm with his left. She let him take hold. Then both stopped and stood statue-like as dusk dissolved into a gathering blackness. And though it appeared that Alda struggled fervently against her body's own desire, she grabbed Michael close and did not let go of him until full darkness enveloped them. Michael's heart beat two times to hers at first. Then, as they both relaxed, one against the other, the poundings in their chests shifted to one steady rhythm. Michael cradled his mother in his arms as she had once nestled him in hers.

Elios left them then, going inside the cottage to light the torch that would guide him back to his chapel and humble rectory.

"We must trust in the Lord," he said to his sister as he came back outside, and drew the Sign of the Cross on his nephew's forehead, kissing Michael on both cheeks, as well.

"You have no children!" she chided him, pointing a forefinger close to his face. "No wife and no children!" Then she calmed herself once more, even laughed, though ruefully. "At least I can trust you will tell me to trust in the Lord." She patted her brother's cheek in the torchlight. "Be careful I don't lose you, too," she said. Elios started down the rocky path to the road leading to the village.

"God go with you, Michael," his uncle called. "I pray I may see you in Paradise."

Michael realized he would miss Elios. His uncle had taught him his letters in the Latin of the Roman Church ("Remember, Michael, my father and mother traveled here from the Sorrentine Peninsula. That is why your mother, you, and I are obeisant to the Pope."), the stories of the Christian martyrs, and—despite his priestly vows and precepts and his faith in the crucified Jesus—even the legends of the pagan gods and goddesses who ruled before the Son of God had made Himself flesh. When Elios spoke the three words, "Son of God," his voice took on a sonorous majesty not unlike his nephew's sacred utterance, "the Venetian fleet."

"Thank you, Uncle," Michael answered, his voice quivering like a gathering mist. He bowed his head at his uncle's blessing. Even if he himself could not understand Elios's unalloyed and unquestioning faith in a God who, as far as Michael could tell, was as ruthless as He was said to be benevolent, he worried that without his uncle's placid assurances he might be less able to navigate the waves of waters more powerful than the inconsequential lappings of his natal cove.

Mother and son watched the priest go, then walked back to the cottage. Alda started to speak, "When...," but decided instead on silence.

"Dawn," Michael told her nonetheless.

Once inside the cottage, without preamble of any kind, Alda, fully-clothed, lay down on the straw pallet she used to share with her husband, while Michael, having already filled a sack with a few changes of clothing, his fish-gutting knife, and the thumb-sized wooden Easter lamb that Theodore had carved, one for each of his sons, made ready to go.

"Mama," he said.

His mother did not stir. Hands across her flattened breasts, black eyes shut, thin lips still, uneven legs motionless. Only her chest moved, one long breath at a time. Her son stared, committing her flesh to memory.

And though she kept her eyes squeezed closed, thinking, "He will not stay with us, Theodore," Alda let her son cup her wrinkled chin in his large, calloused hands. He slipped out of the cottage to arrange a bed for himself behind the rock shed where his father lay. Perhaps Theodore would come out and give him his blessing. Michael did not sleep, but, alert and wanting, waited.

Just before sunrise, at the piercing cries of the first birds, Michael rose and, resigning himself to a solitary departure, moved as quietly he could, barefoot until he reached the edge of the family's clearing. And though he had promised himself he would not look back after he pulled on his ankle boots, he did. His heart quickened. His father had at last emerged from the stone shed. Seeing Michael turn, he dropped to his knees on the grass and, unclenching his fist, slowly raised his right arm in a blessed farewell. Attempting a smile through her tears, Alda, too, waved with two broad sweeps of the air. Then she stood over her husband, enclosing his stooped and quivering body in her brave, unambiguous arms.

Chapter 2

4 June 1401—MANFREDONIA

"Tomorrow we sail," Zen announced, "so tonight we revel!"

A fulsome cheer greeted his proclamation, and Zen removed his well-worn shirt, raising it above him like a conquering flag of state. Michael saw once more the long scar that decorated the recruiter's chest as, cat-like, Zen leapt up onto a long wooden table so all could see and hear him.

In a relaxed pose and jovial mood, contrary to his otherwise purposeful and efficient demeanor as a recruiter for the Republic, Zen played the part of host of the largest dock-side hostel where the bulk of tomorrow's rowers—they totaled one hundred and eighty in all—had gathered. Some were new to the task, others veteran oarsmen from lesser city-states and regions than Venice; the fair-haired and the ebony-skinned; some reticent fellows and others voluble clowns; they were a motley assortment about to be transformed into a cohesive and formidable engine of Empire. But not tonight. Not until they boarded the galley at the height of the tide tomorrow. The hostel, in fact all the port's hostels combined, could not accommodate the swarms of men, so dozens of waiting rowers lined the rooftops of the insufficient way stations along the pier. Alive with men whose spirits thrilled with anticipation, and perhaps apprehension at the incipient voyage's challenges and dangers, the rooftops drew the attention of the gulls, who swooped in, diving among the rowers to snatch the detritus of food the men consumed, it appeared, continuously.

"Michael," Zen motioned with his flag-shirt, directing the young man to him.

Michael had been standing atop the stone wall eating a piece of grilled cod between garlicky slices of crusted bread, saying nothing, but instead observing the others who would be his ship mates. A few spoke in languages he did not understand. One, an older, wizened fellow, talked to himself, waving away the flies that circled his full head of white hair. Still another juggled three oranges until a third man—his friend, Michael discovered—snatched one of the oranges while it was in mid-air, then sat cross-legged on the rooftop, cutting the peel so that it became one long festive ribbon. No sooner had the man dropped the peel onto the roof than a gull, swooping, took it up and away.

"Coming!" Michael replied, swallowing the last of his supper and licking the garlic flavor from his lips.

He hopped off the wall to make his way around the various clusters of energetic men who conversed and laughed together. Making sure to take his rough sack with him, he removed his fisherman's protective woolen cap from his head and stuffed it among the clothes. Then, knotting the two ends of rope that would secure the contents inside, he slipped his left arm through the sturdy circle and held the sack close to his side.

"Right away," he called out again, eager that the noble-born Zen should find him compliant.

As he approached the pony-tailed, sinewy recruiter, he paused a moment in genuine surprise. Standing next to Zen was a man who appeared to be a human boulder. He was a square of flesh and bone. A gold pectoral cross, large enough to be a bishop's, hung in the middle of his chest, tufts of red trunk hair curling around it. His head was shaved and his eyes bore through Michael, two vivid bolts of blue.

"Bronislav," Zen reached his right arm toward the rock of flesh, "meet Michael."

The boulder smiled broadly, revealing a full set of square-filed teeth that showed nearly white against his deeply bronzed skin.

Though beads of sweat bubbled on the man's squat shoulders, some six inches lower than Michael's broad ones, they did not dissolve and turn to small streams of water, so straight, stolid, and still did the man stand. They quivered instead, liquid pebbles upon the great stone slab.

"I am pleased to meet you," Michael said.

Michael reached out his hand to Bronislav, who grabbed it with both of his, holding tightly, like a vise.

"You and Bronislav will share a bench with Jacopo, an experienced Venetian that even The Death has refused to befriend."

Zen laughed at his own witticism and wrapped his flag-shirt around his neck. Michael wondered if he would meet this Jacopo tonight. In the meantime, he felt his hand going numb and stared down at Bronislav's thick legs. They made his own long limbs, strong and practiced though they were, seem slight and unworthy.

"Jacopo will spy on you to see if you are to be trusted or determined an enemy of the State. And Bronislav will protect you from your own ignorance."

Again, Zen laughed, but now not in jest.

"You see how I take care of you, Michael."

His voice had turned tender, and the recruiter adjusted his leggings, conspicuously moving his privates about as he spoke. Michael felt his face redden, suddenly aware of his own callow crotch.

Then, in a new and threatening tone, Zen continued. "You fail and my Venetian superiors, not to mention my painfully heroic father, will be substantially distressed. And I will feel their distress most keenly." Here, his privates now evidently placed to his liking, Zen turned his attention to his upper body. He crossed his arms in back of himself against his spine and let his neck wrench so that his eyes looked heavenward, mimicking the effects of the torture known as the strappado, for which the Republic's Council of Ten was ubiquitously known to employ.

Zen shrieked sham cries of pain as he feigned the rope ripping his shoulders from their sockets. Michael had heard his uncle tell of men confessing to crimes they had not even imagined.

"The rope is most persuasive, I am told," Elios had said. "It presages Hell's eternal damnation, and perhaps not only for those who suffer the torture, but also for those who administer it."

Twitching and writhing in his bombastic, contrived pantomime of pain, Zen continued, "Do not fail me, Michael, for if you do, you will surely endure the rope with me."

He dislodged his arms from his back and, in an instant, reached up and grabbed Michael by the throat. Bronislav immediately let go of Michael's hand, then lowered himself and butted the backs of Zen's knees with his massive head so that the recruiter crumpled. Michael's sun-burnt neck felt the hot indentations of fingers.

Outwardly stone-like, while inwardly roiling, Michael stared down at the fallen Zen, confused by the recruiter's double dealing. Rising slowly, Zen next let out an oddly convivial hoot, first pointing at Michael's gaping mouth, then congratulating Bronislav, putting his hands together repeatedly in sustained applause.

"Nicely done. Nicely done," he bowed to the Slav.

"Thank you," Bronislav said, returning the bow. Then, looking up at a bewildered Michael, he instructed him, "We"—here he shook a pudgy forefinger at Zen's ruddy face—"are not enemies, not enemies," and let his sausage arms drop either side of him. Then, his voice firm as a remonstrative parent's, he reminded Zen, "The boy must be fit to row. We will hurt him only if he proves an evil shipmate or a traitor to Venice." He smiled broadly at Zen, but at the same time shook his right forefinger at the recruiter's face. "You must leave him alone. Remember why you find yourself here. You must leave him alone, I say. You must leave him to me. Finis," he concluded, resuming his earlier pose.

Unclear what Bronislav meant when he admonished his better and why Zen did not rebuff the bulky oarsman, Michael nevertheless hoped that the Slav's protection would bear itself out. Bowing to Bronislav in thanks, Michael steeled himself as Zen came close once more.

Then, as if a priest performing a marriage, Zen—his manner now solemn and sacramental—placed one hand on each of the men's shoulders. His left arm reached up to rest upon Michael, while his right lowered to land on Bronislav. He stood cockeyed, spreading his leather-booted legs apart for balance. And Michael—tall and muscular, with ebony hair and eyes to match—promised fidelity to Bronislav of Ragusa—the squat, sturdy Slav with whom he was destined to share a bench.

Then, as if his previous, disturbing antics had never transpired, "Andiamo," Zen the chameleon trumpeted, waving to the entire group. "If you wish to join me for feasting up in the hills, follow me." He made for the patterned stone stairway. "Otherwise, take your pick of the more indelicate, shall we say, pier-side offerings."

At his words, some of the men laughed raucously, the orange-peeler cupping his hands beneath his own make-believe breasts while his friend fell to the rooftop, sprawled on his back, and spread his legs wide. He thrust himself upward against the sky, then wriggled his legs above him like some beetle turned topsy-turvy in a storm.

"What are you going to do, Jacopo?" Zen called out, it appeared, to the harbor-side wall.

Alert to a new development, Michael followed the recruiter's gaze to a long-legged man who was lying atop the balustrade with his tunic's hood over his face. The man rose up slowly, shifting his body into a half-moon curve, letting his legs unfold onto the roof. He stood and let the hood drop, then shook himself so that his tunic untangled itself. He next bowed to the recruiter in mock humility, drawing a few chuckles from the two Venetian jesters who had stopped their antics to observe. He stood upright, then, and in a military pose, offered, "I shall stay at this pier, signor, as the ladies, whether of the hills or of the dock, offer the same pleasures. Their services are cheaper here, and I will have fewer steps to stumble come morning."

Again, the other two Venetians laughed.

"But before I give myself to the most delightful sins of the flesh, this evening with the daughters of Eve rather than the sons of Adam our vessels provide," he continued, now dropping his mock-humble pose, "might I meet my bench mates for this voyage?"

Zen left the stair way, nodded to Michael and Bronislav, and motioned the two toward Jacopo. The two men stood before him, Bronislav in bemused recognition.

Jacopo was the color of an earthworm, his body as supple as one, too. He looked able to insert and twist his way through narrow crevices, disappearing and emerging at will. He wriggled in sinuous circles around both Bronislav and Michael.

"Aha," he said, and slunk in a prolonged coil around the young Greek. "And how many voyages have you rowed?" he asked.

"None, signor," Michael said, hoping his voice revealed rugged intention rather than lack of experience.

Jacopo looked to Zen in mock or real dismay, Michael could not be sure.

"And how, might I ask, have I injured you to deserve him?"

Michael felt the urge to kick Jacopo in the groin. Zen had pronounced Michael suitable to row. He had assured him, "If The Death, battle, or the wrath of your superiors does not kill you, you should do quite well." Michael had taken him at his word.

Zen laughed. "You know I like you to train the young ones," he said. "Teacher that you are, and so often were to me in the days of my youth."

Zen bowed to Jacopo in a grand gesture.

"Yes," he returned, in a tone Michael had never heard until now. It was as if Jacopo's voice were a thick liquid that oozed. "I taught you just behind the main altar in San Marco, if memory serves. As an altar boy, you enjoyed the rigor of my courses, I remember." He smiled and folded and unfolded his fingers as he stared at Zen. Then he skimmed his right hand along Michael's back as he continued speaking. Michael tensed.

"I see your muscles are taut, ready for the discipline of our voyage," he said.

Michael said nothing, but resented the lingering impression of presumptuous hands through his shirt.

Jacopo made another circle, this time around the Slav.

"And him?" he asked, pointing down at Bronislav. "Why him again? We already trust this Slav, even if his Ragusa is not Venice's most docile outpost."

Bronislav showed his teeth again in a smile.

"Hello, Jacopo. You must remember the pleasures of our most recent voyage together," Bronislav said. "At least you and I came out of it alive, not like the third of our bench, the unfortunate Volo."

"Yes," Jacopo, replied. "The pirate's poisoned arrow made for his quick and tidy departure. Your piss pot, on the other hand, was never empty, and you farted incessantly from the beans! I look at you and my nostrils register excrement." Here Jacopo inhaled deeply, feigning a swoon.

Zen laughed raucously, but Bronislav was not deterred. He held his cross between his hands.

"A rower must drink rainwater when the meager wine turns to vinegar, as it always does. And the man who cannot fart soon dies. In and out, drink and food must come in and go out. That is the way to stay alive. Finis."

He let go the cross and raised his right hand, palm out, to Jacopo, who placed his own palm against Bronislav's. Jacopo gaped at the discrepancy in size, pointing to Bronislav's obvious superiority with his left forefinger so all who watched could marvel with him. If the Slav's hand were a lady's fan extended, Jacopo's was but her glove that could hardly mask a face.

"Am I a dwarf, do you think?" he asked the Slav, taking his hand away and shrinking downward and into himself as he spoke.

Bronislav dropped his own hand.

"Your brain is even smaller than your hand," he teased. "And a good thing, too, for otherwise you could predict my wallops when you behave as the donkey."

Jacopo feinted at Bronislav, his fingers taking the shape of the Devil's horns.

"Alright, I'll row with you as long as you promise not to wallop me again. I meant only to surprise you, not to have the rat bite you when it leapt from your clothing sack. You knocked me unconscious, you bull of a mate!"

"I cannot promise," Bronislav said, "for if you deserve a wallop, I will surely deliver one." He gave Jacopo a wide smile, then, as if he had almost forgotten, added his signature, "Finis."

Zen paced before the trio.

"You see, my dear Jacopo, I give you Bronislav for strength and purity," Zen replied, "for when your languid lagoon disposition and your propensity for imbecilic humor interferes with your galley's speed."

"Liar!" Jacopo called out in exaggerated horror. "I represent only the most noble virtues of our Republic."

"Hypocrite!" Zen retorted, laughing. "The Council of Ten has had cause to jail you on more than twenty occasions. Not the least for your salacious and irreligious, shall we say, predilections."

Then Jacopo ran at Zen, engulfing him in a hug whose meaning Michael could not tell. But when his soon-to-be Venetian bench mate took Zen's head in his hands and planted a smacking kiss on the recruiter's willing lips, Michael wondered if he had made a mistake. He did not have time to ponder, though, for as soon as Jacopo let go of Zen, he came back to Michael and Bronislav.

"And which of you two might I kiss?" he asked, his eyes amused and probing.

Michael burned in shame. Bronislav rolled his eyes. Most of the larger group ignored Jacopo. Some looked and then turned away. One fellow jumped onto the balustrade and off again, smiling broadly at him, while still others shook their heads in annoyance at the Venetian's sophomoric play.

Bronislav crossed his burly arms against his barrel chest as Jacopo came close to his face.

"You already know my thoughts," he said, as if talking to a likable though attention-starved child. "First off, you yourself told me last voyage out, I am too old for your liking." Again Bronislav smiled. "And, to remind you, I do not relish any of our sex." Michael could not believe his ears. "One God, one wife,"Bronislav continued. "Finis." With one thick forefinger Bronislav pointed to the gold chain and the cross he wore around his substantial neck.

Jacopo came close to the man.

"Really?" he asked him. "You really mean that?"

Bronislav smiled again.

"Yes. I do not do as the Venetian seamen. I lie only with Milaslova, my one wife. I make one child, the first time, only a girl. She died of terrible fever. I pray to one God"—here he crossed himself with his right hand. "I sail. When I come back, I lie again with one wife. I make another child. This time God answers my prayer and gives me my boy, Franto, who sings like an angel, I—"

"Blah, blah, blah. You are like a priest reciting a tiresome litany," Jacopo said. "But one of anything is much too little for me." He paused, then asked, "Is your wife beautiful?"

Bronislav pretended to glower at Jacopo. Then he laughed out loud.

"She is as beautiful as I am," he said, smiling in satisfaction.

Jacopo slapped his thighs and laughed, his staccato cries as piercing as those of a peacock. Even Michael grinned.

Then Jacopo returned his attention to him, and Michael's grin instantly faded. Determined to avoid the jester's uncomfortable eyes, he instead stared at the harbor and the long-sought galley he would soon call home for many months.

"Well," Jacopo said, after tapping his right foot ten times, unable to make Michael meet his gaze. He stepped two broad paces away from the two. "How old are you, Michael?"

"Sixteen," the young Greek answered, still avoiding the Venetian's eyes. He tried to sound like his father.

Jacopo slid around him again.

"Not so young as an altar boy, but new to us, just the same. New to the fleet and unschooled, I imagine, in our ways."

Zen let out a sustained whistle. Michael said nothing and stood as tall as he could.

"Well, then," Jacopo winked at Zen. "We shall see."

The recruiter did not reply, but instead ran his hands across his chest as he had done the first day Michael met him. He stared at the recruit, his eyes focusing on Michael as if he were an arrow's target.

Then, leaning forward toward Michael as if to bow a farewell, Jacopo instead adjusted his boots, pulling at each of them extravagantly so that he stretched his hands over the soft leather from toe to thigh, first on one leg, then on the other.

Michael was disgusted at this second vulgar show. How did this Venetian manage the oar, anyway, with his fingers slim as spindles?

"At any rate," he went on, "tonight I will enjoy the ladies, such as they are."

Zen laughed. He appeared to enjoy Jacopo's cogitations, though Michael could not fathom why.

"Come," Zen called to Michael and Bronislav, "follow me. You will have your fill of that devil"—here he made an obscene gesture at Jacopo—"at sea."

Michael shuddered to think of such a thing as Jacopo turned, again fingering his hood, and slipped away.

Chapter 3

MICHAEL'S DISCOVERY

As they started down the stairs—Zen first, Bronislav next, and Michael behind him, followed by a dozen or so other vociferous men—Michael could not help but wonder who, if anyone, he would be able to trust. His uncle's statement, the one both he and his mother had many times mocked, echoed in his mind: "We must trust in the Lord, trust in the Lord." He would have to trust in his wits tonight, that much he knew. He would need to pay attention and stay close to Bronislav. The Slav seemed his best chance for survival. "Finis," he whispered the word as his laced leather ankle-boots met the cobblestones that would lead the group from the boisterous dockside up into the hills above Manfredonia.

The narrow, cobble-stoned street that snaked upward from the hostel to Zen's promised revels, contrasted with the hot open roof-top from which the men had just descended. Whitewashed dwellings attached one to the other with cloth awnings stretched out taut against the waning sun made the walk bearable, even pleasant. Making sure to keep Bronislav in view, Michael spoke not at all, instead listening to the banter that passed among the men, some of them singing a drinking song in unison as they walked. "Beviamo, beviamo, guardiamo il Paradiso!" From a window two stories above, a crone, whose head was wound with an exotic, stone-encrusted black turban—unconcerned with, or, who knows, perhaps annoyed by the brazen paraders below her—launched the contents of a chamber pot directly over the group, so that the excrement splattered onto the heads of the former orange-peeler and his friend.

"Shit!" the former cursed, shaking his wavy hair the way a dog does after emerging from the water. He raised his fist toward the window, yelling, "Strega!" The crone reappeared, this time making the sign of il mal occhio, the evil eye, down at him as she spat.

"You are a smart one," his friend countered, laughing. "At least you can recognize shit as of now." He scratched his splattered ear and wiped his soiled hand across his left legging. "After a few gourd games, you won't know shit from silk," he said. Then, nodding at his friend's soiled face, he held his nose between his forefinger and thumb in mock revulsion.

Michael had played a gourd game the night his sister had given birth to Mattias, her first son, four years earlier. When the midwife stuck her head out the cottage door, announcing, "Mina has delivered you a boy, a live, healthy boy!" her husband, Michael's brother-in-law Artos, had lifted his waiting gourd up toward the heavens, telling Michael, "We will take turns now to celebrate. The first to fall down will be the loser and owe the other one day's work in the lemon groves." But Alda had come out from her daughter's lowly dwelling just as Michael finished quaffing his fourth swig. At twelve years of age, he was hardly a match for the decade-older Artos. "Artos!" Alda had cried, pulling the new father by his ear as if he were her own rascally child. "You don't deserve my daughter. Go and see her now, and your son, God be with him for the likes of you." Then she turned to Michael, whose unguarded giggles and swaying torso betrayed the wine's unmistakable influence.

A voice dispelled Michael's memory.

"Not far now," Zen exhorted the procession of men.

Michael looked over the recruiter's head, Zen's pony-tail bouncing behind him as if it actually were the rear end of a horse. He saw, just a few yards further, what appeared to be a mangled expanse of land, still bright with the early-evening sun. The Manfredonia of cobblestones had come to an end as precipitously as a cliff, the snaking, shaded street giving itself over to a massive field. The space, a long rectangle edged with low stones, was no longer divided and cultivated, but overgrown with untended vines and rampant weeds. Crooked stalks, desiccated and brittle, lay where wheat once stood tall.

His curiosity greater than his shyness at his neophyte status, Michael sprinted forward ahead of Zen to see what lay before him.

"Wait," Zen called out, "I want to show you something."

But Michael ignored him, instead running toward a lofty edifice he could not yet identify. It appeared to rise out of the mess of abandoned earth in the shape of a jagged triangle.

The ivory-colored structure loomed before Michael. He continued toward it, his sprint turning into a steady-paced jog. The closer he came to the building, though, the less certain he was of its purpose. He could not make out a roof, or windows, or a door. His inquisitiveness propelling him, he darted forward until he could no longer hear the voices of the men behind him. Coming within feet of the construction—easily taller than four village cottages stacked one on top of the other—his heart beat with the eager anticipation of an innocent spying novelty. Then, as the composition of the imposing form became clear, he stopped short, first in wonder, then in shocked comprehension.

"Bones," he spoke the word aloud, though he did not mean to.

He stared. The skeletons, bleached nearly white and worn from countless seasons of sun, wind, and rain, lay atop each other. Fingers that had once been hands. Feet of varying sizes, some still connected to legs, others fallen solitary and mismatched among the variegated weeds. Skulls with sockets devoid of eyes, rib cages that held bowl-sized birds' nests, a brown-and-black-speckled snake that slithered like a parched tongue from what had once been someone's moist mouth and ruddy lips.

"The Death," Michael murmured.

Petros's face flashed before his eyes. This is what his brother had become, but not before the rats and gulls had feasted on his plague-ridden flesh. Not before he had vomited black blood and burst from his insides out with poison. Not before he had understood—for certainly he would have understood—that he was utterly and viciously doomed. And, more doleful still, Michael shuddered to think, his brother must have believed that none who loved him might ever know to rail against his swift and calamitous passing.

"God!" Michael bawled, his ejaculation not so much a true believer's prayer as an apostate's outcry.

He kicked ineffectively at the dirt through the weeds, his soft boots barely denting the long-untilled ground in repeated staccatos of grief.

"Petros!" he cried. In that moment, though he tried to bury the thought as if it were itself an infant corpse, he understood a little of his parents' reluctance at his own leave-taking from Rhodes.

A sound like a rushing breeze distracted him, and he watched a dusty mouse scurry from beneath a child's delicate bone torso. The early evening winds sent dry leaves through shelves of baked osseous matter, making a scratching sound where hearts should have pulsed, florid with the blood of the living.

Michael stepped back from the bones, then forward again, and walked slowly and deliberately around the triangle's perimeter. Craning his neck, he decided to count the number of the dead. But before he reached even eleven, he stopped, for he could not with clarity distinguish one set of bones fully from another. Skeleton had collapsed into skeleton, bone had detached from bone. The pile was larger than any dwelling in his village. It appeared the size of his Uncle Elios's chapel that could easily harbor two hundred souls. It looked like the chapel, as well, the top of the pile minus only the cross that heralded it as a sacred place. It was, in fact, Michael decided, a shrine of sorts. Not the shrine of everlasting life that his uncle and the Scriptures promised. No, this was a shrine of death, of The Death that plagued all—Christian and infidel, ruler and subject, the diabolic and the pure, innocent infant and hoary crone.

"Michael," he heard Bronislav's voice calling his name, but he paid no heed.

Instead he found two thick, dry reeds and, as the Slav approached, he pulled them from the ground and fashioned a cross. Its length, he measured, was as long as his arms. As he knotted the reeds together, the other men trooped by, some ignoring the testimony of bones altogether, a few calling, "Come on, to the harlots!" while the shit-splattered duo shouted imprecations at the ruthless Killer that kept reasserting itself as the cardinal foe of the living.

"Ah, I see," Bronislav said as he came close to Michael, who was for the moment sealed in a solitary dominion of despondence. The Slav knelt and dug into the earth with his powerful hands so that Michael was able to place the makeshift cross in the ground. Then, pushing the dirt around the cross to ensure it stayed erect, Bronislav said, "May they rest in peace." He brought his thick fingers to his lips, kissed them, and touched them to the simple, transitory cross in benediction.

"Amen," Michael answered, as Bronislav stood up, unsure what he meant by his response, but realizing he knew nothing else to say.

"Come, my new friend," Bronislav said, and took Michael by the arm. "It is not yet time for us to be among the dead."

Pausing from their walk almost before it had begun, Michael looked to Bronislav.

"How do you know?" he asked.

Bronislav, now also still, pondered a moment. He fingered his cross, twisting its chain and untwisting it in a silence punctuated only by the other men's voices clamoring ahead.

"A fair question, my friend," he said. "A fair question."

The Slav looked beyond toward the other men, who were now well past the mass grave, hurrying to their own transient and futile oblivion.

"Perhaps because we can still talk with one another, we can still take part in the activity of this troublesome world, and we can still pray—though some have lost heart and will tell you they no longer do."

Again, Michael could find no words. Was Bronislav his Uncle Elios transformed?

Bronislav rubbed the dirt off his knees with his hands.

"Come. We will go now, Michael. We are done here."

Michael crossed himself at the tower of bones. Then, as if he had made a discovery, he turned to his new-found mentor.

"Finis," he said, bowing to Bronislav.

"Exactly," the Slav replied.

And the two left the pitiable remains for the torches, tents, and temptations that beckoned ahead in the incipient night.

Chapter 4

DAUGHTER OF EVE

The sun, a red sphere, dropped into the West, replaced, Michael could see ahead of him, by rows of torches surrounding a large, rectangular platform of stone. Female figures in swaying gowns reached up to light them, and the torches' flames licked the advancing darkness, a company of animated, glittering tongues. As he and Bronislav approached the torches, Michael saw Zen whisper into the ear of one of the gowned women. Her long hair followed the curve of her back, ending, Michael could make out in the torchlight, just below her buttocks. The hair, as light as his was dark, curved around her bottom, and Michael found himself aroused. He took his sack from his shoulder and held it in front of him. The woman laughed at whatever Zen had told her and turned to look at Michael as she did. Michael hoped that his eyes, at least, did not betray him. Michael waved to her, and she laughed again, this time covering her mouth with her hand. Michael thought the sound of her voice as beautiful as the sea shell wind chimes his father made and hung near the herb garden. It tinkled in bursts—Zen whispering breezes to her, she laughing at each murmured brush—punctuating the evening with a gaiety that contrasted with the doom from which Michael and Bronislav had just come. Finally Zen acknowledged the two of them and left the torch-lit perimeter, bringing the beautiful voice down from the platform with him. The woman carried her own small lantern in her hand.

"Michael," she called out to him, and his name billowed like a sail.

"Good evening," he answered, and Zen crowed.

The recruiter assured the woman, as if in confidence, "The lad has shown nothing if not impeccable manners. Please God"—here Zen crossed himself in an exaggerated display of piety –"he arrives safely in Venice after his travels, I shall be able to present him to the doge, his Council, and my own infuriating father as my finest recruit."

"Well, then," the voice retorted—full and smooth, her mouth laden with honey, Michael believed—"I shall enjoy his courteous company. It will"—here she pushed Zen away from her in mirthful revulsion—"be a diverting change of pace."

Zen came at her bull-like, then, grabbing both her breasts and squeezing them with his fingers. She, not perturbed in the least, Michael noted, elbowed him in his groin. "Ow!" he yelled, and grimaced at her discomfiting thrust.

Michael saw that her scarlet gown was sheer. When she brought the lantern to rest between the two of them, holding it close to her waist, he did not—try as he might—look to her visage, but instead at her just-manhandled breasts, whose nipples protruded through the mesh folds of fabric, lifting them up and out. His penis would not be mastered.

"Now, then," Zen intervened, pointing at what Michael tried and failed to hide. "Don't raise your mast too soon, Michael, or your voyage will be a brief one!"

As usual, the recruiter laughed at his own joke.

Michael blushed, wishing for complete darkness, while Bronislav grunted, his own member protruding none too subtly from his breeches as well.

Ignoring the obvious, Bronislav said, "I go instead to the platform now, Michael, where the food is sumptuous and the drink plentiful. After tomorrow and for many days thereafter, you will have only biscuits and beans and, with them soon enough, weevils. You can conjure the harlot without benefit of bread"—he pointed to the woman, who stuck her tongue out at him—"but not our sustenance. Either the food is real or it is not. Unlike this albeit tempting morsel of temporary satiety,"—here he bowed to the courtesan, and she, smiling now, returned his compliment with an ironically decorous curtsy—"what sea and earth offer have not the ability to translate from the imagination." He patted his stomach, bowed to the trio, and made off for a long table heaped with ripe grapes and grilled cod, rosemary-laced flat breads and piquant goat cheeses.

"Finis," both Zen and Michael said by way of farewell to the Slav, and laughed as if of one mind.

Then the woman took Michael by the arm while Zen made his way from them, back up to the platform and his own gustatory pleasures.

"Don't forget!" Zen exhorted Michael's hostess. And the recruiter took from the pouch he carried at his waist a thick bangle of gold that he tossed to the harlot.

Letting go of Michael to catch it with both hands, the woman smiled and placed the bracelet on her left arm.

"I won't," she said, and once again took Michael by his willing arm just as another of her trade called out from the platform.

"Zen!" the second woman cried. "It has been months." And the recruiter lifted her high and close so that her bare legs circled him while he grabbed her rump, pressing it hard in his hands.

Michael's escort pulled his face away from the acrobatic display toward her.

"Zen tells me you are his newest recruit. You have not been here before, then?"

"No," Michael answered, feeling her voice plink around him.

"Have you been somewhere else like this, then?" she asked, not mocking or hurried, but curious, interested, Michael could tell. She was close enough to him that he smelled mint on her breath.

Michael shook his head no, not caring that she would know his secret.

"Well, then," she smiled, the torch still between them. "You shall be my personal guest. Come, first we will follow that mountain of a man—what do you call him?—to table."

Michael felt himself being led, wanting to be led, by this Siren voice with breasts that promised more satisfaction than any plate of food might offer, whatever the Slav had said.

"Bronislav," he answered, his voice already thick and sluggish with unabashed, guileless ardor.

"You may call me Aphrodite if you wish," she said, and coaxed him to a bowl filled with amber liquid. She rested her lantern on the stone table—an altar, it seemed to Michael, among a plethora of similarly lavish altars arranged upon the platform. Dipping a wooden cup into the deep bowl, she filled it to its brim. Sipping from it first herself, she next held the cup to Michael's lips as if he were a feverish child. He drank, tasting instantly the sweetness of oranges. Then, when he swallowed, a burning sensation seared his throat. He coughed. Aphrodite laughed, taking his satchel from him and placing it on the floor of the platform.

"More?" she asked.

He was about to say no when she laid the cup on the table, took his head between her hands, and kissed him hard upon his lips. Then, using her tongue like some slick, burrowing animal, she forced open his surprised lips, the mint and citrus and burning mingling together in a swirling wetness. His mouth, until now a mere conduit of daily sustenance, at once became a new-discovered cave of dark sensations. Liquid motion, flickering swiftness, lengthening thrusts. Wave after wave of serpentine probings rippled over his teeth, his gums, and his tongue. All the while his penis gorged itself and, just as Aphrodite withdrew her tongue and bit hard his lower lip, drawing blood he both licked and tasted, his virility exploded. Stunned with stupefied relief, Michael slumped heavily against the woman. His chin rested on her right shoulder. Both her breasts pressed against his firm torso, and her arms, one in each of his hands, feathered him with wisps of downy hair. His leggings were drenched.

"Well, now, that won't do," Aphrodite whispered, her hands cupping his sopping crotch. "We must get you out of these damp clothes. You are not at sea yet, after all."

She picked up the torch and motioned him with her index finger to follow her. Retrieving his satchel and blocking his crotch once more, he did so. She stepped down from the platform just as six men and the gowned women who feasted with them joined hands, one to another. Bursting into spirited song, they began a snake-dance around the altars. Though Michael looked once toward them—he could see that Bronislav did not join in, but instead sat cross-legged on the floor eating from a plate piled high with fish—he instantly turned back toward Aphrodite. He followed her down three steps and away from the platform into a field of waist-high reeds where a line of small lean-to sheds, each with lantern light emanating from within, awaited what he could not yet think to imagine.

"Come," Aphrodite whispered, and he stooped under the low wattle roof. He could not stand completely upright. No door separated the inside from the outside of the dwelling. Before him, he realized, lay the only object in the room besides the lantern. It was a narrow pallet of straw. He dropped his satchel near to where a headrest might have been.

"Remove your leggings," the voice told him. Wind, rather than breeze, moved the sea shell chimes now.

He obeyed and, again, his desire soon showed itself.

"It is hot," Aphrodite said, throwing off her gown, so that the back of her body revealed itself in the torch's glow. She was a shadow of curves, Michael observed. Her soft roundness starkly contrasted to the sharp, pointed weapons of men. Aphrodite affixed the gown to some nettles above so that her dress became a gauzy curtain against the night. Then she turned to face him.

Michael heard himself groan. He could not take his eyes from the extravagant tuft between her legs. As he stared, she ordered, "Lie down," and he, as if obeying tomorrow's commander, fell back upon the pallet. The rough straw pinched his behind. She knelt, one leg each side of him, took his penis between her hands, and, moistening it first with her tongue, pulled it inside her. Straddling him then, she rotated her hips and bent over him. Her hair blanketed his neck and face. He lifted himself into it, inhaling its woody scent. Taking both her breasts in his hands, he squeezed them until his fingers were tight with grabbing. Greedier still, he took first one nipple, then the other, into his mouth, biting and sucking, as if frantic with thirst. Faster and faster she moved, circle and thrust, until from him came a second welcome rush of release. Then darkness.

"Michael," he heard his name. He did not remember having fallen asleep.

Groggy with sated slumber and heavy with damp contentment, Michael sat up and slowly rubbed his eyes. Darkness surrounded the lean-to hut and nocturnal insects buzzed in an incessant, frenzied chorus. His hands were sticky and the room smelled of undisguised carnality. Tambourines and sharp voices pierced the night, outside and downhill from the hut. A man's loud utterance cautioned someone he called Athena, "Watch you do not fall into the brook." Then laughter and splashing.

Again the voice near him, the honey voice, repeated, "Michael."

Aphrodite stood above him in the dark, naked still. Her hair draped her hips.

"Turn over," she told him, and he did, the straw pricking the tenderest parts of him.

What she would teach him now he did not know. He understood only that he wanted to learn it, whatever it might be. His drowsiness gave way to the febrile thrill of his newly-discovered sensuality. His lips twitched in anticipation. He felt like a healthy animal freed from tedious domesticity.

The woman's hair caressed his back as she kneaded his shoulders and arms with her practiced hands. Muscles he once wished only to row with now felt destined to relax in this pleasing, torpid ease, as well.

"That feels so good," he said, his mouth full of gratitude and wanting. "Aphrodite."

"Yes," the woman answered, her hands massaging now his waist, his buttocks, and his legs.

He tried to turn around, wanting to enter her darkness as before.

"No," she said, "not yet."

Again, her hands rubbed and pulled at the calves and thighs of his long, strong legs.

"Now kneel," she said, and, at this command, Michael's heart beat faster in tantalized anticipation.

She kissed the back of his neck as he obeyed her, her lips moving along his oblique spine, among the evenly-spaced dimples of his now-poised hind haunches, then downward over his tensed legs. Again, his desire evidenced itself beneath his avid, covetous form. She stood, her bare feet disturbing the straw.

"Don't move," she cautioned, brushing one hand sideways along the crevice leading to the most private part of himself between his buttocks. "I must relieve myself."

He did as she commanded and waited, his face flush against the pallet. He inhaled straw, let his lips be pinched with dry twigs. The tambourines sounded far off in the distance. Deep, satisfied groans emanated from the lean-to left of theirs. He pulled taut the muscles of his buttocks, then let them go slack. Twice more, as if exercising the equipment of their pleasure, until her feet again disturbed the straw.

Michael craned his neck to see her. Still naked and glowing with perspiration in the humid night and pungent air of the lean-to, she hummed while she brushed across his head and neck and back a soft length of fabric. Straddling him from behind, then, she wrapped the material around Michael's head, bandage-like, so that it covered his eyes.

"But you are beautiful to look at," he protested, with earnestness rather than complaint.

Aphrodite laughed.

"I want to surprise you," she said, and resumed her humming. "Fold your hands as if in prayer," she said.

At this Michael rose upright. Blind now, he clasped his hands together.

"My goddess," he whispered.

"Yes," she replied, laughing.

As the braided rope wound round and round his wrists, Michael faltered. He might easily have refused Aphrodite's dubious ministrations with one quick jolt of his arms, but he did not. Whatever disquiet alerted his senses (and certainly it did, like a demon whose dank breath befouls a cottage despite the crucifix on the wall) was trumped by unadulterated desire. By the time the woman had completed her work, as purposeful as any sailor securing his knots, Michael, submissive and craving, knelt with his head upon his now useless hands. He might have been a prisoner awaiting some exacting justice.

His heart beat loud and fast in his chest. Though he had thought himself spent with pleasure, he quickened again with expectation. What more ecstasy would this beautiful temptress show him?

"Enter," Aphrodite called into the night.

At her sure command, another person's feet rustled the straw in the lean-to. This tread bore the weight of sturdy boots instead of the woman's unshod soles.

"Who is it?" Michael asked, turning though not seeing. His heart raced. Trepidation quelled his heretofore unmitigated desire.

"A friend," the woman said, her hands again roaming Michael's backside, this time spreading his buttocks apart, teasing his anus with licks from the tongue and a forefinger that probed the narrow aperture. Despite the hot night, he shivered at the pleasant tingling.

"Aphrodite," he said, his tone one of appreciation for yet another incipient pleasure.

But before she could answer, he was rammed from behind.

Like an untested beast unable to fend off a superior predator, Michael, screaming, tried to raise himself up. But an unyielding body kept him in place and a pair of hands, thicker and stronger than Aphrodite's, flattened his neck and head as he fought. Blood dripped down the back of his legs and the smell of his own excrement made him retch into the straw.

"No!" he bawled into the pallet, his mouth filled with vomit and spittle.

"Welcome to the Venetian fleet, Michael," Zen said.

Michael crumpled onto the pallet, drawing into himself, fetus-like. He drew his tethered hands to his crotch. Zen ripped the blindfold from his face and let it fall. Wiping his penis clean then on Aphrodite's gown-turned-curtain, Michael's abuser stuffed his member into his breeches.

"Fresh meat," he taunted Michael. Then, his voice softer, kindly even, "Thank you, Michael. You were a genuine pleasure."

Michael gagged, his throat constricted. He gasped for air, dizzy with shame and futile regret.

Aphrodite, standing just outside the lean-to, said, "Isn't he, though? Such a lovely boy."

"Whore!" Michael screamed. "You are nothing but a whore!"

The woman, pulling her sheer gown over her head, looked down at him.

"Yes, Michael, I am." She blew a kiss at him. "Now you know what that means."

Adjusting the gold bangle on her left arm, she left the hut.

Without pausing a moment, Zen stooped and brought his hand to Michael's leg in an apparent caress. Michael kicked his foot upward, aiming for his rapist's groin, but Zen caught it by the ankle in his hand.

"That was very foolish, Michael," he said, and, still grasping the boy's leg, with his pointed boot kicked Michael in the face.

While Michael writhed, Zen brought his recruit's bare toes to his lips. Then, all the while holding Michael's ankle, he kissed them one by one. When Zen let go, he smiled at the boy. And Michael's eyes blinked without respite in the lantern glow, two pools of irrevocable anguish.

"Get some sleep," Zen told him. "Your galley sets sail tomorrow at noon. Do not be late, or it's a steep fine and the strappado for you. I'll see you at the pier."

Then he was gone.

Blood, excrement, and semen soiled the straw pallet. Bats winged through the trees. An animal scurried above in the nettles. Michael needed to untie his hands.

Alone with only the lean-to's lantern for company, Michael cursed the harlot, Zen, and himself. Then, not knowing what else to do, he begged the only God he knew, the God he now hated, the God who—all else lost—perhaps could save him. In Him he placed his insubstantial trust. Dragging himself off the straw pallet, he bit his satchel between his teeth and crawled with it to the lean-to's aperture. With each move forward, his rectum burned. Gripping the satchel between his jaws so as not to drop it, he then shimmied himself up one of the poles holding the lean-to in place. Bowing under the entryway, then, he walked into the grey fog of almost-dawn. He must find the source of the splashing he had heard in the night. There by the water he would, he promised himself, find sharp branches or a pointed rock against which to set himself free.

Chapter 5

TO SEA, BUT FIRST...

"No one must know," the voice in his head repeated. "No one must know."

His silent mantra had replaced that of the night's whirring insects, rushing bats, and grunting men. The brief quiet before the first birds surrounded him, making him feel both a little bit safe and utterly alone.

Snot, tears, and vomit dampened his face in clumps of regurgitated fish and crust. His satchel bobbing before him, he inched his way through the reeds around the back of the lean-to naked, desperate to rinse the blood and excrement from his buttocks and his legs. He hoped the sun would not rise before he had loosed his hands. He yearned for fresh water to eliminate at least the outward show of his shame.

A whispered call came from inside a cluster of dense, low bushes to his left. Michael decided to keep walking. He dared not be discovered.

As he made his way, the ground sloped downward, all at once reedless and rock-ridden. He walked sideways, right foot down, left foot following, so he would not slip. His teeth hurt from the weight of his satchel. His roped hands, bound in their ironic prayerful pose, still shook in mortified humiliation. After twenty or so steps, he heard the running brook. A mist hovered above it, though some swallows were already dipping from the trees to its surface in search of their breakfast.

"There," Michael mumbled between his teeth, as he made out a ledge of rock that might avail itself to him. His gums ached, distracting his attention temporarily from the vile injury to his hind parts.

He let the satchel drop at the edge of the brook. His teeth chattered in relief and his jaw relaxed, unclenching itself. Easing himself down the now-steep incline, Michael stepped into the knee-deep water, slipping only a bit and managing not to fall on the slick mud. Then, turning and raising his bound hands to the sharpest point of the variegated rock ledge he faced, he prepared to set himself free. Rubbing his hands up and down, up and down, he wore the rope thin and thinner. From time to time, he nicked his wrists on the sharp edge, so that rivulets of blood tinted the rope red. From up the incline, he heard the unmistakable sounds of men greeting each other in bleary satisfaction. He rubbed faster, intent with the necessity of his shame.

Focusing so completely on his task, he was oblivious to the watery encroacher who, all of a sudden and with a forceful splash, had already plunged beneath him. Two strong hands encircled his submerged ankles. Raging once more with fierce and palpable fear, Michael pivoted from the ledge and swung his almost-freed hands around. He pounded again and again upon the underwater skull until, as the hands let go his ankles and the culprit rose from up the brook, he recognized the bulk of Bronislav before him.

"Michael, it is only I," the Slav said, raising his arms in hearty, innocent greeting. Then he tucked his massive head down and inward toward his chest, protecting his eyes from Michael's hammer blows.

Still, Michael pounded, pummeling now the speechless Slav's shoulders and chest, hitting hard with his not-yet-freed hands. Bronislav stood still, his arms still raised, his open hands not fists.

"Michael, Michael," Bronislav called up to him. "What is the matter?" The Slav flinched as Michael's part-worn tether scraped his face.

Then, realizing what in fact had happened to the boy, the Slav abruptly shoved Michael backward so that he fell into the water, landing on his buttocks, submerged up to the neck. He appeared to be in a haze of incomprehension.

"Now, then," Bronislav spoke, his voice taking on the practiced calm of sober experience.

While Michael struggled unsuccessfully to stand, the Slav unscrewed what looked to be the bottom of his large chest cross, pulling from it a thin knife, its size that of the long needle sailors' wives used to sew together pieces of their husbands' leather vests.

"Lift your hands," he ordered Michael.

The boy complied. With one stroke of his knife, Bronislav freed him.

Instantly, and without a word of thanks, Michael lifted himself from the water, surveyed the surrounding foliage, and ripped a leafy branch from one of the trees that banked the brook near him. Rubbing it roughly over and over again across his buttocks and legs, his haste and harshness ritualistic in nature, he shut his eyes as he scourged himself. His hands a frenzy of scraping that lasted as long as Bronislav's monotone alphabetical doxology to the saints, Michael finally opened his eyes. He stared into the moving water of the brook, however, rather than meet Bronislav's piercing eyes.

The Slav lumbered out of the water and plopped himself, with an audible thud, on the brook's bank, his own solid nakedness pure and patient as Michael scrubbed. He did not speak. His doxology completed, he shifted to the Lord's Prayer, his words a murmuring rumble against the rushing water.

Soon he eased himself up and trudged away from Michael to a flowering bush where he had spread his clothing. Unbeknownst to him, Michael at last raised his eyes to follow him. The boy watched him as he dressed, though he never stopped scrubbing. When Bronislav had finished, all except for his sandals that he carried, he walked back to the brook's bank. Michael still persisted with the branch.

"You'll take your skin right off," Bronislav warned, his voice friendly and straightforward.

Michael did not answer.

Bronislav saw the boy's satchel, reached into it despite the vomit-laced rim, and pulled out a pair of clean, worn fisherman breeches and a rough woven shirt.

"Come," he stood and held out the clothing.

Michael looked up at the Slav. Turning in the water, he tried to see behind himself.

"You are clean," Bronislav said, his voice assuring and apparently untroubled.

Michael let go of the branch, and it floated away with the swift, bubbling water. He submerged his head, rubbing his black hair with his fingers. He slicked it back, away from his face, and patted it down so that it flattened. Combing it with his fingers, he arranged it so that the full strands framed his face to his chin. Then he took some water into his mouth, gargled and spat. He did so two more times, finishing off his toilet by rubbing his right forefinger throughout his mouth. He scrubbed each tooth one at a time, then swept his gums and the cavity of his mouth, gagging a bit as he finished. Finally, just as Bronislav had prayed to the true Virgin five of her prayers, his voice lifting at the Mother of God's name, he walked out of the brook and up the bank.

As he did, Bronislav turned his back. He spent considerable time putting on and adjusting his sandals, twisting the leather ties around his ample shins and knotting them not once, but twice just below his knees.

"Thank you," Michael said, and the Slav turned back to face the boy.

No longer naked, Michael was nonetheless still wet beneath his clothes. His shirt stuck to his arms and torso. His thin breeches sported blotches of dark water. His cheeks were swollen, and his chin was turning black and blue. He licked his bitten lips with his tongue, rubbed the water out of his eyes, and stared at the ground where his boots somehow lay side by side.

"I got them from the lean-to when I came for you," Bronislav said. "Most go to the brook after the whores. Only not right away, like you."

Michael said nothing, but stared at his boots as if they would offer some counsel.

"We will leave now, before the others," Bronislav said. "That way we can get ourselves a real breakfast before tomorrow's allotted biscuit and beans."

"I am not hungry," Michael replied.

His voice sounded as if it had been in disuse for a long time and was just again beginning to attempt speech.

"I know," Bronislav said. "Nonetheless, you will eat."

Bronislav pointed to Michael's boots and the boy put them on, holding onto a tree trunk to support himself, first with one arm, then the other. His wrists were still raw and red with the impression of the rope. When he was done, Bronislav began to walk, motioning to Michael to follow. He nodded toward the satchel, which Michael lifted and threw over his shoulder, following the Slav up the embankment. The two rustled the reeds as they walked.

Michael felt nothing but tired. If he were to lie down and wait patiently, he could simply die. The animals would eat his flesh and the sun would bake his bones. Like his brother Petros, he, too, would be transformed into a skeleton of death. His sinning flesh dissolved and his ignorant frame bleached to pure whiteness, he would never again fear another's mastery or the result of his own unbridled, dizzying lust. Then and only then would this deep and heavy sadness fall away.

"I'll just stay here awhile," he said aloud, mostly to himself.

Bronislav turned.

"You cannot. Commander Loredan will arrest you. He will keep you tied up on board until our ship returns to Venice, where he will then submit you to the strappado. As your shoulders are ripped apart, you will of course reveal the source of your troubles. And finally you will be left to rot in one of the piombi."

Bronislav fingered his pectoral cross-cum-knife as he spoke.

Michael sighed the sigh of a person resigned to a future of despair. He decided to sit down despite Bronislav's words. But before he could even bend his knees fully, the Slav grabbed him by the arm, slapped the side of his head (though without rancor and as if to awaken one asleep), and ordered him, "Come with me now," his voice ringing with authority as the sun rose.

Like a neophyte altar server obeying his decades-old bishop, Michael followed the Slav. If he could force his own grief-laden steps to match Bronislav's optimistic ones, he might be able to keep on walking.

Reaching up to examine Michael's purpling chin with his hands, the Slav asked, "Was it Jacopo who found you after all?"

Michael, as sorrowful as he had ever felt, shook his head no. Bronislav let go his face. They continued walking

"Who, then?"

Bronislav's voice was without accusation or disdain. They passed the line of huts, empty now save but for one snoring man, if sound rendered the truth.

"Zen," Michael told him, flushing in abysmal self-reproach.

Bronislav grunted.

"He's an unsavory one," the Slav said. "That is for certain."

"I thought you liked him," Michael said.

Bronislav replied, "I must work with him. That is all."

Michael said nothing, but tilted his head to Bronislav to see if he would tell more. The Slav talked as they walked, his voice steady in its narrative of Zen's ignoble actions.

"He has been banished from Venice and denied a ship's command for having abused our own captain's niece. He broke off his betrothal to her over a quarrel with her paternal uncle and his son, her cousin. I do not know the details," Bronislav continued, panting a bit as they climbed the rise. "All the captain has told me between voyages is that The Council requires Zen to hire a goodly number of oarsmen like yourself if he is to recover his status and set right his family's honor in the Republic's eyes." The Slav stopped, took a breath, and scratched his chin. "So much for that when the captain learns of your treatment."

Michael gave a start. "I shall not tell the captain. Surely Zen would find me if I did."

Bronislav looked at the shaken young Greek. "You may not tell him, Michael, but he will find out."

"But how?" Michael asked, brushing his lips with his fingers. He winced.

Bronislav scratched his chin once more. "This is a fact you must know about Venice, my boy. Everyone harbors a secret or two. But no harbor is impenetrable."

"You sound like a riddler," Michael said.

Bronislav chuckled. "Riddled, perhaps. But this much I know after my years of service to the fleet." He faced Michael square.

"Think of the Republic as a spider's web. Many spiders spin among its strands, one colliding with another, interlocked and solitary both. No one spider is sovereign. Each is subject to the others and the others to him. And the web, the Republic, Michael, holds them all among its twisting and twisted strands."

Michael did not know what to say.

The two walked uphill in silence. The raised platform of stone loomed ahead, its altars now strewn with spilled drinks and half-eaten platters of spoiling food. The harlots were nowhere to be seen, and a cat-sized rat careened from one table to another, rocketing onto the platters to gorge itself with the residues of rotting fish and fruit.

"Ah," Bronislav said, quickening his pace, "I can see the steeple of the church from here. I will ask for the priest's blessing before we set sail."

Their walk went downhill now. They passed the graveyard of bones where Michael could see that his handmade cross, though crooked from the buffeting of night's breezes, still stood.

"Here we are," Bronislav said, as the field met the cobblestones of Manfredonia.

He stopped, reaching up to Michael's shoulders so the boy stopped, as well.

"We commit sin, my boy, but we can learn forgiveness, too," he said. "I have, Michael. I have required forgiveness many times. And no doubt will again."

Michael tried, though without success, to keep his emotions in check.

The two walked down the snaking streets. Most of the windows were still shuttered in the early morning. Only a black dog, eyes closed and body prone in apparent sleep, raised itself, blinking once to view them as they passed.

"Good, I smell fish frying," Bronislav said, "and garlic." He grinned. "First to the church. Then we will eat."

This time, Michael did not contradict his friend.

"Just remember three things," the Slav told him, as they both jogged down the cobblestones toward the steeple and the harbor. He panted as he spoke, his words thick with sober care. "Always keep close and in secret one of your knives." He paused from his running to catch his breath. "Do not trust any Daughter of Eve, as comely in her flesh as she might be." He held up three fingers and gulped the morning air. "And, though I regret to have to say so, never turn your back on a Venetian sailor unless you mean to school yourself in the transgressions of Sodom."

Michael nodded his head, an eager if altogether tardy student.

"Finis?" he asked Bronislav, trying to smile at his gracious friend.

"No," the Slav replied, "not this time. This time, Michael, you begin."

Chapter 6

MICHAEL GRABS HOLD OF THE OAR

Three bodily sensations accompanied Michael as he made his long-anticipated walk to the end of Manfredonia's lengthiest pier to present himself to Commander Pietro Loredan, one of Venice's most celebrated nobili. First, the invisible Sign of the Cross scratched on his forehead by the jagged thumbnail of the aged parish priest to whom Bronislav confessed before this, his seventh voyage. "Be brave, my son," the priest had told Michael after Bronislav's sacrament was achieved. "You will be sorely tested, both by nature and by man." Michael, too ashamed to ask forgiveness for his own recent iniquities, had kept silent but for a soft "Amen." Secondly, the lingering burn in his anus that made him twinge as he tried to stride confidently along the pier like the native Venetian rowers. His own status as a sworn rather than born homo da remo would never match theirs, or could it? Thirdly, and as jarring as an unexpected thunderclap in the night, the sight of his nemesis, Zen, standing beside Loredan. Disgust rose with bile from his stomach, and Michael forced himself to swallow again the just-chewed fish cakes he had eaten at Bronislav's insistence.

"Steady," Bronislav murmured behind him. "It is Loredan who captains you now. Be worthy of his trust."

Plagued

The renowned Pietro Loredan di Alvise was to command the guard galley newly-launched from Venice's burgeoning shipyard, the Arsenale, to protect Venetian grain ships from the rival Genoese as well as from any marauding pirates. Later in the journey, he would see to the Republic's formal acquisition of the island of Corfu, the sea power's designated "Door," or central command post, to the far-reaching Stato da Mar.

Michael steeled himself, drawing his torso upward so that he rose to his full height, and donned the persona of the meritorious seaman he hoped to become. He nodded back at Bronislav as the procession of rowers, each being greeted personally by Loredan, suddenly halted.

"Seize him!" the commander shouted, and two black-hooded men standing either side of the gangplank, grabbed a shocked rower, binding his hands behind him and hustling him up and onto the galley, where—from halfway down the pier Michael strained to see—they lashed him to the mast. One man punched the fellow in his stomach while the other slapped him repeatedly across his face until his head hung down. Then they returned to their parallel posts, standing straight and still, and the parade of greetings continued. Though he could not imagine he had cause to fear similar abuse from them, Michael felt a wary caution the closer he moved to their post. His heart pounded against his shirt, not so much for fear of them or pity for the bound man, he had to admit, but more at the proximity of his now-sworn enemy, whose own recent affronts to Michael's previously untested body were all too vivid a memory. He must not let his distress be apparent. If Zen ruled him now, Michael knew his dreams would be forever dashed. He readied himself. Bronislav's words must conquer his own trembling. He must convince the captain of his worthiness, even if he did not yet believe in it himself.

"Captain." He bowed to Loredan, the man's nobility immediately apparent in his regal bearing, his pristine doublet, his gleaming sword, and the supple leather of his high black boots.

Loredan stared deep into Michael's eyes. Equal in height though not inheritance, Michael stared back, consciously ignoring Zen.

"So, this is your recruit from Rhodes?" Loredan asked Zen without taking his eyes away from Michael's. He spoke as if he did not already know the answer.

"Yes, Captain," Zen replied curtly, clicking his boot heels together. He, too, Michael sensed, still focusing directly on Loredan, must have taken care of his toilet today.

Loredan took up Michael's hands in his, examining closely the calluses on his palms. Michael tried to hold them steady, with limited success.

"You have been practicing," the captain said, a broad smile revealing healthy teeth. He was clean-shaven, too. Michael remembered his uncle telling him that the Venetians forebade their men beards in the islands of the Aegean. "Too Greek, their Council tells them," he had said, even as he rubbed his own hirsute face.

"Yes, Captain," Michael answered, bowing slightly again.

"Good," Loredan said. "May your rehearsals serve you well on our voyage. " Then he ran his fingers, their nails filed and clean, across the rope burns on Michael's wrists. Michael winced and held his breath.

Commander Loredan let go the hands, turning and pointing to Zen. Michael pressed his arms tightly at his sides.

After what felt a lifetime, Commander Loredan asked, "And how has my newest recruiter here, a descendant of one of Venice's late and glorious doges and son of a war hero"—here he paused so that his words hung suspended in the late morning air—"prepared you for this voyage?" Loredan waited, but Michael kept silent. "Did he have anything to do with these marks?" He gestured toward Michael's wrists. "Or with the fresh plum growing on your lower lip?" The captain's own lips became one straight line across his face after his question.

This time Michael attended to the warning signal that coursed through his brain. Loredan's questions were a test, a test he must pass to board the galley without a sullied start. He bowed once more, buying time with the choreography of courtesy and imagining what his brother might have said.

Forcing himself to look directly at Zen (though the recruiter's visage and Satan's might as well have been one and the same to Michael), he said, "Captain, Signor Zen has taken a personal interest in me. He has attended to my every need. The marks, I regret to say, are my own fault. A failure of strategy during a game of tug of war."

Here, as Loredan murmured, "Hmmm...," Michael turned the story-teller Petros once had been.

"Was Zen part of the game?" Loredan continued.

Michael did not pause.

"No, Captain. Just a group of recruits like myself from among the hostels. Waiting to board ship and drinking too much wine."

Loredan pressed on.

"Did your team at least win?"

Michael shook his head ruefully.

"No, Captain. The loss belongs to me. I did not control the rope." Sweat trickled down Michael's back as he tried to harness his shaking. His hands twitched and he bit the inside of his lower lip. He hoped Loredan would believe him.

Zen's posture remained rigid. His eyes gave Michael no sign of recognition.

"So, then, Michael, how will you alter your strategy for the next game?" Loredan asked. He watched Michael look at Zen.

Now, for the first time, Michael spoke with genuine certainty and confidence. His brother's spirit was surely with him.

"I will control the rope, Captain Loredan."

Zen's feet shifted on the dock.

"I see," said Loredan.

A pleasing flutter, not unlike a swoosh of wind, suddenly loosed and cooled the hot knots in Michael's stomach.

"Well, then, as long as Zen continues, as you say he has, to maintain the trust of the Republic, his family, and myself, he will remain in his position for another round of recruiting."

Zen made a slight bow toward the commander.

"Thank you, Captain," he said.

Sure he had passed the test, if Bronislav's steady breaths behind him were any testimony, Michael continued, his next words perhaps a bit brazen. "I look forward to a time when I may return the degree of his care, should God will I survive this and other voyages in your service."

Loredan laughed and slapped Michael on the shoulder. Zen remained still.

"Michael of Rhodes," he said, "I welcome you aboard our galley. If you row as aptly as you have just spoken, you will no doubt enjoy, though perhaps I should more honestly say 'endure,' a satisfying tenure with us."

At this the captain turned to Zen.

"As for you," he said, "after you recruit the next group of rowers, you are to return to Venice, where you and I will come before The Ten. Should my report be positive, perhaps by then The Council will grant you command of a ship. Do not give us any new cause to act otherwise. Remember your duty to the Republic, to your family, and"—here he brought his right forefinger to his chest, cleared his throat, and said finally—"to me. Do not forget, I now uphold my late brother-in-law's interests and those of his widow, my sister Elena, and his daughter Marina, my niece and your former betrothed. You have abused each of them. If signs of your continued ignoble actions, such as those imprinted upon the one standing before me now, continue, and still you do not fear the lion of our Republic, know that I am its more menacing twin."

Loredan's face was scarlet and Michael burned with shame. Zen clicked his heels again.

"Yes, Captain Loredan," he replied.

Michael grew brave in the captain's presence.

"Good–bye, Signor Zen," Michael said, trying to capture Loredan's tone with his own voice. "Until we meet again."

Zen did not acknowledge his recruit's farewell, but stood unmoving, as if he had just gone deaf.

Then, as Commander Loredan gave him leave with his extended arm, Michael sprinted past the black-hooded duo up the gangplank in spite of the lingering sear in his body. Against the mast, the galley's prisoner was unconscious. His head fallen into his chest, his eyes closed, and spittle glistening on his mouth, the man drooped, his broad hands roped behind his back. Feeling a momentary, discomfiting kinship with the fellow, Michael blinked and hurried past him toward the hold, curious what the prisoner had done to deserve the captain's harsh displeasure.

"Bronislav," Loredan bellowed heartily below, "I am pleased to see you again. Your presence gives me hope for a safe and successful voyage."

"Grazie, Captain," the Slav replied. "I am glad to be of service again." Then he followed Michael onto the galley, his own steps slow and measured, indicative, no doubt, of his good sense to parcel out his strength a little bit at a time.

"Coming to our post?" he asked Michael. The two stood just past the mast, and the Slav made the Sign of the Cross toward the roped rower.

"In a moment," Michael answered.

"I go, then, and wait for you," said Bronislav, and he walked in the direction of the first mate, who waved him on.

Ignoring Bronislav's departure for a short time, Michael turned his attention from the ship to gaze back out at Manfredonia. His eyes scanned the dock, then followed the close-built dwellings up into the hills. In the twenty-four hours he had spent here, everything he knew of life had changed. As Commander Loredan continued greeting the other rowers, Michael looked straight down on Zen. From this vantage point, the man was nothing but small. He had shamed his own father and dishonored the captain's family, incurring the displeasure of the Republic. He had required a harlot to abuse a stupid boy. He had hidden himself like a thief in the night. And noble by birth though he might be, he had had to resort to a rope tied by a woman to trick his naïve recruit. How weak he was. How insignificant.

"Ha!" Michael crowed.

"Which is my bench, signor?" he asked the nut-brown dock master who stood with the galley's scrolled manifest in his hand.

"Number Five," the man said, scanning Michael's person from head to toe. "With Bronislav of Ragusa and Jacopo of Venice."

"Grazie," Michael said.

The functionary nodded. Then, as if an afterthought, he added, "I wish you safe voyage and protection from every plague."

Rucksack in hand, then, Michael strode to his length of polished fir where, after two years of practice and more than a decade of unabashed desire, he sat down next to the ready Bronislav, his seasoned mentor and patient friend.

"Bravo, Michalli!" Bronislav applauded, as the young Greek, smiling now in anticipation and wonder, dropped his scant and sullied belongings beneath il bancho and wrapped his eager, supple hands around his own Venetian oar.

Chapter 7

STATO DA MAR—OCEAN STATE

"One half hour more!" Aurelio Calli, the proder, the galley's senior oarsman, bellowed out his call.

They had been rowing steadily since leaving the Manfredonia dock, one and one-half hours earlier. At the proder's words, each triad of rowers reiterated the report to the bench forward from their own. Then, relieved that respite would soon be forthcoming, they recommenced the gong-like chant that kept them from laying down their individual oars. The galley creaked and groaned with rocking. Fatigue as heavy as anchors plagued the oarsmen's strapping torsos and their tenacious arms in the final thirty minutes of their two-hour sensile, one man to every oar on board. Michael was wedged, not only beneath the trireme's low parapet that protected its rowers from the elements above, but also between Bronislav and Jacopo. While the Slav was able to look out and down at the frothing water, and the Venetian could turn to the deck, taking in the words and movements of the ship's passing society, Michael had little room to spare for motions not essential to the sensile and suffered the close heat of his bench mates' exertions. He imitated their synchronic movements in hopes that doing so would prove the solitary charm to keep him from fainting or, worse still, from losing grip of his oar.

Calli kept time by the hourglass, its fine sand of ground marble from the mined quarries of Carrara, its luminous glass transparent ampules fired in Murano's blazing furnaces. The implacable device, as deliberate and authoritative as any one of the Republic's written decrees, measured the oarsmen's efforts, quantifying each rower's Herculean expenditure of muscle, sweat, and will.

"Bene," Bronislav panted, even as his breaths aligned with Calli's measures. "Soon we will cease our work. Then we can eat."

Michael nodded, wanting absolute stillness more than food. But he was too tired to say so aloud. He let his eyes wander to Jacopo to hear what opinion he might offer.

But the Venetian did not respond to Bronislav's words. In fact, his eyes were closed and his fingers, long and slim as they were, wrapped snugly around his oar like some delicate bracelets on the arm of a graceful noblewoman. He appeared to be in a sleep-like daze. Despite his seeming detachment from the rest of the rowers, though, Jacopo moved to the proder's beats with steady, rhythmic precision. Michael's own movements, he knew, were jerky and tentative by comparison.

Every rower faced the stern of the galley, rose in unison with the others from his bench, and stepped onto the low footboard beneath him. Arms taut, Michael, like the rest of them, brought one foot to bear on the footboard. Then he pushed the oar's end toward the stern, forcing its blades forward. With each push, he and every other rower held the second of his feet flush with the back of the bench before him. When the oar blade dipped into the water, he pushed off the bench with that second leg and off the floorboard with the first. All the men pulled with their backs, straining the muscles of their trunks so that they literally fell back onto the benches. Then their oars rose out of the water in a coordinated rush of froth and spray. The galley divided the waves. Venice penetrated the seas. Only then could the men exhale in momentary relief. Michael felt his lungs deflate with every single completion. But before they fully collapsed, it was time once more to inhale deeply, to suck like nurturing mother's milk the ubiquitous air that replenished his chest with the invisible blasts required to master the oar again.

"Sisyphus," Michael exhaled, feeling the hiss of the "s" between his clenched teeth. He remembered his uncle telling him the story of the man climbing and climbing in a never-ending physical effort to reach his destination.

"Dieci e basta," the proder called. His resonant voice rang, his tested authority ("Thirty voyages," Bronislav had told Michael during one of the pauses) the basis of his oarsmen's trust. Each arduous stroke was his responsibility and every rower's duty. The antiphony between them, no less sacred than the holy interchanges between priest and choir in churches, kept the galley afloat and on course, freeing the captain's voice and mind for matters of commerce, battle, and honor, all in the service of voracious Venice.

"Dio," Michael uttered, barely able to enunciate, his teeth pressed with effort, the muscles of his mouth, neck, and shoulders tensed with strain. His hair, streaming sweat, stuck to his head, encircling his face like a sodden ebony helmet.

Soldiering on despite a waning confidence in his ability to succeed at a profession requiring such an onerous expenditure of strength, he marveled that he and the others had been pulling their oars without a single respite since departing the coast. Only when the hourglass's sand had disappeared from the uppermost ampule would they dare put down their lengths of heavy, varnished wood. No amount of practice with his bags of dirt and stones, he now realized, could have prepared him for the spiraling roil and drag of the tide beneath the galley's timbers, for the oppressive wooden parapet that constrained his lanky body, for the inevitable shudder and thump onto unyielding plank that followed each counted stroke. His body quailed. His eyes blurred with the salty spray, regardless of how much he blinked and squinted. Surely his tightened flesh would snap. He forgot himself, flinging back his straining neck to accuse the very heavens he could not see for the barrier over his throbbing head.

"I break!" he howled, juvenile and selfish in his cry, as if he alone suffered the bodily anguish of every other rower who manned an oar.

"Michael," Bronislav admonished him. "Do not waste yourself so foolishly. The Captain will deem you mad and useless."

Jacopo opened his eyes, turned to Michael, and, without interrupting the cadence of his movements, said, "Do that again and I'll make you a eunuch with my nicely sharpened dagger."

At his words, Michael looked down at his weary crotch. He was overcome with gloom.

"What did you think this would be?" Jacopo continued. "A ride in a gondola? Your father's fishing boat? You are an idiot."

Bronislav grunted in agreement. Chastened, Michael kept to the beat and was silent.

Calli's voice called out again, "Six strokes more."

Loredan strutted by, studying the oarsmen bench by bench. As he passed, Michael could see his feet and legs and, if he scrunched down and twisted his neck, all the way to his head. Gathering from the proximity and distance of his voice and the clap of his heels on the timbers, Michael could tell he sometimes stopped. Twice he called out, "Steady, steady," along his way. When he reached the mast—not seven broad steps from Bench Five, Michael calculated —the lashed man, his consciousness evidently restored, sputtered through his beaten face, "Captain, have mercy on me. What have I done to deserve your wrath? What have I done, Captain, Captain?"

Michael did not hear Loredan reply. Instead the captain's footsteps reversed and he came closer to Michael and his bench mates once more. This time his pace was a stroll. He stopped. "Excellent," he praised them, waving in at the trio. "An excellent start, oarsmen." Whether or not the galley would successfully complete the Republic's scrupulously planned itinerary would depend upon the uniform discipline of the men, their variable health, God's inscrutable will, and the vacillating weather He used from time to time to exercise His erratic vengeance.

"Four strokes to go." Bronislav's voice matched Calli's.

As if by some secret, silent conjuring, the two previously-hooded men joined the captain by Bench Five, this time without their head coverings. Michael adjusted his body to see as they passed that they were shirtless as well. The thinner one sported a head of hair that resembled cut, dried apricots, and several jagged scars snaked across his back. The broader-shouldered man had no hair at all, so that the sun gleamed off his leathery skull. He rubbed his hand over his pate as the captain spoke. Visible to Michael at each man's waist were the handles of ballock knives, not unlike the one Petros had won from a Scotsman in a game of dice. The ornate metal balls sitting either side of the knife hilts provided yet another unwelcome reminder to Michael that his very manhood might be in perpetual danger, whether on land or at sea.

"Release him," Loredan said, "then chain him upright to the hold's outer ladder wall, wrists and ankles apart."

The Republic's henchmen set about their work. The prisoner jabbered and questioned them without ceasing, and soon his words became muffled, as if his mouth had been stuffed with some sort of rag. When he was out of the way, Loredan approached the mast again, giving the order to hoist the lateen sails. A cabin boy, "Roch," Michael heard Loredan call, obeyed his command. Bounding by the benches like a frisky goat, Roch, Michael could tell by the sound, hoisted first the alboro, the larger mast, then the albora de meza, the mast only half the fourteen paces of the former. The boy bleated as he worked. Glad, Michael guessed he must be, to come out of the dark and into the oscillating air above the rowing benches. Michael heard the sails hoisted, their triangular thrusts and cresting a welcome promise of imminent ease. As soon as the lateens caught the wind with quick, smart snaps, Calli ordered, "Men, lay down your oars."

One hundred and eighty bodies, or, to be exact, one hundred and seventy-nine, unless the lashed man's place had been filled by another, slumped upon the benches slippery with their sweat. No one spoke. Even the proder, his voice close to hoarseness from his recent vocal enterprise, went silent.

Michael's body trembled with fatigue. His shoulders ached, his back muscles throbbed, his fingers cramped, and his legs wanted space to lie prone, raised, and undisturbed for a very long time. But his piss pot and mangled rucksack, along with those of Bronislav and Jacopo, filled the space beneath their bench. The three might as well be prisoners of the crowded Bench Five until the proder declared, "Up men. At ease on deck."

In the instant it took him to release and secure his oar in its thole pin and open his eyes, Jacopo leapt off the bench and disappeared toward the stern of the galley. Bronislav, on the other hand, once he was assured of his oar's stability, let himself sink into the bench, placing his head on the wood behind him and extending his squat legs out toward the wood before him. He snored.

Ducking his own head to avoid hitting the parapet as he rose, Michael stood in the late afternoon sun and tried to make his legs adapt once more to walking. They did, though not without some purposeful rubbing at both knees and ankles. The young Greek emerged awkwardly from his designated place like some stubborn, ragged weed that wanted sunlight.

Chapter 8

SUSTENANCE AND SUFFERING

"Water line," called the armiraio, the man responsible for the crew's discipline. "Last bench first, taking turns either side of the ship, two draughts per man from the mug."

The men gathered from all parts of the deck, forming two lines either side of the galley's midway. They had had three hours to rest. Initially drained from their rowing, they now suffered stiffness from napping on hard wood and the sear of the sun on their flesh. After Calli's order to cease their grueling toil, their bodies had littered the poop deck, some facing the sky, others snoring sideways on the durable planks. A few had returned to their benches, claiming the entire length of them as their own beds. It was almost dusk. Some of the men steadied themselves immediately, balancing on two legs. Others shook first one leg, then the next, to uncramp and stretch their muscles. Jacopo raised his limber arms skyward, unfurling them like two flags. He flapped both limbs up and down, hopped a dance with his legs, and opened and closed his mouth as if yawning. Sweat dropped from him as he moved.

"Oiled dough," Michael muttered to himself. "He looks like oiled dough."

Michael envisioned his mother's feast-day flatbread, how she pressed the black olives into the flour-and-water ball she mixed soon after dawn, kneading it with her knuckles, pressing it firmly with her fingertips until she successfully subdued its opaque bulk to translucent thinness so that it crisped evenly over the fire. As it heated, she drizzled dark oil over it, transforming it from the color of parchment to umber crustiness. How the oil always sizzled and the smell of browning garlic emanated from the cottage like an invitation to table! He wished he could taste some now.

"Come on, move along, one at a time," the armiraio urged.

The moans reminded Michael of cattle lowing. He listened to his shoulders crack as he worked them up and down, trying to untangle the muscles that, even though they no longer wielded the oar, remembered their labor.

"Ahhh," groaned Bronislav.

He stood, rotating his entire body, making swooping circles with his head. Then he spun his arms, trying to avoid hitting Michael as his hands rounded the air, opening and clenching his formidable fists. Finally, raising himself onto his thick toes, he dipped from his waist, five times left, five times right.

"Better," he said, his groan becoming more like a jungle cat's untroubled purr of contentment. "Always it is better when I unravel, when I circle." He talked to himself, his voice soothing, as it might have been, Michael imagined, were he consoling his son Franto after some injurious event. He sounded the way Michael's father did before Petros had died.

Michael saw that the wait for water was akin to the communion line at Father Elios's annual Easter celebration. On that day everyone, even the men who routinely scorned the sacrament as their women's excuse to rest from the daily toil of the household, went to Holy Mass. They took Christ's body—though it always tasted to Michael no different from his family's daily bread—into mouths used to cursing it. Here on the galley, too, men who regularly disdained water in favor of fermented drink, now pushed their way to the stocked wooden barrels whose contents, even at the start of the voyage, tasted at best of some stagnant pond on a heavy August day. But, just as consuming Christ's Risen Body assured their souls' salvation in case of sudden death, drinking the galley's barreled water promised their bodies immediate, if not permanent, protection from physical desiccation.

After the water, which was not nearly enough, Michael realized, having gulped his two mugs greedily, he chewed on a doughy biscuit which opened like a bowl and into which the cook had spooned a mixture of garlic, oil, and beans. Four bites later, Michael was done. He licked his fingers, sucking each one that offered a remnant of crumb or oil. He was still hungry.

"Attenzione! Attenzione!" the armiraio cried. "All are to gather before the prisoner. Everyone, now, before the prisoner."

The rowers shuffled to mid-galley, where Captain Loredan stood directly in front of the shackled man. The sailors of higher ranks, both noble-born Venetians and cittadini, Venetian citizens of the Republic's second social tier, formed a tight half-circle around the captain. The oarsmen, prodded by their disciplinarian, squeezed together in five tight rows so that they faced their superiors.

"Be seated," the captain ordered.

The rowers sat.

"Gesu," Jacopo blurted. "I did not look at the face before this."

Either side of their bench mate, Michael and Bronislav put their heads close to him to better know the cause of his surprise. Jacopo was so tardy boarding, he almost had had to leap onto the galley. He must have hurried right past the mast, relieved to have yet again escaped a steep fine or worse for not honoring his contract with Loredan and the Republic.

"He rowed with me to Corfu the last voyage there," Jacopo whispered. "He, Vincenzo, who rows from Bench Seventeen this trip, and I. I know his crime, though now I wish to our Savior I did not."

Michael looked about to see if others talked as he did. He did not recall meeting anyone named Vincenzo.

"What? What did he do?" Michael whispered. If others spoke, they also did so sotto voce, so as not to attract the captain's disapprobation or worse, a flogging for lack of discipline.

Just then, a Franciscan friar, if his robe could be trusted, walked from the water barrel to the pinioned prisoner. A large man, he moved his brown-draped bulk first left, then right. His breathing was labored, his mouth agape. Removing the rag stuffed in the man's mouth, he brought a mug of water to the prisoner's parched lips. The prisoner drank greedily, choking a bit, so fast did he quaff the liquid.

"Grazie, Padre Martino," the fellow croaked. The priest kept the muffling rag in his hands. He stuffed it into the mug and laid them both down on the deck, where he, too, finally sat, lowering himself tentatively onto a three-legged wooden stool. Like the others on deck, he watched the captain, waiting for Loredan to address them all. The friar's brown robe fanned out around him. His knees, spaced evenly, made a substantive table top for him on which he folded and rested his tightly clasped hands. Gray chest hairs had crept up from under his habit and now curled raucously over the neckline of his cowl. His red-jowled face and thick lower lip betrayed nothing.

Loredan watched the friar. His visage, too, was devoid of expression. When the priest at last was settled, the captain drew himself up, his chest expanding like a sail billowing in the wind, and placed his hands behind his back. He paced unhurriedly from one side of the main deck to the other as he spoke.

"First off, benvenuti a tutti," he said, "and my thanks for a seamless start to this important voyage." He moved his right arm over the assembled men, acknowledging and applauding their initial effort. He even smiled and nodded, Michael observed, to someone crouched low in the front line. Others must have noticed, as well, as not a few necks stretched to look. But Michael could not see well enough to be sure who the man was.

The cabin boy shimmied up the mast. Half way up, Michael saw, he paused to listen, his frizzed blond pony-tail lifting in the wind. He could not have been eleven. His legs, bare from the knees down, sprouted no hair. And not only was his face beardless, but his visage still retained the rosy, round cheeks of a well-fed prepubescent boy. Only the considerable length and breadth of his feet predicted his future stature. They jutted out from his thin ankles and, when he walked bootless, thwacked the deck timbers like the webbed feet of a creature from the deep.

Michael found himself drifting away from Loredan's voice. He wondered if the boy would one day row, too. He stared upward at his feet twisting about the mast.

Bronislav nudged Michael with his shoulder. "Attend to the captain," he said. "Pay attention."

Loredan continued. "As you know, we have been instructed to formalize Corfu's acquisition by the Republic. Therefore, barring unforeseen happenings of any kind, we are to proceed with watchful haste to the island that our doge and our Council have named la Porta, the Door. Corfu opens the whole of the East to us." Here he unclasped his hands and extended both his arms up and outward. "It is up to us, I shall say, to persuade—he drew out the word for an ironic effect that even the novice Michael did not miss—the Corfiots once and for all that Venice is their best protection and ultimate defense, most notably from the Turks and other infidels."

Bronislav yawned, covering his mouth with both hands. Everyone on board knew the Corfiots would comply, that they had neither the will nor the military force to protest. Nonetheless, Venice, whether represented by Loredan or any other respected member of the nobili, would make a spectacle of the takeover. On direct orders from The Council and the doge, this galley's men would set foot on Corfu as if they were in a grand parade from the Council chambers to Piazza San Marco to enact a new law. Michael stifled a satisfied laugh at Bronislav's apparent boredom. At the same time he wondered why Jacopo persisted in clasping and unclasping his slender fingers. The Venetian appeared as jittery as the Slav did torpid. The captain grew silent, even though he still kept his eyes on the men. If anticipation were an object to be felt, Michael believed he and the others must be touched by it. His own face itched and the expectation he felt appeared to make all the other oarsmen's bodies twitch, too, with waiting. Michael scratched first his chin, then the flesh between his nostrils and his top lip.

The captain paused to wipe his brow with his red silk kerchief.

"Now, you cannot have failed to notice that one of our intended rowers, one Ricardo Benis, has been relieved of his oar and is shackled here before you."

The prisoner lifted his head, his eyes wide open, his shirt sodden with sweat.

Until these words, the rowers had been sitting in a variety of poses, some with legs crossed crab-like, others with limbs splayed out in front of them, still more with knees pulled to chins. Now, as if on cue, they straightened. They lifted their necks upright and directed their eyes in line with the captain's. When Michael glanced upward toward Roch, he saw that the boy, too, pressed his head beyond the mast, forward of his body, and held himself completely still. All strained to hear.

"As our veteran oarsman Jacopo Serci is well aware"—at the pronouncement of his name, Jacopo flinched once and his hands grew still mid-clasp—"Ricardo Benis rowed our last voyage to Corfu. To that point, he had been a most able and obedient son of the Republic."

Now Benis turned his head to the friar. The friar motioned him not to speak, relieving his priestly palms of their prayerful pose to lift his hands and hold his right forefinger to his purple lips. His knees came closer together under his brown robe-table.

"However, late last month, just before we sailed for Manfredonia from Venice, The Council heard the testimony of five witnesses, among them Jacopo Serci." The captain pointed to Jacopo and, as if an exercise in harmony, the corps of rowers turned to the Venetian, who directed his eyes downward and fiddled once more with his hands.

The captain paused. Michael looked to Bronislav. The Slav did not move but to put his right hand on his cross.

Turning to Benis, the captain continued.

"The Council has found that Signor Benis is a thief and, because of his repeated thievery, also a murderer."

"No," the prisoner shouted. "He was dying anyway! Alba had a fever. He would not have lived anyway! Ask Jacopo Serci. Ask him yourself."

The rowers sputtered and grumbled among themselves, those who knew Jacopo gesturing at him, while those who did not merely stared.

"Silenzio!" the captain bellowed and, instantly, the only audible sounds were those of the creaking wood of the galley, the waves against the ship, and the constant rush of the wind.

"According to the various testimonies, Benis stole the food of his Corfiot benchmate, Christos Alba, who, early in the voyage, went blind from a great fever."

"But Captain," the prisoner protested.

The friar stood, the hem of his brown robe lifting from the deck and unfolding itself against his legs. He removed the rag from the mug, then ambled left and right again to the prisoner. Standing before Benis, the friar waved the rag in warning. Benis shut his mouth. The friar trundled back to his place on the stool.

Jacopo bowed and tucked his chin under his neck, as if to force it into his lean chest.

"Each meal time, after taking from the cook the mug and the biscuit rightfully Alba's, as he had been ordered to do," the captain paced once more, "Benis consumed portions of or the entire meal himself."

Michael stared at the deck. He was already hungry on the first day of their voyage.

"Eventually, according to sworn witnesses, among them, as I have indicated, Jacopo Serci, he gave no food at all to the sightless man, despite the man's pleading from his lonely pallet in the sick bay."

"But how did you know?" whispered Michael. He, too, kept his head down. "And what of this Vincenzo you mention?"

Jacopo answered softly, though he did not turn his face upward to look at Michael. "I lay in the sick bay, too, for three days with a clot in the leg." He rubbed his left shin.

Michael nodded.

"The day The Council called me, I wished to God that the doctor's log had been lost or the clot had not dissolved and I, too, had died," Jacopo continued. "If I had not told them the truth, I'd be next to damned Benis right now."

Michael looked to Bronislav, who nodded in agreement, his cross moving up and down on his torso.

The captain paused, his words enveloping the rowers like a threatening thundercloud.

"Therefore," he continued, and reached out his arm to the armiraio, who handed him a scroll rolled in a red banner of the

Republic. "Therefore," he said again, unrolling the scroll and reading from it, "I report to you The Council's decision."

The crew inhaled together, their intake of air marking both expectation and inevitability. They listened as the captain read:

"Let the sight of the setting sun on the first night of this voyage be Ricardo Benis's last vision."

Benis's bowels gave way and he soiled his breeches. His urine flowed onto the deck. The obese friar stood once more and, panting from the exertion, moved his stool away from Benis, lifting his brown robe to avoid the urine as he did. His face still betrayed no emotion. His feet, however, did not venture any more from under his habit.

Loredan continued.

"As soon as the golden orb dips below the horizon, his eyes shall be put out by the executioners of the Republic."

"No!" Benis screamed. "No!" His arms and legs rattled their fetters.

The rowers squirmed uneasily. Michael realized his own troubles were, by comparison, small. Jacopo lifted his right forefinger to his lips, rubbing it against them as if to apply a salve. Bronislav held his cross and mouthed a silent prayer.

Loredan went on, his voice devoid of any passion, as calm and clear as his command.

"In addition, the prisoner shall be offered no sustenance until he, too, dies from starvation. He shall endure the same fate he caused his fellow."

Now Loredan handed the scroll to his armiraio and placed his hands on his hips. He spoke directly to the rowers, not needing, evidently, to read the final words of The Council's sentence.

"Finally, upon arrival in Corfu, Alba's widow will be given Benis's full compensation for this voyage. She will do as she wishes with the convicted's body—whether it be dead or yet alive. She will, then, become fully cognizant of the perfect justice and merciful graciousness of our esteemed Republic."

Benis wept unabashedly and begged, "Mercy, please, have mercy on me, Captain."

Bronislav took hold of Jacopo's arm.

"Go now, go. Waste no time, you should go back to the bench. Be still and unobserved beneath the bench."

But the Venetian did not respond, instead sitting motionless where he was, his head now in his hands.

"No," he said, after a pause long enough for Bronislav to shake his arm as if to awaken one asleep. "No."

"Alright, then, we will stay with you."

Michael nodded at Bronislav's words, which he felt were feeble consolation to Jacopo and a command to himself.

The oarsmen rose. One of them, the orange peeler from the Manfredonian rooftop, Michael saw, kicked Jacopo's behind none too gently.

"Slime," he said, "watch yourself. I thought we had made a pact. If you kept quiet about him, I would be silent about you."

Michael pretended not to have heard, keeping his face utterly still. What had Jacopo done? Was his endangered secret worthy of Venice's justice, too? What did Vincenzo know? Michael looked to Bronislav to see if he might offer some answers. But the Slav's face was as still as sleep.

The cook flung buckets of salt water beneath Benis so that his urine mingled with sea wash over the deck. Still holding his robe up with one hand, the priest came close to Benis and made the Sign of the Cross on the prisoner's quaking forehead. Then the two men who had seized Benis as he boarded the galley emerged together from the ship's prow, parting the congregation of seamen with steps sure and measured, their heads hooded in black once more. Each wore a pair of tight-fitting leather gloves and rested his right hand on a shiny knife handle that warned of the lethal edge beneath his black tunic's belt. Both belt buckles bore the resplendent emblem of the Republic's lion forged in fire, the animal's majestic ferocity only slightly less convincing in the artisan's hammered metal than in its native feral turf. Benis looked like a human rag. Michael wished one among the crew possessed the fortitude to knock the condemned man unconscious before his ordeal. But who would dare?

Before he could contemplate becoming or search for such a reckless maverick, Michael was taken up as if compelled by an invisible force. The oarsmen, man for man but for Jacopo, who still sat cross-legged on the deck, rose, turned as one and faced the western sky, waiting and watching in fitful silence as the red sun, foretokening a hot day for the prisoner's dismal tomorrow, sank as it must into the waves.

"Now," Loredan's robust voice cut the air, and the men turned in unison to watch the functionaries of punishment strike.

"No!" Benis screamed, and the two hooded men, looking directly at him, counted, "One, two, three," then lunged.

The combined thrusts of their first-rate knives proved a model of practiced synchrony.

Blood and viscous matter sprang from Benis's eye sockets. Pieces hot and wet sprayed outward, glomming onto the clothes and exposed skin of the men closest to him even as the gore dropped and clung to his own shirt and breeches. His hideous screams pierced the air, his sharp, gasping ululations the unmistakable torment of one irrevocably damned. His chest heaved as if his heart itself would break through its clattering ribs. From above, Roch bleated like a lamb, then half-slid, half-fell off the mast, vomit dripping from his boy's mouth as if it were glutinous clumps of spoiled manna from a displeased heaven.

"Finito," the henchmen said to one another, their voices subdued as they backed away from Benis. They did not study his mutilated oculi, nor did they acknowledge the vexatious cacophony that, as was customary, accompanied their work. Instead, each wiped his gory blade with identical cloths that, when they were satisfied, they let drop into a barrel of salt water the armiraio had placed near the friar's stool. They might have been cleaning the evening's tableware at one of the noblemen's palaces. They did not remove their hoods. Instead they walked around rather than through the assembled sailors. Their steps no longer rang with the brisk, uniform, obedient clack of obligation to Venice. Instead their sluggish tread signaled the weary shuffle of two ordinary men whose unpleasant, sanctioned duty had, at least for the moment, been sufficiently and competently rendered.

Loredan strode to his cabin. Darkness fell. Jacopo was gone. And Michael longed for home.

"Come," Bronislav said. And the two made their way back to il bancho.

When they arrived at their post, they found Jacopo lying down, nearly under the bench with the piss pots, where Michael's place should have been. His rucksack covered his face.

"Michael must lie here," Bronislav said, poking the Venetian with his foot. "He is newest man."

"No," Jacopo countered. "Leave me alone."

Bronislav grunted.

"It is all the same to me," he said. Then, pointing to Michael, he went on. "Then you must lie close along the gangway, perpendicular to the bench as close as possible so no one steps on you during the night."

Michael nodded.

"I take il bancho. Oldest one of our triad. My reward." The Slav chuckled.

Michael, his eyelids twitching despite his effort to appear calm, nodded again. The galley lurched and swayed. Benis still howled, his agonized bays a terrifying mix of bodily torment, garish revulsion, and unremitting horror. Dizzy and losing his balance, Michael grabbed the edge of the bench and lay down.

"Sleep, you must sleep," Bronislav said. "It is the only way. We row again soon after dawn."

"Alright," Michael answered, but despite his palpable fatigue, he could not. Trying to lull his body into at least a semblance of quietude, he held his hands against his ears and let himself swing and toss with the ship. He raised his eyes upward, trying to stare at the heavens, but they blinked rapidly. Then, as if to calm and comfort the same eyes that had witnessed Venice's exacting justice, he covered them for a time with the mask of his two hands. But darkness was also daunting. Finally letting his hands drop to his chest, he clenched them tight and stared straight up at the constellations. He contemplated the unlikely possibility of rest. Contentment, let alone even temporary relief, he imagined, was perhaps too much to expect. If his experiences since leaving his tedious, unappreciated home were any indication, even a momentary respite from hardship might be presumed a rare and singular gift.

"We must trust in the Lord," his uncle's distant refrain joined the chorus of Bronislav's guileless snores, Jacopo's troubled groans, and Benis's agonized lamentations.

"Dear Lord," Michael whispered into the night. He breathed his prayer, questioning himself even as he uttered it. "Dear Lord," again he mouthed the words. But as his eyes closed, it was not God who answered him. Instead, Petros swooped down upon him from above, a gigantic, joyous bird, freed and fit and flying. "Michalli!" he called, smiling and dipping his wings in welcome greeting. "Michalli!"

And the galley slipped unaccosted through the night in a calm sea, only its human cargo subject to the unremitting tempests emblematic of our kind.

Chapter 9

DEBTS

Michael lurched awake. Cold metal skimmed his neck and a hand redolent of urine clamped shut his mouth.

"A sound and you will be gulls' meat."

The whisper was a snake's hiss.

His heart racing, Michael nodded and raised his hands, forcing his palms to open though his fingers tensed and wanted to be fists. The voice's arm pulled him up from his uncomfortable resting place aside Bench Five.

"Here," ordered the voice, pushing him out and away from the bench.

Michael stood to the right of the speaker, rubbing his eyes to adjust to the darkness. The night was illuminated by the brilliant constellations far above, where Michael wished he himself could fly. He dared not speak and tried unsuccessfully to match a name to the angry face in shadow beside him.

The man leaned down and kicked Jacopo's feet, causing the Venetian to flip from his stomach-down position to combat-ready pose—knees bent, soles outward, hands turned to fists, eyes fast blinking to identify and appraise the enemy. Only Bronislav's lusty snores contradicted the night's unexpected intrusion. It was as if the Slav slept eternally, already committed to his heavenly galley, his slumber the permanent rest to which every man is fated and some men untimely go.

"Hear this, you son of a whore," the man spit into Jacopo's face, his whisper harsh. "You put Benis out of his misery before you even think of chewing a piece of your own breakfast biscuit, or I'll be certain Loredan knows you buggered his sister's son, Lucca Loredan Venier, as sure as you saved the child from drowning."

Jacopo made to stand, but his enemy, the orange-peeler, Michael now realized, pointed his knife at him and blocked the way.

"Why so concerned about another spoiled brat of the nobili?" Jacopo hissed back. "Has Lucca become your little lover?"

At this the orange-peeler brought the point of his knife down to Jacopo's neck. Quick as a cat, the Venetian grabbed it with both hands, wresting it from the fellow and turning it back on him.

"Grab him," Jacopo shouted at Michael, but before the young Greek could decide, the orange-peeler thwacked his arm across Michael's face and ran.

"Bastard," Jacopo muttered, then, rising and crouching at the same time, walked from under the bench's hard awning and stood beside Michael. He tucked Vincenzo's knife into a pocket hidden inside his leather vest. "The boy would have drowned. It was Carnevale. He owes me his life. That is worth more than the cost of a quick poke, I should think." He laughed, no doubt justifying his actions to himself even as he related them to Michael. "He is surely some abacus school tutor's boy by now, if he is even yet of an age to leave his nurse." He paused. Then he cleared his throat and whispered, more to himself than to Michael, "So young, not more than six or seven years in this world. Slim and tight and fine as a Murano cylinder." Jacopo's voice smacked of satisfaction. "Hmm, I would like to enjoy him again." Then he chuckled and said, louder than he ought, thought Michael, "Damned delightful." He pulled his cloak around him, hugging himself. His voice became conspiratorial. "You, Michael," the Venetian continued, as if Vincenzo's potentially lethal interruption of their sleep was as common and as insignificant as a cough that wakes, "how about you? Have you ever tried a boy?"

"What do you think?" Michael growled. He sounded like his father berating him.

Chuckling, Jacopo slunk under the bench again. "I'll burn in Hell, I know," he continued, his whispers wet with spit. He unfolded himself under the length of the bench so he lay face upward. "But, truly, Michael, I can't help myself. They don't yammer like the women do, never require a seat and a mug at a bar, and if they cry or whimper, I can take them in my arms to comfort them."

Disgusted and determined to counter Jacopo's disturbing apologia with worry about Vincenzo's threats, Michael asked, "What will you do now?"

"Go back to sleep," Jacopo replied, pressing his enemy's knife flat against his chest.

Confused by the Venetian's seeming lack of concern over Vincenzo's threats, Michael shrugged his shoulders and, following Jacopo's example, lay down once more on his narrow slice of deck between il bancho and the gangway. Soon the Venetian's breathing became regular and his legs, prone to twitching, Michael had observed earlier, relaxed.

"Ach," Michael groaned and grimaced as his bottom rested against the heaving wood. He turned on his side, facing the bench and his bench mates as he tried to sleep.

Still snoring, Bronislav shifted from one side to the other on il bancho. His sonorous exhalations, uninterrupted during the entire troublesome encounter, restored the calm that had prevailed before Vincenzo's visit. They mimicked the rhythmic rocking of the galley, transforming the boat into a grown-man's cradle. His arms tight across his chest as he tried once more to sleep, Michael remembered his own father's snores when all of them—Theodore, Alda, Petros, Mina, and he, had slept together. How safe he had been then! A long time ago, it seemed. He closed his eyes, falling into the dream that would sustain him for many years at sea, the dream he would see and hear to block out what he could not or would not bear.

It is winter and I am but four years in the world. My Rhodes is not the island of history and myth. There is nothing colossal about it for me. It is simply the place of my family. We are together. The damp makes our bones ache, and we hunger for hot soup. The wind howls over the water outside. Pieces of it —"knives," Mama calls them—pierce the whitewashed walls of the cottage despite the tarp coverings over the windows. Mama arranges the dry twigs so the fire will last the whole dark night. Papa lies one side of the three of us, Mama the other. They touch hands over Mina, Petros, and me, each reaching out one arm to grasp the other's. Mina, who is older than I though younger than Petros, nestles her face into my neck, her long hair covering me like a blanket. Mama sighs, sometimes whispering "Dio" in her sleep. She rubs her feet together, making the coverlets, three of them, one on top of the other, move above us as the waves do outside. Here I am safe. There is no screaming, only the smell of garlic and wine from Papa's mouth. When it is morning, Mama will get up first, groaning her prayers. Papa right after. He will go outside and get more twigs. I will hear them talk in whispers, then I will sleep again until Petros jumps up and nips my neck with his teeth. "Michalli! I will get you!" Mina pushes him away, but he does not go. He nips my neck again and again until I reach out and grab his fingers.

"Stop, Petros."

It is not quite dawn. Petros still bites.

"Stop," Michael repeats, and uses his hand to slap at his brother. But Petros does not leave him alone.

Michael grabs for his brother's fingers, instead latching his grip onto something long and taut that pulls hard. He hangs on and opens his eyes.

"Ai-eee!" he yelled, but did not let go, even as the rat's paws scratched the deck and its long whiskers shook.

Angry, he yanked the tail. It was a piece of live leather fighting him.

"I'm stronger than you," he said, and he yanked again. Fully awake, he remembered where he was, that rats were as certain a part of the galley's population as its crew.

In a frenzy now, the rodent squealed in swift, rhythmic bursts, then turned and lunged at Michael. But Michael, still holding its tail, grabbed with his free hand the piss pot closest to him under the bench and smashed it over the rodent, stunning it into submission with a crash and an odiferous drenching. The rodent shuddered, then fell quiet and quivering. A second rat, something thick and pink and mottled protruding from its mouth, ran toward the first rat's distress. Then, evidently understanding the futility of fighting for its now-unconscious compatriot, the second rat stopped short, sat bolt upright before Michael and its fallen fellow, and paused to chew on its prize.

Michael watched transfixed, thinking of his own insufficient breakfast to come, until, as veritable morning paralleled the dawning in his mind, he realized that the rat was devouring a human tongue.

"Look!" He turned to his bench mates to share his unsavory discovery.

Jacopo, he had not noticed until now, was missing. Bronislav stirred and rubbed his eyes, paying no mind at all either to the rodents or to Michael. Not until Roch dashed by, up and down the gangway, crying, "Vincenzo has cut out Benis's tongue and killed himself!" did the Slav register surprise.

Michael made to yell after him, "But Jaco—," then thought better of it, and cut off his bench mate's name.

He watched the second rat push what was left of—could it be? —Benis's tongue into its busy mouth with its forepaws. It ate with rapidity, its sharp teeth shredding and mincing the still-pink meat. When it was done, it blinked and dropped its forelegs again to the planks. Then, nudging its unmoving mate with its snout to no avail, it twitched a moment this way and that, then dashed toward the cook, who was just now carrying by the morning's biscuits in the rough-hewn sack that the weevils counted as home.

Michael moved his own tongue over his teeth, feeling its moistness, realizing how it let him speak and swallow.

"Jesus," he said. "Jesus."

Bronislav sat upright and let his legs fall down from the bench.

"Saying your prayers, are you?" He scratched his bald pate. "Sometimes, my young friend," he went on, yawning and stretching his arms outward and then to either side, "sometimes your prayers are all there is to say."

Michael stood up and kicked the unmoving rat away from him. He crawled under the bench and took his fish-gutting knife from his rucksack. He finished the rodent with one long gash across its neck. Then, with Bronislav watching him, he took another of the piss pots, this one full of Jacopo's turds, as well as his piss, and poured its liquid contents over the rat to wash away the blood.

"What a mess you make," Bronislav scolded.

"Breakfast!" the armiraio called. "Then two hours rowing."

Bronislav stood up.

"We eat," he said. "Despite the events of the night."

Michael turned from the dead rat.

"You heard," he said, his voice a declaration, not a question. "You saw Vincenzo here."

He stared at the Slav.

Bronislav pulled on his boots.

"Of course," he answered. "What a racket."

"But you never stopped snoring."

The Slav stood, just an inch between the top of his head and the wooden awning.

"Of course not," he chuckled. "I am a good actor, no? An actor. Not a witness."

"I guess so," Michael replied. "You had me fooled." He felt angry at Bronislav, at how his mentor was not surprised by anything.

Bronislav stepped over the rat onto the gangway.

"You must learn not to be so easily fooled. You must learn to be able to fool. Otherwise you will become the fool. Listen to Bronislav, Michael. Finis. Except now you must clean up this mess."

Michael sighed. "And all you want to do is eat."

The Slav ignored his words, instead focusing on his own.

"We keep what we know between us, our secret. No Council questioning me or you. Just listen, watch, and be quiet."

He looked at Michael for confirmation. The young Greek nodded. Then, unable to restrain himself, he asked, "But do you think it was really Jacopo who did what Roch said? Jacopo had Vincenzo's knife. I watched him grab it."

Bronislav placed his right palm over his mouth and offered his left to Michael.

The young Greek turned away. As he did, Bronislav spoke.

"Watch your own tongue does not suffer one of Venice's more bloody customs, at least among its pugnacious young, and in some instances, not so young men."

"What do you mean?" Michael asked.

Bronislav, fully awake and ready for breakfast, replied, "A wagging tongue wags no more if it is cut out."

"Very well," Michael answered, his natural curiosity checked for the moment by judicious circumspection.

"Good," Bronislav replied. "Now let us eat. We cannot row otherwise."

And Michael understood, though it humiliated him to do so, that eating was exactly what they would do.

Chapter 10

CHOPPY WATERS

The galley crossed south and east, far now from Manfredonia, into and through the Adriatic on its journey to Corfu. Its rowers lost sight of one shoreline only to gain that of another. It felt good to wield the oar. The rhythm, the forward motion, the expectation that, at least for one hundred and twenty minutes by the hour glass, no unsettling fracas would force itself upon Michael and his fellows, transformed the grueling pull and thrust into an almost palpable peace. The oarsmen sang. Their voices became one voice that entered the air as the galley did the waters, filling both with the energy and the potency that was Venice.

Morning sun flared upon the waves. The sky stretched azure above the galley, though gray-black clouds threatened just above the horizon. Sea birds squawked and swooped, and Roch, when Calli counted the last three strokes, sprinted from one end of the ship to the other, "Wine at lunch today, wine!"

Only then did Jacopo let his cowl fall. He had slipped into his seat on the bench moments before the first stroke was called, cloaked.

"Dio!" Bronislav cried, forgetting to collapse after his last expenditure of strength. He clutched his heavy oar.

Michael stared open-mouthed at their bench mate, his own oar held in abeyance. Time might have stopped and Michael become a statue.

Jacopo's eyes looked like slits, so swollen was the flesh under them. His cheeks, their flesh usually nut-brown and taut, now plumped, two balls of dark dough under his eyelashes. Red scratches streaked his wiry neck.

"What happened?" Michael asked. He still gripped the oar.

Setting his own oar into its thole, Jacopo tried and failed to move his neck in circles over his torso. He winced and massaged his neck instead with his long fingers, a number of them, Michael could not help but notice, bruised a greenish blue.

"Vincenzo," Jacopo began, but Bronislav interrupted, his vocal intrusion a brusque command.

"Basta, enough," he ordered Jacopo, his voice as firm and certain as any captain's.

"Yes, of course you are right," Jacopo agreed. His fingers twitched by his sides, by choice or by nature, Michael could not guess.

"But why basta?" Michael asked.

His two older bench mates laughed, Bronislav directly at Michael, Jacopo, caustically and at neither of the other two, so intently was he nodding down at his fingers as he held them outward for inspection.

"What you have not heard you cannot know, oh, Innocent One," Bronislav told Michael. His tone was that of a patient, ironic schoolmaster.

Jacopo pulled his cowl back over his head. He stared at Michael's earnest face.

"In other words, Stupido, if you are ever called to testify against me, you can claim ignorance honestly," the Venetian said. Then, his voice full of undisguised resignation, "Not that your doing so will matter." He stood, hunched until out from under the parapet, then he stretched upward. "The Council will see to it that you say what they desire." He rubbed his lower lip with one long forefinger, as Michael had seen him do when Benis's sentence was read.

Michael shuddered, fearful that he would crumble at the mere suggestion of torture.

"You see what I did," Jacopo said. "I told them the truth." Jacopo spoke phlegmatically, a moist sigh emanating from deep within his lungs, and pulled the cowl close around his face. "And all the gowned bullies did was sit with me at a table beneath the plinth and the rope. The devil! I am as weak as my bastard of a father told me I was. I can master only boys, not men, not even myself." Then, as though his bench mates could not hear him, he muttered, "Would that I could master myself."

He kicked the bench, then left their post, storm clouds gathering directly above the galley as he went.

"What do you think..." Michael began, turning to Bronislav.

"Shhh," the Slav answered. "I am tired and must rest." He lay along the bench, and immediately began to snore.

Shrugging his shoulders, Michael crawled under the bench, found an overshirt in his rucksack, pulled it over his clammy trunk, and made his weary, curious way onto the deck to see what he could discover.

The looming storm clouds, now right above the galley, opened over him and rain fell as if poured from a monstrous, heaven-directed bucket, pelting the deck. Where Jacopo had gone, Michael could not imagine. No other oarsman rested in sight. Rain had made them willing prisoners of their benches. But agitated and confused, Michael needed to stretch and walk. So he hunched his shoulders against the wind and wet and strode the deck, first the starboard side, then the port. But for Roch, who crouched beside the cook's bench, he was alone.

"Ciao," Michael nodded to the boy and kept walking.

Roch nodded back. Then he stood and followed behind. He was a full two heads shorter than the young rower, and his bare feet thumped on the planks. Turning to him, first in puzzlement, then with approval, Michael noticed for the first time that Roch's eyes were round pools of green, wide open, as if poised in constant wonder, unable to shut out the observable world. Water droplets hung from his eyelashes, one drop pelted off and replaced by another in quick succession. Roch did not flinch from the liquid assault. Michael admired the boy's poise, while he himself did not hesitate to sweep his hand across his own eyelids every few moments.

"What's this?" Michael asked as the two walked, pointing to a narrow red rectangular tent, the tall mast rising through its center, that presently hid the prisoner Benis and the body of Vincenzo from view, Michael guessed.

Roch looked around, motioned to Michael to follow him, and held a finger to his lips. He gamboled like a goat, while Michael, with a heavier tread, followed fast behind him until they crouched by water barrels close to the carpentry, as far from the captain's quarters as possible.

"You are the one from Rhodes," Roch said.

Michael nodded.

"My captain speaks of you. He says you are smarter than a Venetian."

Roch flapped his feet up and down on the planks. Michael blushed, embarrassed to do so in front of a pup.

"Are Venetians smart?" asked Michael, recovering what he imagined ought to be his higher-ranking composure.

Roch hunched his shoulders upward so that his chin appeared to drop into the groove they made.

"I don't know," he said. "The chained one certainly was not." He pointed to the tent mid-galley where Benis no doubt still suffered. "Or the one who killed himself. Vincenzo."

"Are you Venetian?" Michael asked.

Roch stood up straight then. "Of course," he answered. "Captain Loredan allows only Venetians to serve him in his cabin." He stuck out his chin and his feet became still, as if a solemnity had come upon them.

"Is that so?" Michael countered, smiling from his crouch and looking up at the boy. "Then why does he have me?"

Roch knelt now, bringing his hairless face close to Michael's stubbly one.

"Because," Roch whispered, cupping his mouth with his ruddy hands, "because of The Death, of course. Too many Venetians, like my own mother and my father, have died." He sighed. Then he paused and, pointing at Michael's chest, said, "But not now. Now he has you, and he wants to keep you with him because you are better than Zen. I heard him tell the armiraio." His feet thumped the deck again. "I did."

"What does that mean, 'better?'" asked Michael. He could learn much from this boy. Perhaps he ought to befriend him.

Roch, still kneeling, spoke in a rush. "It means you will not be Zen's boy, that you will never let him bugger you again."

"Ai-eee!" Michael rose in a flash. He spat in disgust and burned with angry shame. Everyone knew. Everyone must know. His stomach churned and he glowered down at Roch.

Though he covered his face with his arms as if to ward off a blow, the cabin boy did not flinch or jump away, but instead knelt stalwart beneath Michael. However, the young Greek did not hit him. Instead, his voice shaking with fury, Michael demanded, "Did he do that to you too, then?" He was irate, and grabbed Roch, shaking him by the shoulders. "Did Zen bugger you, too?"

Roch stared straight at Michael's chest and said nothing.

"Did he?" Michael asked again, this time mastering his anger and letting his tone go soft. He drew a long breath inward and knelt to the boy.

Roch nodded his head and looked down.

"He and some others," he whispered. His lips trembled.

"Who?" Michael asked. "Who else? Captain Loredan? Did he? Does the captain bugger you?"

He felt ire rising through his torso again.

"Never the captain," Roch said. "Not even once. This captain, he is not like some others I have heard about. This captain does not even show his private parts. I must empty his bucket only after he leaves his cabin. I have never seen him naked."

"I see," Michael said.

Roch paused, then continued.

"Some say he is injured, that he is ashamed of a deformity. Or, I have heard from others, too, that he has sworn a vow, that he has promised not to do the deed with boy or man or woman so that he will not be taken by The Death."

Michael said nothing.

Roch looked up at him.

"But really, I do not know. Only I am glad that he does not use me that way."

Roch still looked at Michael. His eyes were wet with a liquid not the rain.

"But I mustn't tell," he said, "I must never tell. They will throw me in a sack and drown me if I tell even the friar in Confession." He thwacked his feet in a rhythm that betokened urgency. "I have seen them do it to another." Michael watched a shudder course through the boy. "They did it to Mattias, the carpenter's apprentice. He tried to fight them. They seized him when he tried to go to the captain in the night to tell him. When he did not report to the carpentry in the morning, Jacopo told the captain he had flung himself overboard, gone mad from a vision of the Devil. When his mother met our galley at the pier, they told her he had died of a fever, that his last words were 'Mama, Mama.'"

Both Roch's feet thumped the deck's boards.

Michael stood, the indignation within him like the steaming fog that now was enshrouding the galley in a thick, grey smog. Was this mighty Venice, too? Perhaps he had made a mistake. Could his mother have been right? What did his humble father Theodore know?

"Come," he called to Roch. He strove to speak as Bronislav had spoken to him in Manfredonia. He would be calm and soothe the boy. "Let us discover the meaning of the tent and the captain's decision to serve wine."

"You will help me, then?" Roch asked, as Michael loomed above him.

Michael did not know how to answer.

"Will you?" Roch's eyes bore into his own.

"Roch!"

Loredan's voice pierced the miasma that pressed upon the deck.

"Vieni, come, Roch!"

The boy leapt into action.

"Si, Captain, I come, I come!"

As the boy ran toward Loredan's voice, disappearing into the murky distance, Michael started back to Bench Five.

"Wait," a voice called to him. It was Jacopo, his head emerging from under the temporary tent. He slithered out from under the thick russet folds of patterned fabric and slowly raised himself to face Michael. He stood so close that Michael could not tell his breath from the fog. Jacopo looked like a snail in shadow, so curved into himself was his posture.

"I went to beg his forgiveness," he said. "I needed Benis's forgiveness." Then Jacopo, no hint of the sarcastic clown in his tone or demeanor, crumbled before the novice recruit. "But he was dying. Shit, Michael, he was nearly dead."

Puzzled, Michael stared at stooped Venetian.

"But how?" he asked.

Hugging himself tightly, Jacopo spoke.

"Vincenzo and I fought. I came upon him not long after he had cut out Benis's tongue. Made the poor bastard drown in his own blood."

Jacopo's body shook, his quivering voice matching his twitching frame.

"Benis was spitting red, choking, unable even to gasp. 'Forgive me,' I pressed myself against him, felt his heart stop and start, so fast, too fast. 'Forgive me,' I begged."

Now the Venetian wept openly and raised his bloodied hands toward Michael. Gone was any sign of lewdness or his aping way.

"Then, after but two—I will never forget the sound!—desperate, I tell you, desperate gurgles from deep in his throat, he was dead."

His voice became a whisper.

"So Vincenzo and I fought."

Jacopo shuddered, then closed his eyes. His body quivered, Michael supposed, with memory still fresh.

"But why? Why did Vincenzo cut out his tongue?" Michael pressed for an answer.

Jacopo opened his eyes, rolled his shoulders forward so that his chin touched his chest, and paused before he spoke.

"Because Benis wanted to confess to the friar. Because he had asked Vincenzo to fetch the friar. And Vincenzo knew he was part of the confession."

It was Michael who whispered now.

"What did they do?" he asked.

Jacopo rubbed a long finger across his lips.

"What did we do, Michael. *We*," he said, taking his finger from his lips and jabbing at his own chest. "What we do every chance we get." Jacopo hugged himself. "I am damned," he whispered. "Even with Vincenzo dead, I damn myself."

Michael ran his hands up and down the sodden tent cloth, seeing in his mind's eye the dead men within while staring at Jacopo without. A trio of wrongdoing. But what was their crime?

"Jacopo, how ill was your deed that Benis needed to confess?" Michael asked, stopping the motion of his hands, focusing instead on the Venetian's face.

Jacopo laughed, the sound of his voice in the fog a phlegm-ridden cough.

"The worst kind," Jacopo grunted. "Against innocence," he said. "Against the most innocent of all."

Michael did not understand. He wanted to understand.

Jacopo sat down on the deck. He crossed his legs and held his head in his hands.

"But he, you, all of you, would have been forgiven," Michael said. His uncle had told him that. His uncle had promised him the sacrament would transform sin to forgiveness if the penitent were remorseful and pledged to sin no more.

Again, his hands ran the length of tent, the red fabric flocked in gold with the lion of the Republic, the lion that Michael knew brooked no miscreants, be they noble or not.

Jacopo looked up at the young Greek.

"You are ignorant, Michael, completely ignorant."

His voice had reclaimed its usual sardonic tone.

"What do you mean?" Michael asked.

Jacopo held up his right hand so that Michael could lift him. The Venetian smelled like old blood and new fear. He stared close into Michael's eyes.

"A priest's forgiveness is one thing," he said. "A spy priest's forgiveness is but another route to torture and the gallows."

In the same instant he heard Jacopo's words, Michael pictured both his uncle and the friar. What would Elios do? Could the friar be one of Venice's spies? Might Jacopo's assessment of the Franciscan be true? How could Michael find out, let alone be certain of any discovery?

"Watch to whom you confess, my boy. Or, better yet, keep your sins to yourself."

Michael stood quiet, thinking, but unable to reach any conclusions.

"Did Vincenzo kill himself?" he asked finally.

His question stabbed the fog, puncturing it so that daylight might break through.

Jacopo did not answer. Then he laughed again at Michael.

"What do you think?" he answered.

Michael shrugged his shoulders.

"I don't know," he said.

Jacopo played with his hands, tossing an imaginary sphere back and forth. Michael watched. Then the Venetian stopped, grasped the imaginary ball for a time, and flung its vaporous self to Michael, who made as if to catch it.

"And I'm not telling," the Venetian said. "Only that Commander Loredan found Vincenzo's knife in the son of a bitch's hand, the mark of its blade a match for the slash across his throat."

Then the Venetian slumped, as if all the air had gone missing from his lungs. Michael took him in hand at once, as he ought, as he must, although he did not want to. And the two bench mates, the younger one holding the older man's arm, shuffled together through the hazy swirl. Less sure of the facts than he had been before his questions, Michael now was barely hopeful that their slippery footing on the vaporous deck would lead them both wherever they needed to go.

Chapter 11

THE WEATHER CHANGES

When the fog lifted, just as Bronislav had promised, Michael inhaled Corfu. The heavy salt nebbia rose and dissipated into a sky on the way to azure in the warm Ionian sun.

"Myrtle," Bronislav spoke matter-of-factly. He breathed deeply, folding his large hands on top of his lap and closing his eyes, as if by doing so, Michael imagined, he could consecrate the spicy fragrance in memory.

The captain had dropped anchor hours ago, as soon as the fog obscured the Ionian coast. He had been traveling close to shore, "coasting," as the experienced sailors said, making it possible to escape the eerie, dangerous drifting in the fog that could send a galley off course, sometimes to rocky islands and smashing ruin.

Now that they could see clearly again, the oarsmen on Benches Four and Six, front and back of Michael's bench, resumed the games of chance they played between rowing and sleeping hours. The men's voices rose and fell, goading, groaning, and mocking, vacillating with the vicissitudes of their wins and losses.

"So much noise," Bronislav murmured, and again inhaled the myrtle fragrance, his broad chest rising with his uptake of air.

Jacopo had taken his predictable position, face-down on the deck, head hidden by his cowl. When Roch approached, his long feet, dry now as they met the deck, Jacopo barely moved.

"The captain requests the three of you join him in the tent," the boy said. He looked to Michael as he spoke. Neither Bronislav nor Jacopo indicated any interest in his message. "Hurry," he said, turning to go as he did. "You must not keep him waiting."

Bronislav opened his eyes, rubbed them with both hands, and turned to Michael, whose own face was animated with curiosity. The Slav shrugged his shoulders, as if to indicate his lack of knowledge about what was to ensue with Loredan. Without rancor or force, he kicked Jacopo's feet to rouse the Venetian.

"Shit," Jacopo muttered, and pulled his cowl tighter over his head.

Bronislav nudged him again. "Come," he said. "Duty requires it."

The trio made their way to the recently erected tent from which Jacopo had emerged earlier during the thickest fog.

No myrtle fragrance greeted them when Roch let drop the thick tent flap he held aloft to let them in. Rotting human flesh overpowered what should have been the welcoming bouquet of the captain's just-poured wine. Right before them, inches away from their feet, Vincenzo's scarred body lay wrapped in nothing but a fish net. Adjusting his eyes to the tent's shadows, Michael stared first at the fellow's crossed hands and feet. But then the jagged slash of a monster's grin across his neck drew and held his attention completely. It moved with the rocking of the galley, a taunting smile, a reminder of the sinister secret Michael wished he did not harbor. The tent spun. His knees weakened. He would have fallen were it not for Bronislav's steadying hand.

"Good, you are all here."

Loredan spoke as if all were well, as if the stench of rot did not permeate the air they now all breathed. He sat at a tray-sized narrow rectangular table, seven tumblers arranged close together in a row, each one filled with wine. One side of him stood the stout friar, his hands hidden within the folds of his brown sleeves, his eyes focused on the tumblers rather than the other men, his lips neither smiling nor frowning. On the other side towered the two executioners, their faces, too, offering no hint of Loredan's agenda. Behind the captain and against the wall of heavy fabric rested a new-carved coffin, the top portion of its divided lid opened to reveal Benis's mutilated face.

The captain spoke.

"We will make a procession to Corfu dock in the morning. You will all accompany me."

Now Loredan stood.

"Friar, after introducing Jacopo as one who served justice, and showing the punished Benis to his victim's widow, you will commit the now-deceased rightfully to his God, he having certainly paid for his sins."

The captain handed the friar and Jacopo each a tumbler.

"Grazie," the priest answered, his voice a reassuring rumble.

Jacopo nodded, his hood in place despite the hot and fetid air inside the tent.

"Executioners, you will display the body of Vincenzo, this most unruly Venetian and ignoble suicide, to the assembled Corfiots. Then, without benefit of the friar's blessing, you will relegate him to the deep, his soul unworthy of salvation."

Loredan handed each of the two his wine. Michael watched the friar's face for a sign, but none was forthcoming.

"Michael," Loredan pointed to one of the remaining tumblers for the young Greek to take up, "You will accompany me as my personal aide, wearing a tunic of the Republic."

Michael felt himself spin again. He spread his legs to balance himself.

"You will address Benis's widow as if she were a member of the nobili."

Michael nodded.

"Now, then." Loredan raised his drink. All stood, holding their drinks, but for Bronislav. After a lengthy pause, Loredan spoke again, this time his tone more personal than official.

"Ah, my unflappable Slav, for you awaits a surprise."

He handed Bronislav a tumbler.

"Would you like to know it?"

Bronislav bowed from the waist.

"As you wish, Captain." The Slav did not assume an intimacy equal to his superior's tone.

Loredan considered.

"Let it wait then. That way you may savor the anticipation."

Bronislav smiled and bowed once more.

"So be it, then, my Captain," he said.

Loredan looked to his wine. The others followed his lead.

"Wait!" he exclaimed, "I must not forget." And, taking the last tumbler from the table, he motioned for Roch to take it from his hand.

"Really?" the boy asked. His webbed feet thumped on the deck.

Loredan nodded, a slight smile crossing his face.

The boy nearly spilled the wine as he lifted the tumbler with his two hands while one splayed foot bumped against a table leg. At his ineptitude, the friar allowed a chuckle. Kindly though it seemed, Michael watched the priest's eyes.

"To Venice," the captain said.

"To Venice," the others repeated, and they drank.

When they were done, Loredan nodded to Roch to lift open the tent flap. They were dismissed. The executioners left first, followed by the friar, who, at the Slav's whispered request, made the Sign of the Cross on Bronislav's forehead. As Jacopo followed, Roch sneezed, and the tent flap dropped, so that Jacopo's cowl was knocked from his head. The Venetian hurried to pull it back in place, but was too late to avoid the captain's notice.

"Jacopo, to what do you owe those injuries?" he inquired. Loredan's smile was just short of a smirk.

The Venetian's face was mottled with black and blue splotches and a screed of red scratches marred his cheeks and neck. Hardly anywhere did the nut brown of his natural color show itself. He appeared, instead, a human canvas portraying recent tactile hostilities.

He paused, but only for an instant, one foot outside the tent, the other in, close to Michael, who was most eager to breathe fresher air.

The Venetian looked at the young Greek, then at Loredan.

"Michael will tell you, Captain. Michael knows what happened."

At Jacopo's words, the captain turned his attention to the young oarsman. His face showed interest and curiosity, his almost-smirk reduced to a simple anticipatory smile.

Michael's stomach flipped up and down, up and down, as if it understood and shared the frenzied ruckus in his mind. He was trapped. He could name Jacopo the murderer he likely—no, certainly—was, or he could let him remain blithely free. The truth, something his Uncle Elios had assured him was absolute and irrevocable, had now become his own to alter.

"Tell him, Michael," Jacopo urged, smiling himself now.

The captain waited while the wily Venetian wrapped one of his slender, muscular arms around Michael's sturdy waist.

"You are my bench mate, after all. There is little about me you do not know." His voice sounded reassuring and kind. Again he smiled at Michael.

Michael looked out past the tent flap, where the air flowed clean and fragrant with myrtle. Where he longed to be and breathe. Instead, he inhaled yet another lung's worth of the still, foul atmosphere inside the fatal fabric enclosure.

"Rats." He heard his own cracking voice break the stultifying silence. "I caught a rat and threw it at Jacopo's piss pot and hit him instead. The rat clawed Jacopo when he fell."

"Perfect!" the captain snickered, and poured himself more wine.

"I hope the pot was empty," he said, and took a sip of the dark red liquid.

Blood. The word coursed through Michael's brain. So much blood on a voyage so brief, a voyage so outwardly calm, a voyage without so much as a quick skirmish with pirates.

"No such luck," Jacopo replied, holding his nose between thumb and finger at the alleged memory of excrement. Letting his arm drop from Michael's waist, he stared grinning at his bench mate.

"Ha!" Loredan laughed. "And the rat, Michael, did you at least kill the rat?"

Michael had already played this game before boarding the galley. Only this time his lie, the lie he knew he would tell, did not concern only himself and his own ignorant shame.

The captain looked to Jacopo, who returned his gaze with one just as direct. Michael could tell by now that each was playing a part, both waiting and watching to see how he would play his own. Was this what it meant to be Venetian? To dissemble? To invent on the moment? How could he hope to survive? The young Greek's shoulders slumped in momentary defeat and his heart skipped several beats in his chest.

"No, Captain," he said. "I did not kill the rat." Then he added sotto voce, "Though I should have. I should have then and there."

Michael looked behind the captain to Benis's abused corpse, finally casketed in rest, then down at Vincenzo's tied and wrapped in fish net. His own soul, he was certain, was rotting now, as did both men's flesh. And Temptation incarnate, Jacopo the Venetian, had seduced and doomed him with a facile smile and a genial invitation to lie.

"The rat got away, Captain."

Michael's voice broke entirely.

"I let him get away."

Both Loredan and Jacopo guffawed, as if brothers, while the young oarsman bolted, running the length of the galley. Michael rammed a fist into his mouth, trying unsuccessfully as he warded off calls of greeting from his fellows, to subdue the futile sob that heralded ignominy.

Chapter 12

CORFU

"Now, Michele," his captain intoned, priest-like, as he rose to his full height from the collapsible wood-carved throne that Roch had centered on the cobblestoned walkway connecting the dock to the town. On either side of him stood the executioners, dressed in the sober black cloaks of their office. If they suffered from the press of the afternoon sun, their erect positions never told. Ramrod straight, they stood poised to execute Loredan's commands.

Michael stepped forward, five broad paces in front of the captain, and bowed from his waist to Alba's widow as he had been instructed beforehand by Loredan.

Her face was veiled, her long, modest gown looked the color of wheat, so much lighter was it than the attire of the Venetian men, whose black tunics attested to the Republic's preference for sober and uniform serviceability rather than seasonal sensibility. Commander Loredan himself had seen to Michael's dress.

In his quarters before the group boarded the tender to Corfu, Loredan had told him, "You shall wear Venice, whose islands are soon to become your new home." And Roch had motioned for Michael to lift up his arms and take on an ebony tunic whose mustard-colored lion of Saint Mark bared its teeth across a woven, dark magenta applique on the chest. "There," Loredan had said, apparently pleased as he turned Michael full circle. "Now you are 'Michele.' That is your new Venetian name, the name by which you will answer to me."

With a jolt, his father's face appeared before him and Michael realized that Theodore would have felt Loredan's words a stinging slap. He would have growled in protest. "You are a Greek!" he would have insisted to his son. "A Greek!" Gone, too, but for in his dreams, would be Petros's familiar childhood half-taunt, "Michalli, Michalli, I am coming to get you!" Michael would miss it, and crave it in hard times. Would he—Michalli, Michael, the boy from Rhodes—now keep his birth, his name, and his family only in memory? Did service to Venice require he renounce his very self?

"Michele."

Loredan's brusque call now commanded Michael's attention once more.

The young oarsman rose from his bow to face Alba's widow, who waited before him.

The moment he did, Loredan handed Roch a small wood-carved case. The cabin boy, one of Loredan's scarlet scarves tied around his neck, brought the case, heavy though it was for him, to Michael's hands.

"Grazie," Michael said. The case burdened his hands, so full it was with Venetian coins.

He opened the case and showed it to Signora Alba, who, blocking the sun with her right hand, stared into it. At the sight of the plenty within, she wobbled, and a thick, mellifluous sob rose from deep within her bosom. Quickly shutting the case and holding it close to his side under one arm, Michael held her erect with the other. She tried to manage her breath. After inhaling a few times and wiping her brow with her veil, she succeeded, and her chest rose and fell steadily, albeit in a rhythm more rapid than Michael's own breathing.

"Signora," he said, his lines having been rehearsed with Loredan earlier. "Signora, you find inside this casket proof of the perfect justice, unwavering honor, and certain generosity of the Venetian Republic."

At his words, the woman curtsied and opened her mouth to speak. But Loredan stood before she uttered a word and said, "Signora, the doge and all his representatives thank your husband for his service to Venice. He has been greatly wronged. And, as my assistant Michele will now show you, we ask for your preference regarding the disposition of the man who wronged him."

Attentive to his cue and still holding the case, Michael motioned with his free hand for the woman to approach the executioners. They stood at the edge of the dock, guarding Benis's remains.

"I wish to see him," the woman said, her voice tremulous. The water lapped against the dock and a motley crowd gathered in a half circle around her.

Two old women stood to Signora Alba's left, one with a humped back and a swirling head of stark white hair, the other barely balanced by two crude canes, her hands gnarled but her visage open and alert. Four young fishermen stayed well behind her, their faces burnished by wind and sun. The shortest of the quartet held a net over his shoulder. Another displayed on his sandy tunic the remnants of his catch's guts. And the last two—brothers, no doubt, so similar were their features and gestures—swallowed their lunches of crusty bread stuffed with squid, before they folded their hands in a quasi-prayerful pose. Finally, a person of noble stature both in bearing and attire appeared from behind a succession of myrtles. He appeared to be a cleric, his ankle-length white robe and pointed leather slippers a stark contrast to the others' humble apparel. Taller than everyone else in the group, he tucked his right hand under a chiseled, shaven chin and pressed his forefinger against an aquiline nose. He stood straight and rigid as a pole. Ignoring the others, he nodded in a clipped fashion toward Loredan, who, returning the nod with one of a more supple nature, stood.

Loredan motioned to the functionaries. In a swift movement either side of the casket, they lifted the upper portion of the lid. The widow approached.

"Dio!" the woman cried, hiding her face with her hands. Michael steadied her again, all the while keeping his grip on the valuable case of coins.

Benis's gouged eyes and mauled mouth now coursed with maggots. He was alive with death. Michael held his breath, but did not avert his gaze. Instead he stared at the wriggling creatures. Were they the eternal life his uncle spoke of? Was one's body mocked even in the afterlife? Were he himself not dressed in the lion and conscious of his duty to his captain, he might have given over to the nausea that rose within his chest.

"Now then," Loredan spoke, causing Michael to shift his attention from the living death to him. The captain came to stand between Benis's casket and Alba's widow. "I ask you, signora, if you would like to impose further abuse yourself upon this man. Or, should you prefer, our executioners will see to his burial in sacred ground, he having now paid for his crime."

Taking her hands from her mouth, the widow said, though she could hardly be heard but by Loredan and Michael, "Set the coffin alight and throw it into the sea. I cannot see him burn in Hell. The fire you make must be enough."

Loredan cued the executioners and they set about their task. As they busied themselves, the woman took the case of gold from Michael and, grasping it tightly against her breast, backed away from the Venetian party, stopping where the dock met the cobblestones of the port. The two old women followed and stood one either side of her while the fishermen dallied, watching the executioners work. The white-robed cleric, acknowledging none of them, each of whom had deferred to his status with a Sign of the Cross at his approach, remained poised and aloof. From time to time he ran his thumbs over his nails and gazed at his hands, making sure, Michael surmised, that they evidenced the same observable purity of his dress.

Flames burst from the now-floating coffin while Signora Alba wailed the customary widow's lament (somewhat feebly, Michael observed, given her more robust response to the coins). The friar murmured prayers in his growling voice. Loredan wet his lips with his tongue. Jacopo and Bronislav stood in their inevitable poses—Jacopo hooded, head curved into his neck; Bronislav, thick arms crossed over his chest, his cross-with-hidden-knife gleaming over them like a shield. Roch, closest to the water, shaded his eyes from the sun and thwacked his right foot again and again onto the stones where he stood, unaware, Michael sensed, of his own repetitive motions. And Michael, already sated with death, watched with a steadfast gaze as Benis, Signor Alba's nemesis, met his final doom. A man whose own appetites had condemned him was now himself devoured.

Chapter 13

MICHAEL MEETS CLARIO CONTARINI

"Clario," Loredan bellowed when the flames at last subsided and Signora Alba had disappeared from view. "Don't tell me you are actually a priest! What does your family say?" The captain laughed broadly and strode toward the man who stood like an alabaster pillar and waited for him to approach rather than meet him halfway along the path.

"Alas, my friend, it is my family that has ordained me one," the man answered. His voice was shrill, not unlike the caw of a gull. He stretched out his hand, palm down, and Loredan grasped it.

"They believe holy orders will protect me from my failings, such as they are, or are imagined to be." He let Loredan's hand drop. "Of course, what my progenitors really want to protect is the Contarini honor, or at least the face of it." Here a series of small, pecking coughs interrupted his apologia, and he covered his beak-like mouth with the ringed hand that had just enfolded the captain's.

"At any rate, because of my canonical status, I am saved from both commerce on the high seas and marriage to some vapid, virginal ragazza of the nobili," he said. "I do take some solace in that." He coughed once more. "Neither the mercantile nor the marital status is to my liking," he continued, "both enterprises espousing the same principles." His peaked, and perhaps charcoaled, eyebrows rose at his pun.

The captain laughed and wrapped his arm around the clergyman's waist. The priest did not appear to mind. In fact, he smiled close-mouthed and tipped his head close to Loredan's face.

"The ragazze are not all so bad," the captain countered. "I have enjoyed not a few myself in the past, before The Death warned me against them."

He locked eyes with the priest.

"Why, you might have one of my nieces, one of my sister's daughters." The captain laughed broadly once more. His hands left the cleric's waist and he clasped them together.

"At least you'd be sure of a generous dowry. And, my brother-in-law, Cantuccio Venier, being dead, God rest his soul and damned be the Devil's own plague, I'd be certain to let you have your pick of the four girls. Perhaps Marina, the one wrongly unbetrothed by that bastard Zen. What an embarrassment for my sister, Elena! She has not left her apartments since, not even for the revels of last year's Carnevale, when her son nearly drowned. And don't think Zen has not paid for his betrayal. Don't think he will not continue to pay should I have any say in the matter."

The captain had forgotten himself, Michael could see. His entire body vibrated with fervor on behalf of his family's besmirched honor. But quickly he recovered himself.

"My apologies, Clario, I go on too much. But you understand, they are my sister and my niece, without Cantuccio to protect them. And Zen, well, he should have done better by them."

"Ah, our families," Clario countered, "blessings and burdens. Splendid advocates or detestable vilifiers. Which are they?"

He turned a substantial ring around and around his finger.

"In my case, signor, both, their solicitude as variable as the moon." He pointed skyward. As he did, he brought his hand to his mouth and kissed the ring. "Of course, I shall be glad to assist your niece in any way I can. Perhaps preside at her nuptial Mass, when the occasion arises."

Loredan bowed to the cleric.

"As priest, then, not husband?"

Clario scowled. The captain nodded, and covered his mouth with the palms of his hands.

"Alright, I promise, no more."

"Correct. Priest, not husband. I am unfit for that role. Of this fact I have been duly apprised by a lady, my own blessed mother, whom I am powerless to dispute or defy." The cleric's caw diminished to the cloying whine of a bird with a mutilated wing, and he looked downward, his eyes fixed in place longer than custom accorded. In fact, so long did his gaze linger that Michael counted ten laps of the wavelets on the dock and heard a church bell clang the half-hour.

"Well, then," Loredan said, with apparent recognition of Clario's momentary melancholia. He again put his arm around the cleric's waist and, head to head, they spoke only to each other, the captain's booming voice and the cleric's strident one lowered to whispers that betokened calmer and more intimate conversation.

Roch gamboled from the water's edge and motioned for Michael to lean down to him. Cupping his right hand over Michael's left ear, Roch whispered, "That one, the priest, he is a member of one of the most important families in Venice."

"Yes?" Michael inquired, his tone encouraging the boy to tell him more. "Why, as you say, so important?"

Michael pointed toward the water so the two could talk where Loredan and the unlikely cleric could not hear them. Jacopo, Bronislav, and the executioners had made for the town, Loredan having exhorted them, "Until dusk, you are free men." Only the friar remained behind. Having lowered his lumbering frame onto the grass away from the dock, he, after great effort, lay prone in the shade of a myrtle grove. His body resembled a brown mound of soil awaiting spreading by some gardener. He appeared to sleep, his mountain of flesh rising and falling with each sonorous breath.

"Yes," Roch went on, walking backward so that he faced Michael. Now and again, the young Greek had to push the boy's left shoulder away from the water's edge so he would not lose his balance and fall into the harbor. "His grandfather was a hero against the Genoese, in Chioggia with Pisani. Already then he was an old man. But still he fought." Roch hopped up and down with excitement. "The Great Council had to force him to become the doge." The boy stopped. "They threatened to take away all his property in Padua if he would not consent to his election. Imagine, he did not want to be doge, so humble he was, in spite of his fame."

"È vero? Really?" Michael asked. He smiled at Roch's zeal. Like himself, he realized, the boy could forget himself in a story. Petros would have enjoyed regaling him.

"Yes," Roch replied. "And this one," he pointed now to the man Loredan had called Clario, "is his grandson. Perhaps he will be a doge someday as well, even if he is a priest." The boy paused to consider. "But it will have to be a long time from now. He is too young yet. The Council does not elect the young, as they, we," he corrected himself, "are too prone, the captain tells me, to accept bribes."

"I see," said Michael. "And what else do you know about the Con—?" he began, when a swift gust of wind from the sea almost knocked them over. A trio of gulls, each bird itself buffeted, oscillated over the distant figures of the captain and the cleric, one or more of the birds defecating directly onto Clario Contarini's head so that he screeched an obscenity that Michael had only recently learned from Jacopo.

At the fracas, the friar woke, sat up, and, inferring what had happened, laughed out loud and slapped his knees over and over in evident delight at the cleric's shat-upon head. Until then, Michael had never seen the Franciscan smile.

"Shut up!" Clario cawed at him, ignoring Loredan's own enjoyment of his trivial misfortune. Then, recognition filling his eyes, he spat at Friar Martino, "Shut up, you disgusting piece of lard. You glutton. You are not my school master any more."

Michael recoiled at the cleric's outburst, while Roch covered his mouth with both his hands.

The friar bent his head, turned on his stomach, then struggled to his feet by pressing his hands palms down on the grass and lifting one leg at a time. He panted.

"True on both counts, my dear Contarini. I am no longer he who attempts to teach you the precepts of the Church or the language of the Mass. And I am most assuredly, most sadly, a man burdened by an immoderate propensity for the comestibles our Lord provides. You speak the truth. You are in the right."

The friar spoke as if the cleric were his friend. No apparent anger accompanied his words. His implacable demeanor, Michael saw, further agitated Clario, who once again twisted his ring.

"In fact, try as I might, I am unable to rid from my mind memories of the magnificent suppers your family saw fit to share with me. The fried zucchini flowers, the olives, the..., all of it." The friar closed his eyes and patted his stomach. He appeared the picture of longing. "How fares your dear mother? When did you last see her?"

From under his pearly habit, Contarini took a handkerchief and wiped his pate, smearing the pasty excrement rather than removing it. He shook his head with perturbation.

"She writes she is well. She is a widow now, wielding a widow's power." Contarini directed his words to the captain. "I have not seen her for the better part of a year." Then he added, "Which is exactly why I term these months 'better.'"

His words snapped as he spoke them. Between snaps he looked at the soiled handkerchief and shook his head at the sky.

"But soon, soon I return to Venice and her onerous oversight, with the music master, Maestro Romano, who, at the widow's request, is to found a boys' choir at San Marco. I am to instruct the boys in all matters not musical."

"Ah, I see," said the friar. His face took on a disquieting look. He clasped his hands together and wrung them. Then he turned away, all indications of his recent humor having disappeared.

At the mention of the maestro and San Marco, the captain became business-like.

"Come," Loredan's now-temperate voice seeming an attempt both to pacify and occupy the cleric. "That is the purpose of our meeting. Let us retrieve the copies of your letters of introduction and recommendation to your mother and Maestro Romano for my trusted Bronislav's son Franto, missives for which I am, and, I assure you, Bronislav's family will be entirely grateful."

Loredan turned away from the cleric and called out, "Roch, come now, Roch, go with Father Clario and bring his papers to me that we may show Bronislav his surprise."

"Yes, Captain," Roch replied, and started toward the two men.

At this, the friar took on a sudden energy and scuttled from the myrtle grove, moving his legs as fast as he could. As if the boy were himself a tray full of succulent meats, he attacked Roch, launching himself at him so that the cabin boy fell backwards onto the ground, surprised and confused.

"Roch, I am sorry," the friar said, his voice full of condolence and remorse. But as soon as the boy tried to stand up, the Franciscan held his legs to the ground by each ankle.

"The sun, the sun has tricked my vision. I am sorry." Still, he did not let the boy go. Roch wriggled to set himself free.

Just as puzzled as the boy, Michael knelt beside the friar. Perhaps Jacopo had been right to warn him about the Franciscan.

"What are you doing? Why do you restrain him thus?" Michael asked. "Let him go."

The friar bore his eyes into Michael's as he still held fast to Roch.

"If that one is an honest cleric, then I'm the doge," he hissed, out of breath from his exertions. "I know him. You must trust me. You must go instead. I'll not allow the boy to be in his company."

Michael stood up. Once more he felt the hammer blows of "danger, danger" in his head. Each time he had ignored them thus far, he had been duped, first by Aphrodite, then by Jacopo. He would not, could not, ignore them anymore.

"I'll go, Captain," he said. "Roch's ankle is twisted."

"Oaf," the cleric again mocked his former teacher. And again, Loredan was amused.

The captain waved his approval, though his eyes, Michael saw, as Loredan moved them from Contarini's face to the friar's and back to Contarini's again, betrayed some puzzlement at the brouhaha the Franciscan had instigated.

Again the voice in Michael's head spoke. He trusts the friar. The captain trusts the friar.

Michael looked at Roch and signaled with his eyes, so that the boy, who, registering some unspoken understanding, immediately grabbed his left leg, rubbing it as if he were trying to stave off pain. How adept Michael had become at lying. How quickly did Roch follow his lead.

"Good," whispered the friar. "Good, Michael." He let go of the boy and lumbered up again.

Unsure if he had decided right or wrong, Michael walked toward Clario Contarini.

"Piacere," he said, and made a slight bow as Loredan had taught him to do when greeting one of his betters.

Contarini looked him over, then nodded.

"Come," he said, his voice's natural shrillness now laced with frustration at Nature's, and perhaps his family's, affronts to him.

Chapter 14

DESIGNS

The rectory was attached to a simple church, both whitewashed. The front door, through which Michael followed Contarini, though of unvarnished wood, showed more grandly for the heavy brass door-knock that hung from the open lion's mouth. Any visitor cognizant of the lagoon Republic would have felt he were entering Venetian territory.

"Wait here," Contarini said, his voice more subdued now that he was inside. "I will retrieve the documents. Sit if you care to." He walked up a stone stairway to the left, his white robe brushing against the striated steps.

The loggia was a long sitting room, made for comfort, Michael saw, with windows lining both sides. The white linen curtains that kept out the sun blew with the warm sea breeze, and the red-tiled floor, devoid of rugs, was shiny and cool despite the heat. Eight wooden stools surrounded a rectangular refectory table, and two long window seats with numerous cushions, most of them bearing what appeared to be a family crest, softened them. Michael heard children's voices from the other end of the room. He followed them. But he found only one boy waiting.

"Buon giorno," chirped a barefooted child in an unbelted white tunic.

"Buon giorno," Michael replied, and bent to shake the boy's outstretched hand. He was no more than six years of age.

The boy's blond curls fell around his face. His skin was unusually fair, as if he did not venture out into the sun. From time to time, he reached under his tunic to scratch his crotch. He did not appear to think his doing so was unusual or out of place.

The boy motioned to Michael and drew him to the table where he had been scribbling, shapes mostly, on parchment. He seemed at ease despite the fact that his visitor was a stranger to him.

The room, Michael realized, was a studio. Framed sketches hung along the walls. The boy was certainly too young to have drawn any of them, Michael was sure of that. They were detailed, the work of a mature artist or artists. There was one of St. Sebastian, his chest pierced with arrows, another of a gowned youth, perhaps just short of Michael's age, whose face was hidden in the embrace of a much older man who wept. This little fellow's hands would not have been able to draw such fine lines or differentiate the shadings. Even now, as he pressed the style against the parchment, his fingers struggled to control the instrument. Yet the boy appeared to enjoy his attempts. He worked as if Michael were not even present in the room with him.

Following the boy's lead, Michael kept silent as well. He walked around the studio.

Piles of blank parchment filled a wooden shelf between two evenly-placed windows that looked down a cliff and out onto the water. Smooth stones lay atop the piles, keeping them from blowing about when a sea breeze rustled in. On another shelf, low beneath the first, a basket brimming full of seashells and six slingshots were arranged in a pleasing display. Behind a glass-doored cabinet with a lock lay an arrangement of small knives, each one with a bejeweled handle.

"Sit," the boy said, smiling, and Michael crouched down on a bench whose height evidently had been determined by that of the little fellow and the others who, along with their voices, had disappeared. The boy handed Michael a metal-point stylus and a piece of parchment dusted with powdered bone. Michael had seen such tools and substances once in the bishop's residence, where his uncle had taken him to deliver the parish census. There the artists had been two aged monks. They had shushed him and shooed him off when he asked what they were doing.

"You are old enough to draw like that," the boy said, and pointed to the wall sketches.

"Old enough, perhaps," Michael said, "but without the skill, I'm afraid."

The boy shrugged his shoulders.

"Try, why don't you? Draw with me," the boy invited his guest, and patted Michael's hand as if to encourage him.

More sketches, Michael saw, lay spread across the low table. Religious pictures: Christ crucified, the Madonna and her Holy Child surrounded by angels, wounded martyrs, long-toothed, wide-eyed, clawing demons.

"Who did these?" Michael asked.

"Cleanth," the boy answered. "He is almost as old as you. He is a real artist. That is what our master says."

"I see," Michael said. "Where is he?"

"Don't know," the boy answered. "Maybe with the master."

"Is Father Clario the master?"

"Yes," the boy said. "He tells us what to do."

He kept at the parchment.

"Do you like to draw?" Michael asked.

"Yes," the boy said. "It is better than posing."

His eyes left his work and instead surveyed Michael from head to toe.

"Am I to pose for you?" he asked.

He stood and made to take off his tunic.

"No, no, you will not pose for me," Michael answered, resting both hands on the boy's shoulders a moment so he would not undress. The boy sat down again at the table.

The young Greek grew uneasy.

"Bene," said the boy." I do not like it."

As he listened to the boy and observed him, seemingly oblivious to modesty and shame, a growing apprehension replaced

Michael's initial curiosity. The young Greek tried to keep his voice steady.

"But for whom do you po—?" he began.

As he spoke, another boy, an exact replica of the first, entered the studio. Unlike his sanguine brother, he was crying and the back of his shins bore red marks that suggested recent slapping.

"Here," his brother said, offering the boy a seat on the bench, his voice soothing, his manner apparently not surprised at his twin's unhappiness. "This man is a nice one," he promised, gesturing to Michael with his hand that again found its way under his tunic. "He talks only."

At once uncomfortable and unsure, Michael longed for his brother. Petros would help him, could tell him what this place meant.

Then the caw, like an alarm.

"Where are you, Loredan's man? I told you to wait here. Wait here, I said!"

Michael flinched. The friendly boy looked alarmed, but continued to rub his brother's arm. His doing so, however, did not assuage the other's distress.

Contarini's unpleasant voice now turned to a veritable shriek from the loggia.

"Where are you?"

The crying boy put his head down on the table and blocked his ears with his hands.

"I am with you," the sanguine boy said. "I am here."

But when the cleric stormed into the room, both boys instantly leapt from their seats, lowering their eyes and standing as close together as they could. Their tunics swayed as their little bodies shook.

"Go!" Contarini commanded them. "Both of you. Wait for me upstairs."

The second boy howled now. Contarini glared at him and raised his right hand. His brother grabbed the crying boy's arm and they went. Their bare feet slapped against the tile floor, then went quiet once they reached the stone stairway. Only the second boy's wail carried down the stairwell and throughout the loggia.

Despite his now indisputable misgivings, Michael apologized in an attempt to pacify the priest.

"I am sorry, Father. I heard children," he said. "I meant no harm."

The priest became still, then smiled and spoke.

"Ah, you like children, then?" he said, not really asking. "The twins are the youngest of six here."

He smoothed his white gown with his pristine hands. His gold ring reached to his knuckle. A scrolled "C" encircled a ruby the size of a swallow's egg.

Michael did not respond, but walked around the table, pointing to the sketches, trying to retain the modicum of civility his apology had coaxed from the cleric.

"I did not know you were an artist," Michael said. He pretended a guileless interest in the sketches. "Are the boys I just met your sons?"

Contarini did not answer him, but instead, in a surprising gesture, banged his forehead once against a massive cupboard that likely held more art supplies, Michael supposed. The two doors of the cupboard opened outward, and one more boy, this one older than the twins, perhaps twelve or thirteen years of age, with black hair pulled back and held by a leather ribbon, hopped out. He was naked and held his tunic. There were fresh scratches along his arms. As soon as his feet met the tile floor, he pulled the tunic over his head and, unlike the twins, looked straight up at Contarini, crossed his arms over his chest, and waited.

"To your work," Contarini said, pointing at the table.

The boy bowed, but in a confident manner that suggested decorous custom rather than frightened submissiveness. He walked to the table, sat down on a stool, and picked up not the stylus the little boy had used, Michael saw, but a pen, which he dipped into a small bottle of black ink. His hands were stained, as was his tunic, no doubt indicating a devotion to his artistic work.

"Hello," Michael said.

The boy did not answer, but instead gestured to him in a lascivious manner not unlike Jacopo might have.

"Why do you do that?" Michael asked, his voice telling his annoyance and disapproval.

He looked to Contarini, expecting him to correct the boy. But the cleric did not. Instead he watched Michael's agitation. He even smiled at the rude youth.

"Observe," the cleric encouraged. "You see that Cleanth, my oldest charge, has no need of erasures. His marks are as exact as my own."

Michael watched uneasily as the boy continued refining a drawing he had already begun. He sharpened the contrast between figures and the spaces they inhabited by outlining the human shapes with the ink. In the scene, Michael saw a half-naked man with a raised whip outside an ornate church. Uncle Elios had told Michael of religious zealots known as flagellants, who abused themselves to achieve solidarity with Christ in His own suffering. "Though they were officially banned from their practice upon the moment of their arrival," he had said, "you will still find in Venice, God willing you arrive there safely, la Scuola Grande di San Giovanni Evangelista which the flagellants founded as a confraternity almost two centuries ago."

Michael looked at the sketch, then at Cleanth's arms. Where had his scratches come from?

"No, by the way," the cleric said, "to answer your initial question. The boys are not my sons. I am not to have sons. They are orphans. I care for them."

"I see," Michael said, but he did not.

"I teach them to sketch so they may support themselves when they leave me. While they are my students, they live here. We are a little scuola, a confraternity, like those that abound in Venice."

"I see," said Michael again.

The cleric paused, all the while watching Cleanth work.

"A very small one," the cleric continued, "but a scuola nonetheless."

He seemed intent to uphold the honor of his studio.

"Well, Father, I must return to Commander Loredan before dusk," Michael said. "Perhaps if you would be so kind as to give me the documents he expects."

Michael tried to imitate the clean, direct tone Loredan took when addressing his men.

Contarini spoke to Cleanth.

"Prepare the other two upstairs," he said.

Cleanth dropped his pen, pushed his sketch away, stood, then snickered at Michael and left.

"Alora," the cleric said, as if he had not taken the slightest note of Cleanth's low manners, and he motioned for Michael to follow him from the art room to the loggia. "I would be remiss to my friend Loredan if I did not provide you with some refreshment before your walk back."

Surveying the studio again in a sweeping glance, Michael followed Contarini and re-entered the loggia, where a stooped, aproned woman was placing two goblets and a plate of fresh cherries on the table. He looked up the stairs, but heard nothing except silence.

"Thank you," Michael said to the woman as she turned away, but she did not respond.

"She is deaf," Contarini said. "A most useful trait in a servant."

He pointed to a goblet for Michael.

"It is only water with the juice of lemons. The children learn to like it."

Michael drank and tasted bitterness. His mother had always added honey.

Then the priest went to a tall-backed chair by the door where the duplicate letters, one of the missive to his mother, the other of his proposal for Maestro Romano, rested, scrolled and tied.

"Tell your captain and this Bronislav that I look forward to meeting young Franto. He is just now six, I am told, and quite a singer."

Contarini's fingers brushed Michael's as he handed him the missives. Then the priest walked over to the table, took a cherry from the plate, and, spitting the pit directly onto the table, swallowed it in one bite.

Even as he heard his voice mouth a courteous, "I will, Father. Thank you," Michael knew he would somehow see to it that Bronislav's son was not left alone with this man.

A thud, followed by a persistent thumping, sounded on the ceiling over them.

Michael looked upward.

Contarini said, "I must leave you and see to my students."

The cleric put his hands together as if in prayer and walked Michael to the door of the rectory.

"Perhaps you will visit me again with your Commander Loredan in Venice when I bring Maestro Romano to San Marco. It is I who will tutor the eight nobles and this Bronislav's son, the ninth boy, as it were. By the third year of this new century, this choir and these boys—my choir and my boys, I dare say—will have become the most renowned in the Christian world."

The cleric raised his arms in a victorious "V," then turned his back to Michael, who watched as he mounted the stairs, unbuttoning his long white robe as he climbed.

Chapter 15

MICHAEL READS TO BRONISLAV

"Read, Michele, now you have returned," Captain Loredan prodded Michael. "Make use of your uncle's teaching." He pointed to the scroll, damp from Michael's perspiring hands.

The captain, the friar, Jacopo, and an eager Bronislav sat waiting on the dock by the tender that would take them back to the galley, then on to several ports along the Dalmatian Coast. At each port, Loredan was to personally exchange missives with specified custodians of the Republic abroad. The documents, each stamped with a waxed seal identifying the sender's office, and all protected in numbered and locked cases whose keys were strictly controlled, would consist of both routine book-keeping matters and precise strategic instructions that arose from the exquisitely-developed spy network for which the Republic was already known and feared.

Shaken from his strange and troubling interlude at the rectory and not yet daring to look directly at the friar (with whom he now wanted a lengthy discussion), Michael had tried without success to compose himself as he walked down the craggy path from the dwelling back to the dock. Now he tried again.

"Where are the others?" he asked.

"Gone back, thanks to the courtesy of some fishermen who rowed them," Jacopo said. "Would that I had arrived earlier so I might sooner sleep off the afternoon's exertions." He strutted a bit, pointing to his crotch and his mouth alternately, and even the captain laughed.

The friar cut short the Venetian's antics, encouraging Michael. "What have you got to tell us?" he inquired. "Bronislav's surprise, perhaps?"

Michael looked to him. "Yes. Yes, I will read."

He cleared his throat and unscrolled the parchment.

"Now, Michele," the captain insisted. "Soon darkness will fall."

Michael propped one leg against a low stone wall and rested the other on the sandy ground just outside of the myrtle grove. Again he cleared his throat, then extended his neck upward as if he were declaiming to a crowd:

> Dearest Mother:
>
> I, your dutiful son, presently a priest of Holy Mother Church and docile servant of you, my deceased father Bartolomeo, and our most noble Republic, write on behalf of one Bronislav of Ragusa, a trusted oarsman of many voyages with Captain Loredan, one of our fellow nobili and a most valued friend of the Contarini family.
>
> Bronislav's son, by the name of Franto, is determined by Captain Loredan and his local choirmaster to be a singer of great talent and even more promise.
>
> In keeping with our mutual allegiance as nobili of the Republic, Captain Loredan and I request your certain influence so that young Franto may become the "ninth boy" in the incipient Boys' Choir of San Marco. Though low-born, a stranger, and a Slav, he would be, as Captain Loredan assures me, an able substitute for any of the eight noble boys (among them, Lucca Loredan Venier, Captain Loredan's own nephew), should plague or any other pernicious calamity strike one. Of proper age (six years in this world), in possession of God-given talent, and tested in his own parish for proven industriousness, he promises to become an asset to the project I am most eager to oversee. The music master, Maestro Romano, has already agreed to this proposal, and a copy of the letter I sent him is enclosed with this one for your perusal.

Here Michael paused and looked to Bronislav, who wept silently and fingered his cross. When he could stop his tears, the heretofore unflappable Slav looked to the captain and clasped his hands in thanks.

Loredan smiled and clasped his hands, as well, in copied response. The two might have been brothers.

Michael continued:

> Through your efficacious persuasions, Franto and his mother, Milaslova, a seamstress of proven competence — here again I have Captain Loredan's word—would be placed in the service of Captain Loredan's widowed sister, the highly regarded Elena Loredan Venier. While Milaslova assists with the linens and apparel of the household, Franto can join young Lucca in his studies and provide companionship and suitable distraction to the family's only boy (among four sisters), in a fatherless household. Bronislav, meanwhile, will continue his voyages as long as he is able. Then (should he be spared earlier death whether by disease or warfare), when he cannot any longer wield an oar, he will, as Captain Loredan has assured me, retain certain and less strenuous employment in the counting house at the Arsenale. In any and all of the matters above, Captain Loredan promises his careful oversight and constant attention.
>
> My sincere and continued gratitude for your continued parental love, your generous and wise counsel, and your immediate intercession in this matter.
>
> With all due filial regard and respect,
> Clario
>
> In the year of our Lord, 16 May 1401
> Chiesa della Virgine, Corfu

"There," Loredan said, as Bronislav rose and stood open-armed before his captain. "Your surprise."

"And my eternal thanks, my Captain," Bronislav replied, and turned to Jacopo with a broad smile.

Without comment and no doubt tired from his afternoon spirits and erotic gyrations, Jacopo stepped down into the tender, Michael following after. Then the young Greek turned and reached up to assist the friar. Jacopo steadied the boat's rocking while the Franciscan arranged himself in the center of the boat.

"You understand now," he whispered to Michael.

"I am not sure," Michael answered quietly. "But what I saw and heard troubles me. I am sorry I doubted you."

The friar did not reply, but waved his hand toward the sea and said, again sotto voce, "We will talk later."

Bronislav, still smiling, hopped down into the boat and reached up for Loredan's hand.

"And when will my family learn of this wonder, Captain?" he asked. Still the Slav smiled.

"They already know," Loredan answered. "They should be on the dock awaiting you when we, God willing, disembark in Venice on the Feast of All Souls. Clario, who is to set sail for home tomorrow, however, will see to their arrangements before then, should we be delayed or, God forbid, lost."

Jacopo, still silent, and already hooded for the night, unlashed the rope and pushed the tender away from the dock.

"God speed us, then," Bronislav uttered his prayer.

"All speed," Michael answered.

"Yes," the friar added. "Yes."

He frowned and moved his fingers from one of his beads to the next and the next with a feverish speed atypical of his deliberate and lumbering nature.

Michael watched the Franciscan pray. He realized he had not even asked the little boys their names.

PART TWO

VENICE

"Consider your origins: you were not made to live as brutes,
but to follow virtue and knowledge."
Dante Alighieri

Chapter 16

2 November 1401—ARSENALE

"Fire!"

Michael leapt from his hard berth along the gangway. His black hair, grown to his shoulders after five months at sea, shook around his head. He pounded Bench Five to rouse the others.

"Fire!" again he hollered.

Though they both woke and sat up straight, neither Bronislav nor Jacopo seemed alarmed by the young Greek's yelling. Instead, the Slav laughed and traced his usual Sign of the Cross over his chest with his pendant while the Venetian pointed a satiric forefinger to the sky where newcomer Michael had expected to see dawn's purple and pink. Where light and brightness should have shone steadily, however, intermittent, rhythmic bursts of black billows rose and spread.

"The Arsenale, oh Stupid One," said Jacopo. "Its furnaces already at work."

Michael did not understand.

"Where they build the galleys," Bronislav explained. "Where we will dock."

Michael still stared without comprehension.

"Where Venice will greet you," Bronislav went on. "Soon, within the hour, you will see it up close with your own eyes."

Michael's bench mates toyed with him. But Michael did not mind. None of the three had died, been mutilated, or murdered. Pirates had not captured them. No one had declared him unworthy of his oarsman's status. The executioners, having had no further need to enforce the judgment of The Great Council this journey, had been off-loaded at Zara where, most assuredly, given their speed and determined looks as they bid Loredan farewell, they sought some other miscreant of the Republic. The likes of a Zen had not again accosted Michael either at sea or in other ports. And, causing him both initial elation and subsequent trepidation, Loredan had told him, "I have plans for you, Michele," after his biscuit and rancid wine last night.

"Michael, wake up," Bronislav goaded him. He stood and slapped his bench mate playfully on one cheek. "Pay attention, I say."

Michael squeezed his fingers into fists as if to prove his alertness, then relaxed them again, satisfied. He repeated the exercise. If the galley were only an hour's time to Venice, he knew he would soon be rowing. But for the moment, he was cold. Advent would soon be upon them, as Friar Martino had reminded them. He shivered, wrapping his arms around his trunk as if they made a cloak.

"Well, I smelled a great deal of smoke," he grinned back at them. "At least I smelled an unusual amount of smoke."

Letting his arms drop and rubbing his eyes, his excitement palpable in his voice, he spoke. "I am at last to set foot in Venice!" Then, more to himself than to his bench mates, "Would Petros were with me."

As Michael spoke, Roch helped bring down the trireme's sails one at a time, his feet, still bootless despite the chill, slapping the deck as he scampered. The galley was just beyond the Lido, the splay of beach and dwellings that lay like miles of a giant's outstretched arm, protecting the Republic's lagoon from the Adriatic and any would-be invaders.

"Up and at your oars, men," the armiraio commanded. His voice, too, sounded rich and full of promise.

Fore to aft and back again he strode. Groans and shuffling. Jostling on the benches. Utterances, "Venice. Home. Home at last."

The triad took their accustomed places—Bronislav was to see his family within the day, Jacopo would no doubt hood himself and arrive almost-late wherever he intended to go, and Michael...? What for Michael?

"You are to remain where the galleys await finishing," Loredan had told him. "Remember, stay there until my valet comes for you."

"Yes, Captain," Michael had answered.

Where did the captain think he would go? Where did he have to go?

The galley had become his home. He had learned how to live as one of three on a bench. Despite his stupidities and his failings, he had survived. And now, just as he realized his success at not failing, his achievement at not falling short, just as his acceptance among this crew of men had been granted, he must, like the rest of them, take his leave. He would become a wandering novice once more. Until his next journey, his next galley, he would need to find and practice his footing among the stones, alleys, and small courtyards of Venice. He would need help. But whose?

But even as he wondered, his musings were disrupted by the armiraio's singular voice.

"Men, take up your oars."

One hundred and eighty lengths of wood were grabbed, adjusted, lifted from tholes, adjusted again, and finally supported by sunburned, calloused hands. Each man stretched his back, his calves and his feet, his fingers and wrists. Each rower sat up as keenly as he could. Whether tooth lost, arm burned, eye blinded, stomach bloated with gas, or spirits dashed by unintended insult or deliberate malice, he and every other oarsman lifted his chest, as poised and masterful as he could make himself.

"Pronto!" the armiraio bellowed, and the rowers inhaled as if with one pair of needful, greedy lungs.

"Uno..."

The thrust and pull of the galley's oars; the rhythm of the armiraio's beat as familiar now as that of his own heart; Jacopo's secret, closed eyes and slim, taut wrists; Bronislav's sturdy labor and steady understanding of both good and ill; Roch's wide-eyed plea; his own trust in the Franciscan friar; Clario Contarini's inscrutable scuola; and Commander Loredan's surprising remove from shipboard sins and brisk interest in his newest oarsman's future all filled Michael's consciousness as he rowed the last strokes of his first voyage. The closer the galley glided to the city, the sootier the air became. When the looming red-brick Arsenale rose into sight, it was through a miasma of soot that stung and scoured Michael's eyes. They wanted to shut, to keep out the stinging pollution and its certain pain. But in the exhilarating moments as the boat approached the dock, the young Greek, so recently re-named Loredan's "Michele," forced them to open wide. He had to see, to look, to take in all that Venice was, threatened, and promised.

"Dieci," the armiraio told them.

They were almost there.

Bronislav began to sing, his cross a pendulum to his anthem.

"God has brought us from the sea," he chanted in time to the beat. "God has brought us from the sea."

Though he smirked at first, eventually Jacopo joined in. He lifted his eyelids once, turned, and smiled at Michael. Then he stuck out his tongue.

Despite the Venetian's antic, the voices-that-became-one-voice, the singular chorus that had first seduced Michael eleven years earlier, caught and lifted his soul like the great galley's sails themselves. He had completed his first voyage. He had seen it through. No soot, he told himself, no momentary tear-ridden searing, no minor charring of the lungs by the furnaces' residues, would deter him from triumph at his arrival.

"Due," the armiraio called.

And Michael heard before he saw the voices of the throngs waiting on the dock.

"Benvenuti!" they called.

There was clapping of hands, whistling, sobbing, too. Bells rang, as if from many churches, while one long, sonorous gong sounded dirge-like from a blackened bell tower he could not make out for the thick smoke.

"Finito," the armiraio called the final stroke, and a cheer rose up from the crew.

Following the lead of those who knew better than he, Michael grabbed his torn and filthy sack of belongings. It appeared that Captain Loredan, as he had at the start of their journey, was speaking to each man as he left. Two lines formed along both gangways and merged to one just before the gangplank's descent.

"Perhaps I will see you," Jacopo said, and goosed the young Greek with his left fist. Michael returned the thrust with a swift knee to the Venetian's groin. "But if anyone should ever ask what you know of me, I beg you to act as ignorant as I initially thought you to be."

"I'll take that as a compliment, Jacopo," Michael said, and swung his sack over his shoulder. As he did, something fell from it, dropping hard upon the deck.

"My lamb," Michael said, reaching down for the wood carving his father had fashioned for him one long ago Easter.

He turned to Bronislav and motioned for the Slav to precede him.

"For Franto," he said. He gave the lamb to Bronislav. "For your son."

The Slav cupped the lamb in his broad, serviceable hands.

"Thank you, Michael," he said. "He will like it."

"Good," Michael said. "I hope it will protect him as it has protected me from death among all life's plagues."

"And for you," Bronislav said, lifting his chain with its cross-cum-knife over his powerful neck. Michael lowered his head so the Slav could set it in place. "Your God and your knife. You will require both here."

Michael nodded.

“I understand now,” he said.

“I know you do,” Bronislav replied.

Michael stood up straight and turned his thoughts from the sea to the sooty city before him.

“Finis, then?” he asked the Slav.

“For now,” Bronislav answered. “For just a little while.”

Then, not caring a whit what Jacopo might think or say, Michael grasped his mentor’s cross in his right hand and bent his ruddy, black-stubbled face to the Slav’s. Through tears that one might not without reason infer were the fault of the Arsenale’s furnaces alone, Michael kissed him on the cheek as a son would his father.

“Grazie,” he said.

And the boulder of a man patted Michael’s muscular arm with a paternal gentleness the young Greek had nearly forgotten.

Chapter 17

THE FEAST OF ALL SOULS

Michael stood utterly alone.

The crowd had dispersed, and the Arsenale itself gone silent and gloomy. Its workers had retreated to their churches at noon to honor the dead, whose spirits, Michael felt, had likewise abandoned him.

He gazed first at the enormity of the city made of bricks, the long lines of purposeful buildings that housed the men who built the ships.

One vessel, soon to be a guard galley, he surmised from its shape and still-unfinished fittings, stood in skeletal form, braced upright in the canal beside him. He felt incomplete as well, his own body in need of significant improvements.

He wanted to be clean, to shave, to sleep on straw again, maybe even alone. To wake without prodding, without needing to unkink calf muscles that were tight and sore. He ran his tongue over his mossy teeth. His mouth felt thick with a damp, filmy down, not unlike that on the newborn chicks he and Mina used to chase. He wanted a stick to catch and roll it from the sides of his mouth, to lift it from under his tongue. Rosemary or mint to freshen his rank breath. He wanted to break and run, to stretch his bare legs across tall grasses. To lie still and watch the sky. He wanted not to stink. He longed for a piece of fruit, some grilled fish, bread without weevils, a tumbler of wine that had not already turned to vinegar.

"I am greedy," he said, his voice intruding on Venice's November. "I want too much."

But at least he could breathe. The furnaces were down now, and the sky had stopped raining soot. However, Michael could not help but notice that it had not cleared completely. Instead, it rippled a luminous, pearly silver, reflecting the wavelets from the slate and verdigris lagoon.

Michael listened and heard the calm water nearby.

"Lapping," he said. His voice again intruded upon the almost-silence. He let it speak again. "Lapping instead of crashing."

Wavelets like the hands of many children patted rather than slapped the slatted dock and the gray stones before and beneath him. Hundreds of liquid tongues licked the wood and rock in a manner that did not betoken storms or rough weather. The lagoon's play against the Arsenale's walkways felt friendly, intimate, promising safety instead of adventure. And after months amid the rush and roil of the Adriatic, Michael welcomed it.

Spreading his legs evenly on the stone path by the galley-in-progress, Michael felt his body still anticipating the rougher rhythm of the waves which had characterized his long journey. His body sought some relief, a rest, an equilibrium more subtle and calm than the sea allowed. He would learn to mimic and match the lagoon, he decided, begin to feel at ease in the small shallows, a gentler pool, a refuge, he imagined, from the deep.

He inhaled and let out a long breath. Again. He felt his chest rise and fall, rise and fall with the lapping. He closed his eyes. "Petros," he whispered, "Petros." As if he were a pagan sorcerer, he called to his brother, imploring his presence. He opened his eyes, looked skyward, but found no sign of the longed-for wings. Then, with a resolution to find at least a small respite between his voyage and his sojourn in Venice, he lowered his tired and tested body onto the undulating dock, crossed his legs, and waited with neither joy nor dread for whomever Captain Loredan had designated to fetch him.

As he drifted into an uncertain but pleasant doze, the sky above him shivered open, and a winging breeze dipped to graze his shoulders. The sleeves of his tunic rippled over his arms, and he brought both limbs together across his chest the way his mother always had. Should there have been an observer to witness this trick of the wind, he would perhaps have wondered at Michael's brilliant, soporific smile at his filial recognition.

Chapter 18

AT THE BARBER SHOP

"Michele, Michele!"

A voice cracking with adolescence woke him, and a hand, not rough, shook his shoulder. Michael opened his eyes.

"Oh," he said, and lifted himself upright. "I must have fallen asleep."

A youth, perhaps just a year or two younger than he, stepped back and gazed up at Michael. The fellow, about six inches shorter than Michael, was dressed as if a prince. Scarlet cap resting atop combed and oiled hair that ended at his chin, black leggings and a magenta tunic held in place by a leather belt with a circular buckle decorated in gold with the letter "L". Soft mahogany ankle boots. Clean hands with polished nails.

"I am Nico, Signor Loredan's valet."

"Piacere," Michael said, and bowed.

Nico laughed.

"No need to bow to me," he said. "I am only the captain's servant, a valet, one who takes care of his personal needs." He laughed again.

Michael shook his head, somewhat embarrassed at his ignorance. Nico appeared to be a friendly fellow.

"Where I come from," Michael said, "a tiny cove in Rhodes, you would be thought of as having royal blood."

"Too bad I am in Venice, then," Nico said. He laughed once more and looked Michael over from head to toe.

"Well, you are in worse shape than I imagined," he said. He held his arm against his nose. "I mean no offense, you understand, but this is the first time I have been sent to meet someone just off a galley, and Signor Loredan always goes to the barber shop before he returns to his palazzo after his voyages. That is where I am to take you. He has seen to the arrangements with the barber, and we will meet him later."

Nico stared at Michael, who stood still and silent.

"You will live with the two of us, he says."

"I see," said Michael, looking at his sack.

Then, suddenly animated at the realization that he would have a place to rest his head, "Does Commander Loredan have a wife and children?"

"He lives only with me and, now," Nico smiled, " with you."

Michael grabbed his sorry sack. Nico looked at it appraisingly.

"I would leave that if I were you," Nico said. "You won't need it. Not if you are to work with me, with us now. Signor Loredan will see to your clothing." He added, "And everything else."

Michael looked into his sack and the scant dirty pieces of clothing that remained.

"Here," Nico said, and reached for the humble woven sack. When Michael handed it to him, he took it gingerly between thumb and forefinger, and flung it unceremoniously into the lagoon.

"Trust me, Signor Loredan will see to everything. He is a generous master. And not quick to anger, I must say."

Michael did not reply, but instead watched the sack floating out and in, out and in from the dock. Another piece of his former life gone.

"Ready?" Nico asked, and with a tentative nod Michael followed, looking behind into the water only twice.

Nico led Michael away from the Arsenale along a stretch of walkway he called la Riva degli Schiavone. It was a place of many hostels and inns, all quiet now. The lagoon was to their left, the doge's palace straight ahead. Just a few alleys before it, he veered right, away from the lagoon into an alley marked Zaccaria. All around him, buildings three and four stories tall loomed above. Shuttered windows indicated la riposa, the afternoon rest, Nico told him. "Besides, it is a holy day, so you will not see people about. They are at church or"—here he laughed yet again—"they are hiding from those who want them to go there."

Michael stared upward, making sure to look down every few seconds so as not to lose sight of Nico. In and out of short and narrow alleyways they walked until, after what felt like a journey of three or four miles, they came to a wooden door with a rounded top and an iron door-knock in the shape of an open scissors around a ponytail of ebony-iron hair.

Nico knocked four times. Michael heard a mellifluous voice singing within.

The door opened and a lean man with a black apron over his gray tunic and blazing bloodshot eyes looked out.

"Ah, Nico," he said, and with a gracious sweep of his arm, he ushered Nico and Michael inside. Then he resumed his song, bustling to sweep some already-shorn locks of hair into a pile, which he then brushed into an iron dustpan and flung into the fire. The pieces of auburn hair flamed up, then collapsed into embers. Michael could not help but notice that though it comprised the better part of the wall and gave off considerable heat, the shop's fireplace appeared a trivial thing compared to the flames and soot of the Arsenale.

The barber turned to face the two, ending his song with a long, bellowing flourish. He smiled and bowed. Nico applauded.

"My name is Dominic," the barber said to Michael.

"Michele," Nico said, before the barber could ask.

"Ah," he replied, and in what Michael came to learn was his most habitual gesture, motioned with the same sweep of an arm that the two should follow him.

Michael adjusted his eyes to the many lit candles that filled the square room, the largest among them on either side of an ornate wooden chair with a lion-patterned cushioned seat. Three steaming pots of water bubbled over the fireplace's flames that had so recently devoured the shorn auburn hair. On a long table between the fireplace and the chair were arranged scissors and combs, brushes and ointments. A tomb-like ceramic tub with clean linen towels draped over its sides was empty, but, now that Nico and Michael had arrived, the barber took a protective glove in hand and, lifting one pot at a time, poured steaming water into the tub, then added cool water from a jug.

"For you," he motioned to Michael. "If you please, get in."

Michael's left eye twitched. He felt unnerved. Even at home he had not washed himself in a tub, but instead down in a narrow cove or, in cold weather, just he and his father by the fire while his mother kept to her pallet. Now he would be naked among strangers. He felt his face redden and hoped that the candlelight's shadows hid his embarrassment. When he dropped his leggings and tunic, Dominic picked them up with long iron tongs and threw them into the fire. They caught the flames and smoked for a moment, then sizzled first into scraps, then into mere shreds of fabric. Soon they were nothing but ashes. Only Bronislav's chain and cross remained on Michael's body and entered the tub with him. Its welcome pressure on his chest accentuated his otherwise unadorned state.

"Ah," Michael could not help himself from groaning with pleasure when the hot water enveloped his filthy frame. Dominic poured some lemon-smelling liquid into the bath from a long beaker of glass, took a sea-sponge from one of the many drawers underneath the long table, and proceeded to scrub Michael's back with it.

"Now, you," he handed Michael the sponge and motioned for him to scrub himself.

His initial embarrassment trumped by the soothing water and scent, Michael did just that. Not since the Manfredonian brook on the morning after his shameful encounter with Zen had he cleansed his entire body. He dipped his head under the water and scrubbed his teeth and then his scalp in brisk, joyous abandon.

The barber ignored him, instead preparing his grooming instruments and humming a melody once more. Nico, meanwhile, sat on a bench across from the fire and helped himself to some breadsticks and wine. He played with a length of thin leather between bites and swallows, using his fingers to configure different shapes between his hands. He appeared to feel at ease in the shop. Perhaps waiting here for Loredan and others was part of his job. Michael hoped it would not be part of his. Such waiting would prove to be dull, of that much he was certain.

"You will have some, as well," Nico promised, pointing to the food and wiping his mouth with a cloth napkin. He raised his glass to Michael.

From an adjacent room, closed off with a door similar to the outer one, but minus a door knocker, came intermittent male voices, some low laughter, and an occasional groan of pleasure not unlike the one that had issued from Michael in his private lagoon of steaming comfort.

Captain Loredan had been good to him. He would try to make him proud. Again, as at the dock, he felt himself drifting off, this time from contentment rather than fatigue.

"Pronto?" Dominic asked.

The barber stood by the tub with a large linen towel ready to dry Michael's soaped and rinsed body and hair. Both Michael and the shop smelled of citrus. Michael stood and emerged from the tub, lifting out one relaxed leg at a time. He shook himself so that water droplets fell from him, dotting both the barber and the shop's floor. The barber's rubdown, quick and sure, made Michael's flesh tingle and glow with unexpected relief. He felt resurrected.

"Now the rest," Dominic said, and, wrapping another dry towel around Michael, led him to the chair where he shaved him, cut and oiled his hair so that it mimicked Nico's, and rubbed his face and neck and arms with more citrus perfumes. Finally, he clipped and filed Michael's hand and toe nails, buffing them with a dry sea-sponge until they looked as luminous as the moon. Only the calluses from his oar would not be mastered, though Dominic massaged them and each individual finger with an ointment, softening skin toughened by work and weather.

"Nico, he is ready," Dominic called to the valet, and Loredan's young man stopped eating and drinking to walk to a carved wardrobe. He opened it, reached inside, and gathered a readied set of apparel exactly like his own, but fitted perfectly, it turned out, to Michael's taller and markedly more-muscled frame. The young Greek dressed.

"Alora," Dominic gestured, and walked Michael to a full length mirror that hung inside one of the wardrobe's two doors.

Michael stared at a stranger. He would not have recognized himself if someone had drawn his image. He doubted his family could have, either. His former self was gone. Only the calluses on his palms, Bronislav's cross and knife, and his mind and imperfect soul remained. To the naked eye, he was purely Venetian. When asked now, he must say he was Loredan's man. When called for, he must answer to "Michele."

The door to the adjoining room opened.

"Michele!" a voice greeted him. "I am told that your captain has christened you such. He must deem you the son he has not yet sired."

Michael turned from the mirror, and was struck speechless.

The voice belonged to Zen.

Michael felt Bronislav's cross-cum-knife against his chest. He would use it if he must.

"Your captain told me you were expected. I am glad to see you again," Zen said. "I trust I will see you often now that you are in Venice, as well."

The recruiter looked resplendent, freshly groomed and wearing festive robes that suggested an evening of feasting and entertainment lay ahead. Michael hated him.

Remaining silent, his jaw tight and his hands turned to fists, Michael glared at the man. Nico watched, his body tensing after Michael's, but offering no words, either.

"Vino?" Dominic interrupted, proffering refreshment to both Michael and Zen.

"Si," Zen answered.

"Non, grazie," said Michael.

As he spoke, Jacopo, still in his sea-ridden state, emerged from the adjacent room, though uncharacteristically without his hood. He pulled his leggings up over his naked arse. Behind him followed Roch. The boy's shirt was torn, his face mottled, and, most noticeable of all, his wide eyes defeated.

"Roch," Michael called out, and went directly to the boy.

At first Roch did not recognize the rower at all. He merely stared up at him. Then, perhaps hoping it was he, he asked, "Michael, is it you? Are you Michael of Rhodes?"

Michael knelt down on one knee and looked into Roch's face.

"Yes," Michael answered. "Yes. I am the same."

And he grabbed the boy's arm and stood.

"You are coming with me," he said.

"One trip to the barber and you talk like a captain," Zen mocked him.

Ignoring the recruiter and before Nico could protest, Michael had taken the cabin boy outside.

"But, what if Signor Loredan..." Nico began, following hard upon the two.

"No matter," Michael said. "Roch stays with me."

"Enjoy him," Zen called from inside. "He was far better than you."

"To hell with the both of you," Michael retorted, not knowing whether or not the men heard him. He would find his captain or the friar. Either one of them could, must help him.

"Direct us, Nico," he said. "Take us to the captain."

So as Nico indicated left or right, pointed to a particular bridge that straddled a narrow canal, or pointed his right arm out straight ahead or down a covered alley, Michael marched ahead of him. Roch kept close to the young Greek's side until at last the three arrived at the alley entrance to the widowed Signora Francesca Contarini's frescoed palazzo, whose public loggia and private chambers overlooked the bustling daily activity on the Grand Canal. It was nearly dusk.

"Signor Loredan and Friar Martino should be here," Nico said.

Michael banged on the massive carved door with the brass plate displaying the Contarini crest.

"Buona sera," a deep voice greeted them, and an older but still vital man in a black tunic and a white fabric cap that covered his ears looked quizzically at the unexpected assortment of youth before him. "What is it you wish?" he asked.

"Captain Loredan is expecting us," Michael said. He spoke as if he regularly visited nobles in their palazzi.

"Ah, bene," replied the servant, accepting Michael's tone and demeanor as the young Greek had hoped he would. He opened the great door wide. "Whom shall I say is calling?"

"Michele," Michael replied. "Michele, Nico, and Roch."

"Come in," the servant said.

"Grazie," Michael answered.

"And to you, as well," Michael bowed to Nico as they followed. "Thank you for bringing us here."

Chapter 19

LA SIGNORA FRANCESCA ALIGHIERI CONTARINI

La signora stood as the unlikely trio entered the mirrored and candlelit great room where she received her frequent guests, many of them, it must be said, seeking her venerable counsel and her valued patronage. Captain Loredan and Friar Martino had been sitting either side of her, each on extravagantly cushioned chairs. She herself had selected a high backed carved seat without any benefit of softness. She was tiny and slim, with the same aquiline nose as her son Clario, but with bright blue rather than hazel eyes. On her stockinged feet, which showed beneath a sky-blue robe with ermine cuffs, were ribbon-laced wooden shoes, the heel and sole on the left foot higher than those on the right by nearly four inches. Without them, Michael instantly realized, the lady would have walked with a serious limp. Instead, she approached quite gracefully. Her hair was coiffed in an upswept style and draped with an intricate lace veil. The veil's open-work allowed her emerald drop earrings to sparkle in the candlelight, which also made her animated face glow. Her complexion, clear and with few wrinkles except around her mouth and eyes, was enhanced by the play of the gems.

"You are Michele, then, about whom Captain Loredan and Friar Martino have been speaking. You will be helping me, I understand, to manage the boys who will comprise the San Marco choir during my son's untimely and unseemly absence."

"It will be my honor to do so, signora," Michael said.

Though he did not yet comprehend the import of one word la signora spoke, Michael bowed to her as if he understood completely, bending from his waist, the quality of his new garments matching his supple and refined decorum. Then he stepped back again. No doubt observing Loredan's approving smile, Nico imitated the new fellow's gestures. Meanwhile, Roch stood silent and still and small. He reeked of sweat and carnality. He scratched his thumbs with his forefingers and stayed close to Michael. His eyes blinked and twitched; he needed to blow his nose.

"Excuse our intrusion, signora," Michael began, and then moved his eyes to the friar. He spoke slowly, his words awkward intrusions into the otherwise comfortable atmosphere of the large receiving room. "It could not be helped. I needed to find Captain Loredan or Friar Martino. Nico"—he gestured to Loredan's valet —"was kind enough to lead me here from the barber's shop. It was there that we, quite unexpectedly, I must say, discovered Roch."

Michael paused.

"Too late," he continued, speaking directly to the friar now, his voice thick with a combination of anger and remorse. "Father, I am very sorry to say, I discovered him too late."

Roch trembled beside Michael. His eleven years, if indeed that many comprised his life on earth, seem to have diminished as his sufferings increased, so that now his timid, skittish attitude resembled that of a much younger, woefully neglected child.

"Ahem," the Franciscan mumbled as he lumbered to stand by the lady. "I am glad you have found me, Michael, as I am just this evening to welcome Roch into our dormitory and classes at the Frari."

The friar came over and patted Roch on his matted head, then returned to his chair.

The boy did not react. However, Michael breathed a sigh of relief at the priest's immediate understanding of his and the boy's predicament. He could not tell whether Loredan understood as well, or had merely decided not to comment or intervene, such remove having been his custom during the five months that Michael had known him.

La signora spoke without revealing evidence of either comprehension or shock.

"I hope Roch will prove a better pupil than my own son," she said. She did not smile, but instead pursed her lips after her words. She looked at Roch's dismal face.

"Have you no family?" she asked. Her voice was direct and kind.

The boy whispered, "Dead. Dead from God's own plague." The boy made the Sign of the Cross on his forehead. "That is why I went to sea."

He looked at Loredan.

"Commander Loredan said I might be his cabin boy. I watched him prepare his galley and I would not go away."

Loredan nodded, "Yes, he was an eager one."

"And Signor Loredan, or Michele, took you with him from the galley?" she asked.

Roch shook his head no.

"Then who?" she continued.

The boy could barely be heard.

"Jacopo," he whispered. "Jacopo told me to go with him to meet Zen at the barber shop. He said there would be biscuits and fruit and cheese."

His lips trembled, but he did not cry.

"Who is Jacopo?" la signora asked.

Loredan answered, and the lady turned to him as he spoke. "One of my veteran oarsmen, and a good one, too. He is the man who saved my nephew Lucca from a canal last Carnevale."

Michael realized his captain did not know what else Jacopo had done to Lucca.

"Then what?" la signora asked, returning her attention to Roch rather than pursuing the captain's comments.

"Then Michael came. He found me when Jacopo and Zen were finished with me and he had Nico bring me here."

The boy closed his eyes. The room was silent, and the captain rubbed his hands over his just-shaved face.

"Jesus Lord," he said.

"But obviously the barber did not groom you," Signora Contarini said.

She did not mock. Michael heard no harshness in her voice. Yet the boy looked at the floor. But for the brief pops of embers in the fire, silence enveloped the room. Then Michael saw her blue eyes open wide with understanding. Again she looked to Loredan.

"Zen," she said, as Loredan paced the room, hands crossed behind his back, visage stern, lips tight. "The Zen your sister so rightly detests?" she asked.

"The very same," Loredan growled. "The Zen who will not be tempered, even by the recent impositions placed upon him by the unyielding communal attorneys of the Avogadori."

Signor Loredan circled the loggia while he talked, his pace quickening as his anger grew.

"After his unmannerly treatment of my sister and niece, he was stripped of his right to captain his own merchant galley for two years and sent to recruit foreign rowers."

Here Loredan paused.

"That is how Michele came to know him," he continued.

He circled the loggia again.

"And Friar Martino has recently told me of more shameful and blatantly illegal practices, not befitting conversation with a lady such as yourself, in which the man allegedly partakes. Practices which his recruiter status, I am sad to say, allows him to expand."

Again he rubbed his face with his hands.

"I see," la signora said. "I believe I understand what you are saying."

She put a finger to her lips for a moment, as if deciding whether or not to go on. Then she did.

"Even a lady such as myself, as you say, has heard that the Avogadori have recently appointed The Council of Ten to seek out and aggressively prosecute those who engage in such practices. So prevalent have they become, I am told, that they threaten the very stability of the Republic."

Again she stopped for a moment.

"Convicted sodomites—'Sodomite' is the Scripture's term, I believe—that is what you mean, don't you?"

"Yes," Loredan answered, his discomfort obvious when he drew his eyes away from the lady, looking instead into the fire.

"Such men are now burned alive in the piazza, are they not?" she said.

The captain tempered his surprise at la signora's knowledge and again met her gaze with his own.

"Yes," he said, "they are. I am sorry, signora, I had not expected your grasp of the situation."

"Understood," she said. "But I am a widow now, without need any longer to blush. Without a husband, I must be cognizant of the world as it is."

She pulled her lace veil closer to her cheeks and said, "Such men abound in Florence, as well. My son has been in their company. I myself required"—here, in an uncustomary expression of dismay, the lady grabbed at her gown and wrung a section of the blue fabric in her hands—"God forgive me, I myself required that he be in their company!"

For an instant, her stoic mien abandoned her. But she breathed once, deeply, and regained her composure.

"Dante has written of them. He, my gifted cousin, has immortalized them."

She let go her gown, her hands fell to her sides, and her shoulders slumped.

"Burned alive and immortalized," she said. "Such is our world."

She sighed, clasped and unclasped her hands.

Then, as if the previous conversation had never occurred, she turned her attention to Roch once more. Stooping so that she was eye to eye with him despite his abused and bedraggled state, she cupped his chin in both her jeweled hands.

"You are hungry," she said, an assumption rather than a question.

The boy did not respond.

"Donato," she called, and the servant who had opened the door appeared.

"Please see to it that this boy is fed and otherwise taken care of. Treat him as our guest. As our noblest guest. Do you understand?"

"Si, Signora Contarini," the servant replied. "I will do you as you request." And he gestured graciously to the boy as the barber had to Michael earlier.

But Roch did not move. Instead he looked up at Michael.

"It is safe, my son," the friar assured Michael, so the young Greek motioned for the boy to go.

Once Roch and the servant were out of sight, la signora resumed her seat, arranged her gown so that it flowed over her shoes, and proceeded.

"Now you will sit with us," she said, and she motioned for Nico and Michael, who was most unclear of his place and his function at the moment, to sit on a velvet-cushioned settee perpendicular to the friar.

"And you will tell me, fully and without omission, what has been going on. Only if you do so may I use my status to assist you and the unfortunate boy."

She gestured for the two to help themselves to candied fruit and colorful liquors on the low table before her. While Nico did so, Michael instead held his palms together and tried to put his thoughts in order. How could he tell a woman, and a noblewoman at that, all that he had learned?

When la signora let her back rest against the tall-backed chair and said, "Go on," Michael sat straight up on the settee and took a deep breath.

Silence filled the stately room. Many candles, some tall and slender, others squat and thick, flickered in the deepening dusk. Though desperate to relate the evil he had encountered, not once but many times now, the young Greek was loath to speak. And despite sitting so close to those who both commanded and guided him, he knew not what to say.

While he hesitated and considered what words he might rightly use, la signora began instead, her calm and steady voice a litany of facts that betrayed little emotion but much authority.

"I know I am only a woman," she said. "But I am the noble Bartolomeo Contarini's widow, forty-six years of age, and a cousin of the great Florentine poet Dante. I read and write like a man, and manage both the servants and the considerable family fortunes. I have no daughters to distract me with frivolous female trifles, and my only son, Clario, who should have become a great artist after his mentor Cennino d'Andrea Cennini in Florence, has proven himself a mere parody of a painter. He is presently held under house arrest and awaiting trial in the civil courts, accused of sodomizing and murdering six-year-old twin orphans in Corfu, scorned even by the canonical superiors and bishop whose own cleric he has claimed himself to be."

Michael gasped. La signora was taken aback.

"Michele?" she said.

"Pardon my outburst, signora. It is just that I met them," he said. "I met the twins."

He put his head in his hands. La signora waited.

"And?" she asked.

"I knew something was not right. They were hurt and frightened. But I did not even try to take them away. I should have taken them away!"

He looked to the friar who, at Michael's cry, folded his hands over his great lap.

Nico stopped eating to listen. His eyes darted back and forth between this new man and la signora, who listened to him as if he were her equal.

Loredan interrupted, speaking to Friar Martino.

"And that accounts for your silly tussle with Roch when I wanted to send him for the missives," the captain said to the friar.

"Exactly," the friar said, and he unfolded his hands.

Apparently unperturbed, la signora continued.

"I assure you, Michele, I can tolerate whatever unfortunate news you have to share with me. Your dispatches and the presence of one sad boy will not, I promise you, rise to the level of disheartening information that has recently plagued me and shamed the Contarini family."

Michael took another breath. With it, clarity flooded his mind. Suddenly he knew. The lady's own words had told him what he must say.

"But they do and they will, signora. What I have learned plagues the honor of all Venetians," he insisted, "both your family and those of all honest nobili, cittadini, and popolani."

Loredan paced again. The friar fingered his beads. Nico listened open-mouthed.

"For me, signora, but not only for me, for Roch and for many others, the trouble began with Zen. But it does not end with him. He is a ring-leader, no doubt. But he is not alone. He is far from alone. Jacopo, as well, my captain, has spoiled one closer than you know."

Loredan stopped, stood still, and listened.

"What do you mean?" he asked. "Who?"

Through the night, then, the young Greek told them all he knew. The fire died down and the candles guttered. A chill November dawn rose, and Roch, the cabin boy, returned to the loggia bathed, dressed, and fed. He was ready now to join Friar Martino's classes so that he, too, like the young Clario Contarini years before him, might learn how to be a trustworthy Christian citizen of the great Republic of Venice.

Chapter 20

TRINITY

"So, it is decided," Signor Loredan told his younger sister Elena, a woman of thirty-two years, who wore her unfortunate widowhood like a girl.

It was the first Sunday of Advent. The captain sat at the head of the table where the late Signor Venier, until three years earlier, had overseen his family's affairs. He had died in three days from a fever no amount of physician's bleeding or his wife's cool compresses and prayers to the Virgin would alleviate.

Elena sat with Signora Contarini to her right and Friar Martino to her left, in the cinnamon-scented dining room of the Venier palazzo, only a short gondola ride away from the Contarini residence, and not far from the Rialto. Michael stood behind Captain Loredan's chair and listened, eager to be dismissed. He wanted supper himself, but Signora Elena had not invited him to join the family. Instead, he was to eat downstairs with Bronislav and his wife, who must by now, he imagined, be impatient for his arrival. He had already stood through the cold meats, a hot broth, and now a tray of sweets, each carried in to the nobles and the friar by a bustling woman Signora Elena called Isa, and a close-mouthed man with a stiff neck who answered to Angelo. Roch was under Nico's care at Signor Loredan's residence, where the valet had promised to teach him to play chess, and Nico would be rowing the boy back to the Frari before the evening bells rang nine.

The two women had listened to plans made by Loredan and the friar, specifying that Michael would escort the eight choir boys, plus Bronislav's Franto, to and from rehearsals and lessons at San Marco. The boys were to practice both morning and afternoon each day through Advent and debut their accomplishments during midnight Mass on the eve of Christ's birth. Signora Contarini would see to their feeding, choir robes, and accessories. All of Venice was looking forward to the liturgical and social celebration.

"I have arranged for Marina to be surrounded by her seven female Venier cousins, none of them yet betrothed or affianced, so that she will not feel so conspicuous," Elena said to her brother.

"It is already a year since Zen duped her," Loredan complained. "It is well past time for her to be considering other suitors," he insisted, as he took a slice of ricotta-topped torta and swallowed it whole. "If she does not, she will end up unmarried and a nun like our own sister."

"You're a fine one to talk," replied Elena, pointing a forefinger at her brother. "Are there other suitors? You, after all, were the one who suggested Zen!"

She pouted, crossing her slim arms across her bosom.

"True, I did," Loredan answered. And Elena babbled on, nattering directly at Signora Contarini about her brother's bad choice and her daughter's lost prospect.

"Where is the girl?" asked Signora Contarini, interrupting Elena. "I would like to meet her. Perhaps I may find a proper nobleman for her."

Elena bobbed up and down in her chair. Michael found her annoying.

"That would be wonderful, signora," she said. "I am sorry she is not with us this evening. She and her sisters are spending two weeks with their aunt, our sister, whom my brother just mentioned"—she pointed to her brother again, this time with a smile—"Suor Patrizia Loredan, who you may know is the novice mistress at San Zaccaria."

Signora Contarini asked, "Is it your plan to have Marina join the convent?"

Elena giggled a bit, then answered, "That is most definitely not my intention, dear signora. But, given the price of dowries and my lot of daughters, I am certain that at least two of them must take the veil."

Her brother patted his sugar-crusted mouth, cleared his throat and said, "We shall see about that, my dear sister. For the moment, let us succeed at getting Lucca singing."

At the mention of the boy, the captain looked to Michael.

"And Lucca," Signora Contarini said, commenting on the boy's absence, "where is he?" The lady sniffed. "Have you given away your children?"

The captain laughed.

"It appears, dear lady, that my sister has decided to make your evening a calm one."

And he passed Signora Contarini some dried figs and nuts.

Michael had not yet met Lucca, either. Tomorrow he would be escorting him and the others to San Marco.

"With his nursemaid, I am afraid," Elena said. "In his chamber. He had a pustule in his ear, and the surgeon lanced it just this morning. I trust by now he sleeps, if the mandragora has done its work."

"I see," said Signora Contarini. "I hope he will be able to attend his rehearsal tomorrow."

Signora Elena patted her lips with her dinner napkin.

"Yes, signora, I will see that he attends."

Michael shifted his weight from one leg to another behind his captain while Signora Elena changed the subject and told Signora Contarini of her recent failed attempt to learn to read music with Lucca as her instructor. When she exclaimed, "I am simply lacking in those intellectual gifts that my son seems to have gained so effortlessly!" Signora Contarini did not even smile.

"I could not agree more," she said, and Signor Loredan looked away, covering his mouth again with his napkin.

"Go," he turned and chuckled to Michael. "You see what I deal with here, why I prefer the galleys. Go, Michele, enjoy your reunion downstairs. I will call for you later."

As he went, Signora Elena asked Signora Contarini, "What will you wear to the choir's debut on Christmas Eve?"

"Garments suitable for the Mass, of course," la signora replied. "It is not Carnevale, after all."

Undeterred, Signora Elena continued.

"Well, I have been planning...," she went on, but her voice rose upward like a dissipating vapor as Michael bounded downstairs as fast as he could.

He had no sooner taken his last step down three floors of the Venier palazzo, the upper stairway constructed of marble, the lower two of simpler stone steps, when he heard Bronislav's familiar voice.

"Finis, I said, finis. No more lifting you!" His mentor's voice sounded jovial and hearty.

Bronislav crouched before Franto in the doorway of the kitchen on the canal level of the Venier home, where Signora Elena, reluctantly acquiescing to her brother's significant prodding and eventually effective financial assistance, had arranged for a suite of two rooms to be set aside and outfitted solely for the Ragusans' use.

"Bronislav!" Michael exclaimed, and the two embraced. It was the first time they had reunited since the galley had docked.

Franto stared up at them. Smaller than Michael thought he would be, given his father's substantial frame, Franto dashed to hide behind his father's girth when Michael reached out his hand to shake the boy's.

"Out, you must come out," the Slav said, and reached around to take his son by the arm.

Just as he did, a woman appeared from behind a movable wooden screen in the kitchen.

"Milaslova, meet Michael," her husband said, and the woman first bowed then shook the young Greek's hands, taking them both in hers.

Michael was shocked into open-mouthed silence by her beauty and youth. He realized he was staring. He remembered Bronislav's joke to Jacopo that Milaslova looked just like him. But she most certainly did not. Her hair, peeking from an amber veil held in place by a wooden headband, was the color of almonds, her lips plums upon a face unblemished and open. Her eyes dark brown, with lashes upturned as if lifting to the sky above. Slim and taller than her husband by just so much that her mouth was even with his eyes, she appeared to glide across the floor, her long orange tunic as bright as her disposition. A fire from the kitchen added a glowing warmth to her welcome.

"Michael," she said. "At last we meet. They have kept you too long upstairs. Come and eat with us, though our repast will prove much simpler than Signora Elena's, I am afraid."

She knelt to Franto and tousled his hair with her unadorned hands. The boy's curls were the same color as his mother's longer waves.

"Help our guest now, Franto," she said. "You remember, don't you? One must always help a guest."

Franto, though a bit wary, finally offered his little hand to Michael.

"Come," he said, "I will show you to your seat."

His voice was a small bird's.

"Thank you," Michael said, and he followed the boy.

In the kitchen, Milaslova had laid a table with four shallow wooden bowls, and now she picked each up, one at a time, walked to the fireplace, and ladled into them a thick fish stew. While she did, Bronislav ripped a long, crusty loaf of bread into four pieces and placed them in a basket, which he instructed Franto to pass first to Michael. Milaslova poured wine into simple tumblers, scooping some water from a corner barrel into Franto's glass. The boy took up his spoon, but returned it to the table when Bronislav motioned with his eyes.

"We must give thanks and remember our dear lost daughter and sister," the Slav said, as Milaslova sat, reached out her arms, and took her husband's and son's hands in hers.

"Please," Bronislav said to Michael, and the young Greek opened a hand to grasp his mentor's.

"Franto," Milaslova cued her son, smiling.

The boy rose at once from his bench, stretched his chest up and outward, and sang.

"Grazie, grazie, Dio bene; Grazie, grazie, Amen."

Though Michael heard and understood them, the words seemed but excuses for beauty sung. Franto's voice, rising and flowing from within his diminutive body, filled the room with a surprisingly warm, rich, confident melody. Michael would not have been one whit surprised had heavenly angels joined them to surround the boy. The Mother of God herself would certainly have smiled upon him. How Michael wished his own stooped mother could hear such a voice. "God in our world," she would have reminded him, as she had when he saw his first rainbow. He bowed his head and whispered, "Praise, thanks, plea, and pardon," the prayer he had taken to repeating silently every day since Bronislav had saved him from himself in Manfredonia.

"Now we eat!" the Slav announced, and the four of them took up their spoons.

At least Bronislav had not changed, Michael was glad to note.

"Delicious, Mila," Bronislav complimented his wife after his first swallow.

Milaslova smiled at him, and Michael thought he saw a promise flicker from underneath her long eyelashes. He felt himself flush, both aroused and moved by what passed between the two.

"Good!" Franto chirped, and all of them laughed.

A trinity they were, Michael realized, as the hearty soup filled and warmed his body the way Bronislav, Milaslova, and Franto were firing his soul. Could it be so? Was such a miracle possible? Could he, too, find this kind of contentment, perhaps even this happiness, on earth, with his own woman and, should God will, their own children, in Venice?

His reverie was short-lived, however, interrupted by a sudden and desperate banging on the door by the kitchen's loading dock.

So quickly did he and Bronislav leap up that they rocked the table, spilling their bowls of stew onto the table's planks.

"Go," Bronislav barked to Milaslova. "Take the boy and go."

Milaslova jumped up, grabbed Franto by the hand, pushed him ahead of her into the adjoining room, and slammed and bolted the door.

"There," pointed Bronislav, and Michael took a poker from the hearth.

Bronislav felt for the utility knife under his belt, strode to the door and asked, "Who is it?"

No one answered, but the banging continued without pause.

Motioning for Michael to stand flat against the wall just where the door would open wide unless he kept it from doing so, Bronislav lifted the metal bolt and eased the door just a bit, enough that an oar would have filled the space. When he did, a bloody hand and a leg shod in the same boot with which Loredan had fitted him, pushed against the Slav's pressure.

"Nico!" Michael cried, and Captain Loredan's valet fell forward onto the floor, blood dripping from his mouth. His cries were muffled with gurgling noises and he held one hand to his face.

Bronislav re-bolted the door while Michael turned the valet on his side. He panted, and with eyes bulging, opened his mouth.

"Dio!" Michael exclaimed.

Nico's tongue had been slashed so that most of it dangled over the valet's lips.

"Jacopo!" Michael knew, even as he uttered the Venetian's name. "Jacopo tried to cut off your tongue!"

Nico nodded and, with his right hand, held up two fingers. He drew the letters "J" and "Z" in the air.

"J! J! J!" he gestured as he panted, slashing upward with his hand. Then, right after, "Z! Z! Z!" bringing his arm to his waist.

"And Zen held you."

Nico nodded.

While Michael deciphered Nico's pantomime, Bronislav ran to a pile of cleaning cloths stacked on a table next to the fireplace, took one, then dipped it into the water barrel. Returning to Nico, the Slav had him press the cloth to his tongue to staunch the blood. While the valet did so, Bronislav examined his trunk, his legs and hands, looking for other wounds.

"Roch," he asked, "Where is Roch?"

Nico raised his shoulders, then used one of his hands to indicate running.

"He ran away? He got away?" Michael asked.

The valet nodded yes.

"Where did he go?" Michael continued.

Again, Nico raised his shoulders and shook his head.

"You don't know?" Michael persisted.

The valet shook his head.

"Jacopo and Zen, do they have him? Did they take him?"

Nico shook his head no.

"Z," he motioned again, then pointed and jabbed at Michael. "Z," then "M, M, M."

"Zen wanted me? Zen wants me."

Nico nodded his head so that his matted hair shook. Then he held his free hand in front of his mouth and shook his head no again.

"And you would not tell him, that is it, isn't it? You would not tell him where I was."

Nico nodded yes.

"Milaslova," Bronislav called. "Come."

"I will get the captain," Michael said, and he ran up the three flights of stairs and into the dining room.

Until the shocked looks of Loredan, Signora Elena, Signora Contarini, and Friar Martino greeted him, Michael had not realized he was covered in blood now.

"Nico has been wounded, come upon by Jacopo and Zen, who were looking for me."

The two men stood.

"And Roch?" asked the friar. "Have they taken Roch?"

"Nico says not," Michael answered. "But he doesn't know where the boy has gone."

"We must find him," the priest said.

"I will go," replied Michael

"We will go together," Loredan said.

"What happened?" Signora Elena asked. "Who are these men? Isn't Jacopo a good one, the one who saved Lucca?"

Ignoring her, Michael and Loredan bounded down the steps while the friar took Signora Contarini's arm in his and, together, they followed, her uneven legs and his stoutness slowing their descent.

By the time they arrived downstairs, Bronislav had already laid Nico on his side upon the table, a bundle of cloths making a pillow for his head so he would not choke. Milaslova had joined her husband, and she had in her hand a long sewing needle threaded with strong, fine linen, the type she used to sew together Signora Elena's leather pillow covers.

"Stay inside," Milaslova called to her son, who peeked from behind the bedchamber door. Her voice attempted calm.

Michael saw that her hands shook, but she stroked the valet's head and drew his eyes shut.

"We will help you," she told him. "I am sorry, but the stitches will hurt."

The captain and the friar each took two candles apiece and held them so that Milaslova could see inside Nico's mouth.

Bronislav pinioned Nico's wrists as Milaslova knotted the thread, then with one hand pressed the dangling tongue back into the valet's mouth.

"His ankles," commanded Bronislav, and Michael held them down.

Milaslova pierced the intact portion of the valet's tongue with her needle and the knotted thread.

The table shook and still more blood spurted from Nico's mouth and nose, covering Milaslova's hands and arms in scarlet. His shrieks were muffled by her fingers, slippery now, inside his mouth as she stitched. She had to hold the needle tightly so it would not slip. She counted aloud as she worked and he writhed, her calls as rhythmic and persistent as any armiraio's. How admirable she is, Michael told himself. His hands kept a firm grip on Nico's ankles. If all were true to their tasks, perhaps the valet would speak again. Perhaps he could lead them to Roch and his attackers.

Because he did not know what else to do, Michael prayed, his words accompanying Milaslova's count, both evocations effective measures to temper, if not defeat, chaos.

"Help us, O Lord of compassion," he said, "We trust in you to help us in the time of our need."

He repeated the words, trying to match them to the rhythm of Milaslova's stitching.

"Help us, O Lord of compassion," a woman's voice spoke now. "We trust in you to help us in the time of our need."

In a far corner, having let drop her dinner napkin from over her mouth, Signora Elena, he realized, had joined him. She moved closer to the table, still out of the way, but within the valet's hearing. On the third plea, Signora Contarini, close by the bedchamber door, raised her voice as well, so that soon, by the fourth repetition, all of them, even Loredan, had formed a mighty, unified chorus.

Despite their prayer, Nico still writhed in pain. Loredan and the friar still held straight their candles. Milaslova still stitched ruthlessly, trying to save the tongue. Bronislav and Michael still held the valet down.

So intent with purpose was each and every one, that none took notice when little Franto opened the bedchamber door, slipped out, and climbed to the fifth step of the stone stairway where he could look down upon the group who hovered over the kitchen table.

He began to sing.

"Dona nobis pacem, pacem. Dona nobis pacem."

The others' prayers went silent. Still Milaslova counted.

Again, he lifted his voice.

"Dona nobis pacem, pacem. Dona nobis pacem."

The company joined his song, turning the simple prayer into a round, the boy's piercing clarity leading them to transcendence in the midst of doom.

All but his mother and Nico were singing. But even as she stitched, Michael saw that Milaslova smiled. And even as he suffered, Nico opened his eyes wide.

Though Michael understood that Franto's voice and song could not begin to erase Nico's ordeal or mitigate his injury, it acknowledged and mourned both in the valet's immediate presence and hearing—a mellifluous, innocent prayer intoned by a little boy, more effective than any theology.

"Amen," Franto drew out his voice. "Amen."

And at Milaslova's nod, Bronislav lifted a shaking Nico and supported him until the young man could keep himself upright.

"Let's go, then," Loredan said. "Let's find Roch."

Chapter 21

RESCUE

He was not at the Frari, not at the Arsenale, nor at Signor Loredan's palazzo, where Michael and the captain now stood, perplexed.

"Roch!" Michael had called, his voice echoing through the canals that snaked around each place that might have hidden him. "Oh, Roch!"

He and Loredan had searched the boats, climbing from one lashed gondola, sandolo, traghetto, and caorlina to the next, lifting tarps, opening fish lockers, peering into cabins. They had bent and crawled under porticos, slid around and between columns, climbed parapets.

Still no sign of the cabin boy.

It was nearly midnight. Venice was still but for a few swift gondole skimming the mirror-like water with one or two passengers, all men, most of them cloaked in black.

Michael stood still and listened. His captain did the same. Lapping and mist. Lapping and mist. Then, like two heavy gears that together moved a pulley, they circled one another slowly, deliberately, grinding to a halt when, their scan completed, their faces finally met.

"Where was his home?" Michael asked.

"But they died," Loredan said. "Both his mother and father are dead."

"Yes," Michael answered, "I know."

"By the Arsenale. One canal away, parallel to it."

"Let's go, then," Michael said.

"We must hide ourselves," his captain told him. "Our tongues, too, may speak too much for Jacopo's liking."

The two covered as much of themselves as they could so that only their eyes and noses rose above the folds of their cloaks. By the time they finished, Loredan and his Michele had transformed themselves into just two more anonymous figures in the night.

His cloak's cowl held in place by a scarf wrapped several times around his neck, Michael rowed the sandolo. It would be a safer vessel than a gondola, the captain told him.

"A fisherman's boat," he said, "not a nobleman's."

They were fishermen indeed, Michael told himself, with the same blind hope of all other fishermen: that something would bite, that they would find what they sought and reel him in.

Just as Nico had directed him from the barber shop previously, so did Captain Loredan point the way now. Their sandolo emerged from the side canal beneath the Loredan palazzo and entered the Grand Canal, the waterway's daytime traffic reduced to their own boat and a cabined gondola traveling in the opposite direction.

Neither Michael nor the captain spoke as the boat slipped passed the Piazza San Marco, the doge's palace, and on toward the Arsenale.

"Dock here," the captain said, long before the great brick city arose.

Michael recognized la Riva degli Schiavone, where Nico had led him to Zaccaria and the barber shop.

"We will walk now. Cover your face and do not say a word, in case we are being watched."

Loredan led Michael away from the broad walkway that paralleled the lagoon. Down the Zaccaria alley they went, then over a small bridge, up another alley, across another bridge, and so on, until, "There," the captain pointed.

The building, although composed of three stories, was small. Narrow, with only two shuttered windows each side of a central wooden door on the ground floor, then five windows on each floor above. The third level boasted a middle balcony. All was dark within. All was silent, as well.

"Here," Michael said, and tried the outer door.

It opened.

The two tiptoed in. Michael's eyes adjusted to the dimness. A skylight above allowed a shaft of luminescence to filter down through the stairwell.

"He said he would watch the boats from the time he could just peer out the window," the captain whispered.

"So, canal side," Michael whispered back. "What floor?"

"I cannot tell you," answered Loredan.

The two felt their way along to the central stairwell, Michael leading the way now with his younger, sharper eyes. Just past where the stairwell ended, he felt and blinked at open space and, turning right and waving his arms up and down, realized that a crawl space under the stairs offered them a place to sit, hope, and wait.

"Here," Michael said, and reached his hand out to bring the captain close to him.

Michael sat down first, crouching. Loredan followed, sitting bunched against the young Greek. The two brought their knees to their chins and wrapped their arms underneath their thighs, positioning themselves so that they seemed fixed twin sculptures.

They waited and listened. Perhaps at first light, they could find Roch's apartment, and maybe they would find the boy, as well.

"Psst." The captain elbowed Michael's arm.

The outer door had opened, letting in a blustery swoosh of damp air. Michael held his breath.

Someone, one person only, climbed the stairs, stopping, it seemed, at the top of the first level. Then, silence and stillness again.

"If he comes back down, we take him, you around one side, I around the other," the captain whispered.

"Yes," Michael agreed. "Otherwise we wait."

"The watch will come with a foreman to see that the furnaces are stoked well before dawn," the captain said. "We will hear them and breathe the smoke. Then, those who dwell here will surely wake."

"Good," Michael said.

He wanted to stay awake and alert, but warm under the stairs, closer to the captain than he had been all night, he felt himself dropping off. He was afraid he might snore and be discovered.

But before his head could drop in slumber, an apartment door opened two stories above, and a torch flamed in the hallway and stairwell. Someone with a heavy tread and a set of keys that jangled and clanked started down the stairs. Step, jangle, clank, pause. Step, jangle, clank, pause. Then the man uttered a sudden, gruff, yet glad cry.

"Roch!" he exclaimed. "Thanks be to God, Roch. You have returned safe from your voyage."

Without answering, the boy leapt up and ran down the stairs, the man's voice calling after him, "Don't go, Roch. It's alright. Come in, come in."

And just as the boy's feet in their shoddy boots (completely wet now, Michael could tell from the way they sounded as he ran) touched the alley-level floor, Michael and the captain grabbed him from either side and held him tight.

The boy struggled to wrest himself loose until he recognized Michael's and the captain's voices.

"You are safe, Roch! You are with us now," both captain and oarsman repeated. "We have come for you. You are safe. You are safe."

The boy relaxed. Still, the man from above came quickly upon them.

"What's this? What has happened?" he asked. "Roch, it's me, Giubbe, Giubbe."

The man studied the captain and Michael through the torchlight.

"Who are you?" he asked. He brought his lantern close to their faces.

"Are these friends, Roch?" he inquired, bending his tall frame down to the boy. "Are these two your friends?"

The boy, drenched and shivering, nodded his head.

"My captain," he said. "Captain Loredan."

Giubbe's eyes opened wide, lit by his torch's flame.

"Signor," and he bowed to Loredan. "My apologies."

"Giubbe," the captain returned the man's greeting. "No need."

"And Michael. My friend," Roch said. "An oarsman."

"Pleased to meet you," Giubbe said.

"I, as well," Michael replied.

Niceties completed, the captain and Michael let go of the boy, and, as if he could support himself not at all, he fell in a heap on the floor. Michael picked him up then, holding him in his arms as if Roch were but an infant.

"Come," Giubbe said, and he led them back upstairs.

When the quartet entered the small apartment, Giubbe's wife, head still covered with her night cap, initially hid herself by a tall cupboard. Then she cried with joy when she saw the boy.

"Roch! Roch!" she called, smothering his face with kisses. But he did not respond, his gaze vague and without recognition. "Roch, it is Clara, Clara."

Instead of responding, as if he at last knew that he was safe, Roch had fallen fast asleep.

"Here, here," Clara cried. "I will take care of him. He must have our bed."

She and Michael propped the limp, wet boy against a chest of drawers. Then, with Michael's help, Clara removed his soaked clothing, wrapping him in her husband's nightshirt and drying his head with a worn towel.

Even as the boy languished, his eyes opening and closing intermittently at Clara's ministrations and supported almost completely by Michael, he allowed Clara to swaddle him. She crooned to him as if he were her own child. "You can sleep now, you can sleep."

"What has happened?" Giubbe asked. His keys dangled from his belt. He still held his torch, and thrust it close to the captain's face, searching for an answer. "He is a different boy. Afraid. Weaker. Not like before. What has happened to him?"

"Later," Clara shushed her husband. "It is not important now. Just that he is dry and can sleep."

"Why don't we step outside," the captain suggested. "We can speak there without disturbing him."

"Si, si," Clara agreed. "I will sit by him. I will keep watch." And she dragged a stool to the bed.

As she did, Michael lifted Roch again, this time from his quasi-standing position. He followed Clara from the chest of drawers three steps across the room to the couple's humble bed, where he laid the boy down on the straw-filled pallet and covered him with a woolen blanket from his feet to his chin. Until then, when he let go, Michael had not realized how light a burden Roch was.

Chapter 22

MAESTRO ROMANO AND THE SAN MARCO BOYS' CHOIR

Though he had slept not a wink, Michael was at Signora Contarini's dock at half-past eight, as per her instructions. She had arranged for Donato to have her gondola outfitted and ready to transport the eight noble putti plus Bronislav's son to meet Maestro Romano so that they might begin their training and rehearsals.

"Buona giornata!" la signora herself called from above.

She was as yet unaware of what had transpired overnight. Michael decided to wait until later to tell her. If Captain Loredan let her know before he did, well, he could do nothing about that. As for him, he thought it of no use to ruin the start of her long-planned dream of the boys' choir.

"I will attend you later, before the noon Mass," she said.

La signora's hair fell loose and long without its veil, light brown strands of it not yet overtaken by the gray, and she waved avidly as she called, having thrown open the shutters despite the cold.

Letting his black hood drop, and pulling down the scarf that had covered all but his eyes, Michael lifted his freed face upward to respond. "I look forward to your arrival," he said.

Suddenly he realized his words were more than simple courtesy. He longed for la signora's company, wanted to be in her presence again. After last night's deeds, he would be able to tell her without a shadow of doubt how reckless and ruthless Zen and Jacopo had become. He would prove his claim that their actions were not random or spontaneous, but instead served as continuous cynical attacks on the Republic's virtue and order. Such ideals, until his own recent humiliating experiences, had been mere words to him. How he had squirmed with impatience and shifted in his seat every time his uncle had spoken them. But after the long night in Signora Contarini's spacious and glittering loggia, he had seen, as she bade them farewell and sent them into the November dawn, her cousin's own *La Divina Commedia* opened on the oak reading table behind the maroon velvet couch. La signora had moved her delicate forefinger beneath the words and read aloud: "You were not made to live as brutes, but to follow virtue and knowledge."

That is what Michael wanted to do. That is what he would try to do.

"Ready?" Donato asked him.

Michael nodded and grasped the gondola's oar, much lighter but requiring no less skill than his galley's heavy one. He dipped it into canal water that did not crash and roil like the sea, but lapped and rose and fell as the result of peripheral tides. As he directed the Contarini gondola, he wondered if the galleys and the high seas were the only places that afforded men the adversities and opportunities to achieve honor. Perhaps, he allowed himself to consider, this singular lagoon city of smaller vessels, some the same size as his father's lowly fishing boat, called for such men as well. He had been a fool. He wanted to tell his father he was sorry.

"Ciao," Donato waved.

Then, with a generous push of the shiny black boat, the servant, shivering despite his woolen coat and furry cap, sent Michael off. The young Greek knew his route—six palazzi, each along the Grand Canal. His first stop would be to pick up Lucca Venier and Franto.

"Bronislav will go with you. And as you row, you must not show your face," Captain Loredan had instructed him. "Stay alert.

Be watchful. Take care that no one but Romano interacts with the boys. We will speak when you return this evening."

Blinking against the wind's occasional bluster, Michael began the first of his twice-daily runs. He dipped and turned the oar into the water, balancing his feet on the flat platform as he stood so that he worked in time with the gentle rocking of the wavelets and the puffing buffets of almost-winter wind.

The putti, he rehearsed their names, were:

Lucca Venier, age six, whose bandaged ear, Michael was secretly glad to know, would single him out for easy observing;

Claudio Mocenigo, age nine—"a complainer and as arrogant as his strutting father," la signora had told him, "but quick to learn and eager for the accolades he will garner";

Alfredo Mocenigo, age seven, the younger brother of Claudio —"He is a genuine delight, with no burdens of a first son," la signora had said, smiling as she did. "He keeps time with his fingers as he sings. I find myself watching his hands even as I listen to his voice";

Giovanni Foscari, age eight—"So solemn, much like his mother. She has him carry Our Lady's beads in a small pouch tied to his belt. Sometimes his cousin, Claudio Mocenigo, that one again, teases him mercilessly about doing so. But, as his mother admonishes him, he turns the other cheek. Perhaps he will become the family prelate";

Giorgio Zanchi, age eight—"A jokester, and a fine one, I am told by his aunt, a choir nun at San Zaccaria. When I last visited her, she told me how he snuck one of the kitchen cats into his nursemaid's bed, tucking the animal all around, so that when the poor servant walked into her chamber, which was right next to his, she heard a frantic mewling and saw such a wiggling under the coverlet that she screamed. To Giorgio's delight, I might add. Watch you do not find him pretending a fit of fainting or dousing another boy's music with ink";

Frederico Zanchi, age seven, the younger brother of Giorgio —"I hope he will enjoy your company. Unlike his older brother, he does not forget his father stays long at sea." La signora had sighed. "He is a sad and lonely boy";

Leonardo Falier, age seven—"This one sings every waking moment. His mother told me she does not really need the nursemaid for him, as she always knows where he is in the palazzo. All she need do is follow his voice";

Sebastiano Zorzi, age six—"He will have trouble reading the music, as his eyes lack strength. Get the maestro to place him near some large candles";

And the ninth boy, Franto the Ragusan—"As you might imagine, some of the nobles are not pleased that a non-noble, let alone a Ragusan, has been allowed to accompany the others." La signora had then motioned for Michael to lean down so she could whisper in his ear. "But they do not say this to me. Donato tells me that they complain to one another as he leads them to and from their visits to see me. As if Franto poses a threat to their sons' futures!" And then she had laughed. "As Captain Loredan admires and trusts this Bronislav," she had continued, "despite his humble and foreign origins, then so must I."

Now, as he turned her gondola toward the Venier dock, Michael wondered what, if anything, the captain had told her about him.

"Good morning, good morning," Bronislav called as the boat approached. He flung a rope, one end fixed to an iron loop on the dock, to Michael, who knotted it on the gondola's forcola.

The Slav stood between Franto and Lucca (whose cloth bandage showed a few spots of yellow, evidence, no doubt, of the surgeon's lancing). While Franto wore a simple brown fabric cape over his deep red tunic and and similarly colored leggings, Lucca enjoyed a fur mantle over his shoulders. Lucca's hands, too, were gloved, while Franto's, like his father's, were hidden beneath the sleeves of his tunic. Bronislav himself might have been a bear from the forests far north of the lagoon, his broad frame covered in dark brown wool, his head encased in a fuzzy hat his wife had fashioned from the remnants of a coverlet she had sewn for Signor Elena's large and solitary bed.

Upon entering the gondola, the boys separated, Lucca immediately assuming the first seat in one of the eight sedie piccole that Donato had arranged in two rows, four chairs each across the vessel's mid-section. Franto must have been instructed earlier, for he did not even start toward one of the chairs, but crouched opposite Michael and beneath his father, tucked under Bronislav's legs on the gondola's floor, protected against the wind and who knew what else.

At each stop, the putti, all dressed similarly, jumped or hopped into the vessel, all but Claudio Mocenigo, that is, who complained to his long-nosed nurse, "I do not want to sing. I would rather stay with my father." But the nurse ignored him, even when he stamped his feet. As she returned inside—blocking her ears with her hands as she went, Michael was amused to observe—Bronislav stepped out of the boat and lifted the fellow into it, reaching under his arms as if he were a sack of wheat. By the time Michael had picked up the last of them, Sebastiano, they looked like a gathering of young mice huddled together, their fur shoulders and gloved hands awaiting whatever piece of cheese might be offered them at lunch, though such respite from their lessons remained hours of effort away.

"Here we are!" Franto announced to his father when he spotted the domes of the basilica.

Bronislav crossed himself, with his right hand only now that Michael wore his crucifix. As he did, Michael felt for the gift beneath his layers of black.

The young Greek eased the gondola toward the city's busiest dock, where a bevy of other boats bobbed in the water. Men of various postures and builds, some with parchment rolled and tied in hand, others gripping metal chests, still others with woven bags of foodstuffs, made their way from the dock either to the doge's palace or the basilica. Their workday, too, had begun.

"Attenzione! Attenzione!" one burly man hollered, as he lifted a sack so heavy, with what Michael did not know, that Sebastiano called out, "Look!" They all watched his body shrink under its weight. The man spread his legs and walked, placing one strong limb in front of the other while his shoulders shifted up, down, up, down, until he disappeared beneath the columns of the ducal palace.

"This way," Bronislav called out after the man had gone, and directed the putti up and out of the boat. Michael made sure to wait until each and every boy, Franto included, walked between the Slav in the lead and Michael in the rear, ensuring their safe passage for the few hundred steps between the basin of the lagoon and the great doors of the basilica.

"Dio!" Franto called out as he entered the church and looked up at its sparkling gold domes. "It is the heavens!" he cried. "The heavens!"

"His first visit," Bronislav called back to Michael.

"Mine, too," Michael replied, unwrapping his scarf and dropping his hood. The basilica's mosaics glinted above, lighting the holy place with piercing shards of brightness. Michael's heart soared and tears sprang to his eyes.

It was indeed as if the heavens lifted golden above them. Shafts of light shot through the high windows and across the cavernous basilica. The altar of gold rose in splendor. Even the floor, composed of heavy patterned stones, projected the presence of God upon the floating city.

"Look, Papa, look!" Franto shouted, pointing to the statues of saints and thrones for the prelates. He spun around and around.

Michael saw that the boy was as besot as he with the splendor of the basilica.

But Franto's cries were soon mocked by Claudio's sneer.

"Shut up, you peasant! Haven't you ever seen this place before? You don't belong with us anyway."

Franto turned and stared at the boy, and Michael could see his lips tremble. But Franto did not answer him. Instead, imitating his father, he crossed himself before heading toward the main altar and the choir stalls.

Claudio laughed, then turned his attention to hopping from one set of floor designs to another.

As the group approached the choir stalls, an imposing figure stood before them.

"Maestro," Bronislav called. He bowed to the musician. "We have brought the putti."

There, dressed in the academic gown that revealed his office and his purpose, stood Maestro Romano, his hair a wild mane of brown waves, his dark eyes bulging noticeably, and his conductor's baton in his right hand. Even as he greeted the boys, he slapped the baton into the palm of his left hand. He counted aloud each time the stick hit his milky flesh. He looked as if his body had never come in contact with the sun.

"One, two, three, four, five, six, seven, eight, and, of course, nine."

He bowed to the boys, as if to an appreciative audience, though the nine, with the exception of Franto, did not bow back. Then he addressed Bronislav and Michael.

"But where is Clario Contarini?"

The maestro craned his neck toward the entryway to the basilica, no doubt looking to see if the cleric had entered and was walking toward him.

Michael answered in haste, "He has been unexpectedly detained, Maestro."

"Ah," Romano responded. "When shall I expect him?"

"I cannot say," Michael replied. "He remains in Corfu at the present."

The maestro struck his baton against his chest.

"Then how do I proceed?"

He banged the baton again. This time Sebastian giggled, earning himself a glare from Maestro Romano.

Michael came closer to him.

"I assure you, Maestro, you may proceed as you and Clario Contarini have long planned. Bronislav," here Michael motioned to his colleague, "and I, in deference to Signora Contarini's request, will act in Clario Contarini's stead until his arrival in Venice."

The maestro considered, lifting the tip of the baton to his thick lips.

"And the two of you will manage the boys when they pause from their musical enterprise?"

"Yes," Michael answered.

"Certainly," Bronislav agreed.

The maestro paused, as if he were mulling over a ponderous decision. Then he removed the baton from his lips.

"Very well," he said. "You will sit there," he told the two men, pointing to a bench upon which sheets of music were piled at one end.

"At your service," Michael bowed.

"Likewise," Bronislav said, and the two did as he instructed.

Michael lifted his hood over his head again, as he had been advised by Loredan, although he removed his cloak and scarf. Bronislav pushed him toward the middle of the bench, between the pile of parchment and his own bulk, so that the Slav's body, rather than Michael's, was the only one visible to those walking along the main aisle of the basilica.

"Putti," Maestro Romano said, and he motioned for them to unwrap themselves from their outer garments and leave the clothing on another bench along the wall behind the choir stalls.

The boys did as he instructed them.

Then the maestro pointed to Claudio, the tallest of the nine.

"You, what is your name? Distribute the robes to the others."

"Claudio, but," Claudio started, but the maestro cut him off.

"Obedience is my first requirement, young man."

Claudio's face reddened, and Michael was glad.

The boy followed the maestro's baton to the throne-like seat upon which the white robes were stacked and folded. He lifted the stack and walked to the other boys.

"By size, then," the maestro instructed and, for a brief time, chaos ensued.

The maestro watched how the boys worked together or not. He did not interfere. After each boy had succeeded in finding a robe of relatively good fit and slipped it over his head, Franto helping Lucca so his ear would not be touched, Claudio said to the maestro, "Done."

"Done, *Maestro*," Signor Romano said sternly.

Again Claudio's face went red, and he breathed a loud sigh that Signor Romano ignored.

"I wait," Signor Romano said, slapping his baton against his palm four times.

"Done, Maestro," Claudio said.

The maestro did not acknowledge his improvement.

"Now, then," Signor Romano proceeded.

Claudio's voice had not sounded the least angelic, Michael noted. And he was certain the maestro was not tone deaf.

Signor Romano arranged the boys by height, looking askance at Sebastiano and tapping his arm with his baton when the little boy picked at his nose. He regarded Lucca's bandage and asked him loudly, speaking directly into his bandaged ear, "Do you hear me?"

Lucca nodded. "Yes, I hear you."

Romano corrected him, "You are to say, 'Yes, *Maestro*,'" He held up his baton and waited.

"Yes, Maestro," Lucca repeated. And Romano patted his head and said, "Good. I hope your injury heals soon."

He called each boy before him, requiring that he pronounce his entire name.

"Two steps only," he said, "and standing as straight as a column." He made them return and start again if they walked even one step fewer or one step more. He modeled the posture he sought from them, lifting his own shoulders up and back every time.

Then he had them sing "La, la, la" across the scale, singing higher and higher octaves until their voices gave out.

"You may sit," he told them after the exercise.

They did so clumsily, some banging their legs against the wood of the seats, others adjusting their robes as they slid to rest. Still others, Giorgio, in particular, chattered with abandon. The younger Mocenigo looked as if he would cry.

"Unacceptable," Romano told them. "Again. Together. As if you are a choir that the world will want to hear, and that other choirs will envy. After all, you are to represent Venice!"

His voice rose in command. He was as much the captain as Loredan, Michael observed.

Four times it took until the boys sat as if of one accord, their final sweep onto the chairs a motion entirely fluid and all but silent.

"Excellent," the maestro said. "Well done."

The boys, even Claudio, smiled.

"Now we shall stand and sing," Maestro Romano instructed.

Only three times did standing need rehearsal.

Bronislav appeared to be asleep for the duration of the "calisthenics," as he called the movements later. But upon hearing the "A—men, A—men," that the boys sang, he opened wide his eyes and stared.

"Again," the maestro commanded.

"A—men, A—men."

"Now with arms relaxed and palms at your sides," he instructed the boys.

"Perhaps he knows what he is doing," the Slav whispered to Michael.

Michael nodded in agreement and smiled.

"A—men, A—men."

"Again," a different, feminine voice called to the boys.

"Signora Contarini." Now it was the maestro who bowed deep and long. "I am glad and relieved, I must say, to see you. I hope your son will return very soon from Corfu."

Donato held his mistress's arm. She was dressed for the Mass in a black veil and an altogether sober gown. But she still glittered from within, pleased, it appeared, to see her dream turning into a reality.

"I, as well," she said.

Then she came close to the maestro, stretching from her shoes, and whispered into his ear.

"Of course, as you wish, signora," he answered.

He walked to the boys, raised his baton, and said. "'Dona Nobis Pacem', you are all familiar with it, I know. In round. Franto first, then Giovanni, then Sebastiano."

The three boys placed their arms in position, stood up straight, and looked to the maestro.

"And," he nodded to Franto, and the boys began.

Ignoring for a moment the physical splendors surrounding them, Michael instead watched Bronislav stare at his son. The

Slav's broad face appeared ethereal, and he clasped his hands as if in prayer. The young Greek listened to the tender voices of the three small boys echo through the cavernous edifice, their nascent artistry, like that of those who had constructed and decorated the basilica itself, enough evidence for him that beauty could indeed rise and flourish, even amid wrongdoing, hardship, and plague.

Chapter 23

TESTIMONIES AND DEPOSITIONS

In an action heretofore unprecedented, and only with The Great Council's unanimous approval, did three of The Ten, otherwise known as the The Masters of the Night, appear at nine in the morning on the Wednesday of the second week of Advent in la Signora Francesca Alighieri Contarini's loggia. Bronislav alone had rowed the boys to rehearsals so that Michael could attend. La signora's great greeting room had been re-arranged to resemble The Ten's court chamber, so that Gaetano Memmo, Orso Aiani, and Marco Dandolo, robed in their somber cloaks, sat in identical tall-backed chairs, cushioned not with the Contarini coat of arms, but rather with the lion of the Republic. With his son Ezio, who daily kept la signora and her household staff supplied with food and other domestic requirements, as well as making repairs to her boats when necessary, Donato had made a trip to the doge's palace for the sole purpose of retrieving the pillows from the valet at the offices of the Avogadori.

The day after Roch's rescue, while Michael had transported the choir boys to their first singing lessons, Friar Martino had verified with Milaslova that Nico would recover from his slashing, and with Giubbe that Roch could spend the day attended to by Clara, the boy's former neighbor and his late mother's closest friend. The friar and Captain Loredan, then, had been able to meet with The

Ten to make a formal accusation naming Zen as strategist and leader with Jacopo and likely Clario Contarini, two of his known associates, of a Republic-wide syndicate of sodomy and ancillary abuses. The two Venetians, they contended, had abused not only Roch, a boy who had not reached his puberty, and—in Zen's case—not only Michael, an older boy not yet of legal age, but many other boys and young men, especially those who affiliated themselves with the Republic's fleet. Clario widened the group's reach to include orphans on Corfu. Loredan and the friar viewed his crimes as especially heinous, as they mocked the very holiness and protection his clerical status assumed.

The evening before their meeting, Michael had recited his entire personal narrative, beginning with his regrettable visit to the whores in Manfredonia; then relating his conversations and encounters with Vincenzo, Jacopo, and Roch on board the galley; recalling in excruciating detail his visit to Clario Contarini's rectory; and finally ending with his discovery of Roch's abuse by Zen and Jacopo at Dominic's barber shop. Friar Martino had written every word the young Greek spoke so that, upon being ushered into the office of The Ten, he and Loredan were able to present to the councilors a complete, dated record of abuses which, to their knowledge, and under oath, they swore to be true. They had shared their findings with Signora Contarini, she being the only immediate relative of her son Clario and, therefore, due full disclosure of the accusations presented. The Contarini family's honor, after all, was at stake.

"Buon giorno," la signora said, her right arm sweeping the loggia as she entered from her private apartment. She was attired as if for a funeral, not a bit of color emanating from her black gown, fringed mantle, and lace veil. She wore no jewelry. Her only accessory was a pair of fitted gloves against the chill. Given the novel and temporary arrangement of the room, she was as far from her own fire as she could be.

The three examiners stood for her, another noteworthy deviation from normal procedure.

"I thank you for making an exception to the Republic's standard practices regarding depositions," la signora said, and she made a quick curtsy to the trio before her. "For acknowledging my position as head of the family, despite my sex, I express my sincere appreciation."

Signor Aiani, who had been designated beforehand to lead the questioning, motioned for the lady to sit in what would normally be termed the gallery, now a line of four chairs directly across from the tribunal and behind a witness's bench. His trademark mole, in the shape of a strawberry, decorated his left cheek. Each witness would be called to the bench individually, with la signora, Captain Loredan, Friar Martino, and Michael listening to all. The three men were already at their places and they bowed as la signora took her seat with them. Left to right facing the tribunal they were: Signora Contarini, Captain Loredan, Michael, and Friar Martino.

"We are happy we are able to save you from more public scrutiny at the doge's palace," Signor Aiani said.

Then he directed his words to the assembled group.

"Let us begin," he said, and he motioned for the secretary, a young man perhaps just one or two years older than an adolescent himself, to ready his writing instrument. The scribe did, resting his right elbow on one of la signora's tables as he prepared to write.

"Signor Loredan," Aiani called.

Loredan stood, walked past Michael and Friar Martino, and took his place in the deposition chair.

"For the record, Signor Loredan, did you witness any of the episodes of sodomy or other abuses that Michael of Rhodes, or 'Michele,' as you refer to him, experienced or saw?"

"No sir, none but the aftermaths of Michael's treatment by Zen, Nico's slashing, and Roch's rape at the barber shop."

"May I?" Signor Dandolo interjected.

"Of course," Signor Aiani replied, and returned to his own chair as Signor Dandolo stood and walked to Signor Loredan.

The interrogator wore mitts on both hands, as if he were going to lift a scorching pan of meats from the fire. He swung his arms either side of him as he spoke, the mitts keeping time with his words.

"Signor Loredan, since you did not witness any of the alleged rapes and/or other abuses, how are you able to suggest, let alone swear, any or all of them actually occurred?"

Loredan appeared unmoved.

"Two reasons, signor," he replied. "The first, I trust Michele. I have had occasion to observe his behavior from June the last to the present day, both aboard the galley I commanded, and now in my household." He coughed once and proceeded. "The second, I saw physical evidence—Michele's torn wrists and swollen lip when he first boarded my galley, Nico's slashed tongue when he arrived bloody and wounded at my sister's home, and—most troubling due to his puer status—Roch's shameful bodily tearings, scratches, and obvious terror when Michael and I discovered him. The boy had been mightily abused."

"I see," said Signor Dandolo.

He put a finger to his lips and paced from one side of the deposition chair to the other.

"Do you believe it is possible, since you did not witness any of the alleged crimes, that one or more of them may have been committed by men other than Zen or Jacopo?"

"While it is possible, signor, I do not believe so. As I say, I have Michele's sworn testimony."

"I see," replied Signor Dandolo.

"And you swear by that testimony. In fact, you are yourself willing to suffer the gravest consequences imposed by the Republic should Michele's testimony, in part or whole, prove untrue?"

"Yes, I am," Signor Loredan replied.

Michael fervently hoped he proved worthy of his captain's trust.

"Even though your first-time oarsman is but a common sailor, and a Greek, to boot?"

Michael remained still, though his stomach churned and he wanted to rise and punch Singer Dandolo.

Signor Loredan stretched out his legs and crossed his arms against his chest. He might have been merely conversing with the interrogator.

"Signor Dandolo, while I understand that your questions are part and parcel of your office, I know an exceptional young man when I meet him, common or noble, Greek or not." He uncrossed his arms and used his right hand to emphasize his words.

"Michele," he lifted his arm and held it aloft, "even as he boarded ship, did not, as he might have, blame another for the bruises on his wrists which—as you have read in his testimony—he instead admits were the result of his own improper and ignorant decisions. His accusation of Zen as his defiler is, by his own reckoning, separate from his own sinful, yet understandable, actions, given his age and the natural sexual energy that accompanies it. He blames no one but himself for engaging in wrongful intercourse with the whore Aphrodite, as he then, in his true innocence, believed the harlot's actual name to be."

Here, even Signor Dandolo allowed himself a chuckle, and Michael felt himself reddening, wishing that Signora Contarini were not present. Captain Loredan let his hand drop to his lap; the lady did not move.

"Also, Michele has gained nothing but trouble and fear for his person, in fact for his life, ever since he has chosen to act in an upright, honorable fashion to protect Roch and the orphans he left behind in Corfu. It was he, Michele, after all, that Zen and Jacopo sought, not Nico."

"Then why did they, or one of them, if indeed they or he did, slice Nico's tongue?"

"As you will certainly recall from Michele's testimony, when Nico would not tell Michele's whereabouts, Zen held him and Jacopo—as he had already done to another aboard ship—slashed him with the intention of cutting off his tongue."

Here Loredan turned to la signora, the friar, and Michael behind him. "It appears as if Jacopo uses only one method of attack," the captain sneered.

"Now then, no need for that," interrupted Signor Memmo from his chair.

"No further questions," said Signor Aiani.

Next it was the friar's turn. He lumbered to the chair, over which his body extended to either side of the seat. He took a deep breath, folded his hands on his lap, and waited.

"Friar Martino, you told us earlier that Michele had made his confession to you before relating his testimony."

"Yes, he did," said the priest.

"Did his confession in any way vary from the testimony you wrote on his behalf?"

The friar looked at Signor Aiani and smiled.

"You know that a priest must not reveal a penitent's words."

Signor Aiani paced the room again.

"Yes, yes," he said, brushing the air with his hand.

"And," the friar continued, "be certain to let the record show"—here he pointed to the scribe—"I did not write the testimony on behalf of anyone, but in order to compose and render a document of truth."

"I see," said Signor Aiani. "And, like Captain Loredan," the interrogator went on, "you are willing to stake your own life on this young stranger's claims."

The priest smiled again.

"I am, signor."

"And why, I ask?" Signor Aiani pressed.

"Because the young Greek is without guile, because he demonstrates neither the inclination nor the practice of gilding his words."

"You are certain?"

Michael squirmed. He had done little but lie since his service to Venice.

The friar reached his arms around the back of the chair and grasped his hands together so that his knuckles cracked.

"I am as certain as my own limitations allow and my sense urges me to conclude." He cracked his knuckles again. "When I warned Michael in Corfu that I would not send Roch to Clario Contarini, he responded as one unwilling to cause harm to a puer. When he assisted Nico in his plight and set out to find Roch in Venice, again he acted with no thought for himself, but only for those more vulnerable than he. I do not think he will ever forgive himself for having left the orphans in Clario Contarini's alleged care."

Michael burned with shame that he had not been smart or sure enough to cross Clario Contarini.

Now the friar stood, even though he had not been given permission to do so by his questioner.

"So, yes, I am willing to risk my own meager life on Michael's testimony." He looked directly at Signor Aiani, then at the two other interrogators in their chairs. "I believe the members of this tribunal would do well not to deem a man's accident of low birth as a necessary contradiction to his decidedly noble deeds."

"Dismissed," said Signor Aiani, with a frown and a wave of his hand.

He resumed his seat, paused, then nodded to the secretary when he stopped writing. The scribe stood and walked to the door of the loggia.

"We are ready," he called out, and Nico, hands cuffed and locked behind his back, was brought into the room between the two executioners Michael had last seen when they left the galley at Zara.

The captain's raised eyebrows signaled his surprise. The friar exhaled loudly and fingered his beads. La signora sat silent and alert, her spine no longer touching the back of her chair.

"Nico," Michael called.

Upon seeing the group, Nico bowed his head.

"Here, you will sit here," the bald executioners placed Nico on the chair. They did not remove the cuffs.

"This youth has this morning been arrested for causing a public disturbance last Sunday evening, resulting in the slashing of his tongue."

"Now, wait," Loredan said and made to stand, but the friar laid a hand on his shoulder and the captain desisted.

"You are Nico, Signor Loredan's man, are you not?" asked Signor Aiani.

Nico nodded and answered, though his "Yes" sounded thick.

"Did you initiate a fight last Sunday evening in the presence of Zen and Jacopo?"

"No," Nico mumbled and shook his head.

"Who cut your tongue?"

Loredan spoke. "Don't you see, he cannot talk. Remove the cuffs, man."

Aiani nodded and the bald executioner came to Nico's aid.

"Again," Aiani asked, "Who cut your tongue?"

Nico spelled out Jacopo's name with his hands.

"Jacopo?"

He nodded yes.

"Why?" Signor Aiani asked.

Again, Nico moved his hands and spelled each word, "Because I would not tell him where Michael and Roch were."

"Wait," said Aiani, pulling Nico toward the scribe. "Give him the pen. Let him write his testimony."

Nico wrote and Aiani read his testimony aloud: "Jacopo slashed my tongue because I would not tell him where Michael and Roch were."

"Was Zen with Jacopo?" Signor Aiani asked.

Nico nodded yes, and made motions to show how Zen had held him as Jacopo cut his tongue.

"Why would you not tell them where Michael and Roch were?"

Nico wrote again, and Aiani once more read his words.

"Because they said they wanted to kill Michael and abuse Roch until he begged for his life."

"And they call themselves men," la signora said, loud enough to be heard by the tribunal.

"Silence!" Signor Aiani bellowed.

She did not acknowledge him.

"That is all," Signor Aiani said. "There is no need to cuff him. His language, such as it is"—here Signor Memmo laughed—"concurs with the testimony."

Then, to the executioners, "You may return him to the care of the Slavs at the Venier palazzo. That is what you wish, Signor Loredan, is it not?"

"Yes," the captain replied.

Nico looked to the tribunal, but made his bow to those in the gallery and tried to mouth "Good-bye."

As he left the loggia, the scribe again went to the door.

"You are called," he said, and, Giubbe entered. He gripped one of Roch's arms while one of the Avogadori's men held the other.

"I am with you," he assured the boy.

"Roch," Michael called out, and the friar stood and joined Giubbe.

"Here, Roch" he said, "I will sit by you."

And, even as Signor Aiani said, "No, no, moving the furniture is prohibited," the friar dragged his chair next to the deposition seat and sat down.

Giubbe and the Avogadori's man went and stood by the door.

No sooner had Friar Martino blessed the boy on his forehead than Roch looked up at tribunal, trembled, and pointed to Signor Dandolo.

"He, he is one of them!" he cried. "When Nico told me to run, Zen called out to him," again he pointed to Dandolo, "to catch me! 'You can have him first this time,' he said.'You can have him first.'"

The boy shook Friar Martino's arm.

"You must believe me, Father. You believe me, don't you?"

"Yes, yes, I believe you," the friar said.

The Franciscan stared at Dandolo. Michael inhaled and clutched his hands together. Signora Contarini's right foot betrayed her otherwise statue-like stillness.

Signor Dandolo stood, glared at the boy, and shouted, "You don't know me!" he yelled. "We have never met. You are nothing but a street urchin and a liar, to boot."

The boy, now taking and wringing a portion of Friar Martino's brown robe between his hands as he stared at his accuser, cried, "You are the liar, the real liar!"

"Sit and be quiet," Signor Aiaini said to his colleague. "And you, boy, respect the members of this tribunal."

He came close to the boy.

"And how could you have recognized this man," he pointed at Signor Dandolo, "or any other man, in the dark?"

He stared down at Roch and raised his hand as if to strike him. The boy flinched.

"Go on," prodded the friar.

"It wasn't dark, signor. Both Nico and Zen held torches."

"Go on," said Signor Aiani. "Suppose it is true that they held torches."

"They did," said the boy, even as he shook. "They held torches. One each."

"But even so, how can you be sure you saw this man and not another?"

He pointed again to Signor Dandolo, whose face remained contorted with rage.

Roch looked to the friar again.

"You must tell the truth, Roch," he said. "Just say the truth."

The boy took a deep breath.

"I know because of his hands."

All present immediately looked to see, but Signor Dandolo's hands, mitted as they always were, had slipped under his sleeves.

"What about his hands?" Signor Aiani asked.

As all of Venice knew, his colleague wore the soft mitts to protect what mutilated skin and fingers remained from burns he had sustained in heroic battle against the Turks.

"He has only four fingers," Roch whispered, "four fingers on each hand. That is what Zen said."

Michael held his breath.

"'You will like how they feel,' Zen said. 'I promise you,' he said. 'Four instead of five. Something new for you to enjoy.'"

La signora hissed.

"Well," she stood. "Remove your mitts."

Signor Dandolo shouted at her. "Shut up, woman! Know your place."

Signora Contarini made her way to Signor Dandolo's chair. No one, not even Signor Aiani, tried to stop her.

"Your hands," she said, her eyes raised to meet and hold Signor Dandolo's.

The man looked to his colleagues. Signor Aiani shook his head no. Signor Memmo stared at his own hands which he placed palms down on his lap.

The fire crackled behind the tribunal. Roch's shallow breaths accompanied his trembling body.

At last, Signor Memmo, the quietest of the three thus far, said, "Quickly, man, quickly."

"You will see," Roch said. "Now you will see."

They did.

In a move as swift as any he had ever witnessed, Michael watched Captain Loredan leap to his feet, grab Signor Dandolo by the arms, and throw him to the floor.

"Restrain him now, Michele," he called.

And Michael removed his own belt from his tunic, wrapping and knotting it three times over the wrists to keep them from moving.

"Make note, make note," the friar instructed the scribe, who wrote with frenzied stokes of his pen.

"Dio! Dio!" he said in whispered exclamations as he scribbled.

"I assume the deposition is over," said la signora.

"Certainly," Signor Aiani said.

"Michele, you and I will take this devil to the jail cells in the doge's palace. I am sure the strappado or some other equally effective means of persuasion will jog his memory about all we have contended."

Giubbe left his place by the Avogadori's man and knelt before Roch.

"We will keep you safe, Roch" he said. "Giubbe will keep you safe."

The friar led the boy and his burly neighbor back to the Frari, where together they broke bread and made plans for Roch's future. The boy walked between them, head held higher now, as they went.

Chapter 24

SNOW

The last Sunday of Advent Maestro Romano had declared a day of rest for the choir.

"You have done well," he told his choir boys. "Now you must rest your voices for your debut performance on the day of Christ's birth."

The boys had applauded and cheered at the maestro's pronouncement. But, over the month of their instruction, even Claudio Mocenigo had come to respect his teacher, and wished him a hearty farewell "until the next time." The boys had learned, although none yet possessed the language to articulate his understanding, that the maestro's orders were not the annoying blasts of an elder, interested only in bleating his own authority, but rather those of a gifted man devoted to them and the handing down of his art. With the day off, Claudio and the other boys would be able to enjoy the holiday preparations for Christmas Day with their families at home.

"You must spend the afternoon with us," Bronislav had insisted to Michael. "We will invite Nico, Roch, Friar Martino, Giubbe, and Clara, as well. Roch and Franto will enjoy making and hanging the decorations."

Signor Loredan had assented.

"You will join Bronislav's family, and Nico will first come upstairs with my sister and her children. Elena wishes to fawn over him a bit since his injury and has ordered some unguents, she tells me, that will perhaps lessen his pains. I have no doubt, Michele, that you will enjoy a better time downstairs than I shall, with my bevy of family nobles."

So, when Michael awoke, at first forgetting he need not hurry to transport the boys to San Marco, he lay back on his comfortable, blanketed bed, not rising until eight strokes of the church bells rang out. He did not need to meet his friends until noon.

He got up, stretched his neck and arms, and went to the window of the third-floor bed chamber he shared with Nico. Nico had no doubt already gone to their master's suite across the corridor to lay out the clothing Captain Loredan would wear to Signora Elena's. Nico's blanket was folded straight across the foot of his bed, and his indoor slippers were missing from the wooden rack where he placed them every night before retiring.

Michael unlatched and swung open the dark green wooden shutters and smiled. Venice was blanketed in snow. A thin layer of white draped itself like altar linens over the gondola, sandolo, and a caorlina below. Lacy flakes fluttered from the sky, sugaring the water of the canal. The points of the wavelets, like Michael's tongue, tasted the netted crystals. Stretching out his arms and his head, Michael let the snow fall upon him. It felt like a gentle blessing, a recollection of purity. It hinted at a time well before Petros had died from plague and before Michael had known and chosen sin.

"Praise, thanks, plea, pardon," he whispered.

On the galley, after his disturbing experience in Corfu, Michael had confessed his own shameful wrongdoings. The friar had bent from his stool on the deck to listen while Michael spoke, cross-legged on the ship's boards.

"I absolve you, In the Name of the Father, the Son, and the Holy Ghost," Friar Martino had recited the sacrament. "Go and sin no more."

"But how, how can I be forgiven?" Michael had asked. "The boys are still there. I should have taken them."

The friar had not answered right away.

"What you say is true, Michael. Some boys are still there. But had you not met them and Clario Contarini, you would not be here confessing now. You would not have decided to seek justice against those who do great harm, and peace for those they injure. Through your good will and your intended future actions, pray God that Clario Contarini and others of his ilk will be locked away from those they seek and find."

Michael had pondered the friar's words.

"Go and sin no more."

He would try.

"I will try," he said to the air now, and again received the snow on his tongue.

And, though he shivered a bit even after he had taken the blanket from his bed and wrapped it twice around him, he found himself still standing at the window, transfixed with wonder at another of the world's small and singular beauties, when the church bells rang nine times.

Chapter 25

AN UNEXPECTED DINNER GUEST

"Welcome, welcome," Milaslova greeted Michael at the canal-level door to the "the little kitchen," as Signora Elena described it.

The main kitchen of the palazzo abutted a canal perpendicular to the one the Slavs used. Here Milaslova acted the proud hostess, as if she were receiving the young Greek into her own snug cottage in Ragusa rather than into the most humble quarters of Signora Elena's palazzo.

"Nico is upstairs, seeing to the captain," Michael said.

Milaslova smiled and reached out her hands to take his cloak.

"I hope Captain Loredan will not keep him long," she said. "Here he can rest. I have made some soup that, when cooled a bit, will both nourish him and soothe his pained tongue."

As Milaslova hung his cloak on a peg among a line of pegs, most draped with clothing in varying states of dampness, Michael saw that Giubbe and Clara had already arrived with Roch, and the three were showing Franto how to mix cloves and dried rose petals and put them into into hand-sized woven sacks that Milaslova had earlier sewn on three sides. Roch, who was in charge of tying the open side of each sack once Franto had finished filling it, wound thin pieces of dark leather round and round the sack tops, then knotted them, finally fluting the woven fabric above each leather string.

"Hello, hello," said Michael.

"Smells good," Franto said in response, inhaling each sack as it was finished.

He handed a sack to Michael who, upon inhaling the powerful clove and faint scent of dried rose petals, agreed.

"Yes, good," he said, and handed the sack back to Franto.

"Here, then," Milaslova told her son. "Place them on the window sills in the kitchen and in our sleeping chamber."

Off Franto went, with Roch lifting him wherever a window was too high, and Clara, her head covered by a pale purple veil, attempted to greet Michael with a peck on his cheek. She stood on tip-toe to do so, and her husband, laughing at her unsuccessful effort, lifted her so that, for a brief moment, she and Michael were face to face.

Clara was as short as Giubbe was tall. They made an odd couple until they sat together on a small bench by the fire. Only then did Michael see that they complemented each other. She was all hovering maternity (though Michael had learned from Roch that the two had no children, an only son having died at birth). He acted the observant, capable mechanic. No matter what needed doing, Giubbe saw to it, while his wife fluttered about him, encouraging, helping, soothing, cooing. When she got in his way, as she inevitably did, he lifted her like a sack and laid her aside. She pouted, though without actual rancor, until he finished his task and once again looked upon her with clear, if tested, affection.

"I will help you with the soup," Clara told Milaslova. "Shall I raise it higher off the flame so it will not burn Nico when he comes?"

"Yes," answered Milaslova. "Thank you."

Both women stood before the fire then, Giubbe having gone off to the other room from which Franto called to him, "Come, Giubbe, come." The women giggled as Clara stirred the soup and Milaslova, leaving her for a moment, sought to discover where Bronislav had hidden the bread he had fetched from the baker soon after dawn.

"I do not hide it, Mila," he always told her.

But he did. He liked to rip it first, before she did, so he could tease her with a piece of end crust held before her mouth. Just when she bit the edge of the crust with her teeth, he took her in his arms. Every time. Then he ate the better part of the loaf, so that sometimes there was no bread left to sop the last of the soup.

"Where is Bronislav?" Michael asked.

The women giggled again, though Michael could not fathom why.

"He will be here soon. He has gone to fetch Friar Martino."

"Oh," said Michael.

"And another package," Clara turned and said.

At her comment, Milaslova shushed the woman, and the two again giggled.

Michael looked about the kitchen, seeing if he might be of any help, if only to avoid further confusing talk with the two women.

"What do you need me to do?" he asked Milaslova.

Bronislav's wife turned from Clara, smiling at him. She wore the orange robe and a wooden headband that kept her veil in place. But today, a festive gold ribbon twined itself around the band. And, reminding Michael of her husband's gift to him, she wore a cross on a chain, the length and size of both properly suited to her slender figure. The cross danced as she gesticulated and spoke, and Michael could not help but notice her firm breasts gracing either side of it.

He looked away, aroused and self-conscious. But, if she saw and understood his pleasing discomfort, Milaslova did not let on.

"Thank you," she said instead. "You may slice the meat." And she handed him a knife that seemed as ferocious as a weapon.

"Here," she added.

Michael accepted the two thick mitts she handed him. He put them on, then went to the fire and lifted a roasting pan from the flames. Inhaling the smell of rosemary and roasted pork, he brought the pan to the long utility table to which Milaslova pointed, and, with two long forks she handed him, lifted the better portion of a piglet onto the table where it steamed while he removed his mitts and readied himself to carve.

"A Christmas gift from your captain," Milaslova said.

Michael savored the aroma and heat from the meat.

"We are here, open up!" roared Bronislav's voice from outside.

"Babbo, Babbo," cried Franto, and the boy came running from the bed chamber.

Roch and Giubbe followed, each carrying a carved boat. Roch also carried the carved lamb Michael had given Bronislav for the boy. Seeing it, Michael smiled and, though he did not want to for fear of loneliness, he thought in a flash of his father and his home.

"Franto says we must fill these boats with good smells, too," Giubbe laughed, "and have the lamb sniff at them."

Roch smiled at Franto's wishes. All but one scratch was gone from his face. His clothes were clean, and, if he shivered today, his shaking was not from fear, but rather from the whoosh of wind that entered the kitchen with Bronislav, Friar Martino, and—Michael blinked twice to be certain—a girl, almost a woman, who looked to be an earthly angel.

"Welcome, welcome," Milaslova hurried to the trio.

While Bronislav took the cloaks, Milaslova took the girl in hand and led her close to the fire, where she introduced her.

"Everyone, meet Dorotea, Friar Martino's niece."

Knife in hand, but imagining it a nobleman's sword, Michael bowed from his waist to Dorotea, as if the girl were Signora Contarini in her snowy maidenhood.

"Dorotea," Bronislav told her, "Michael of Rhodes."

"I am pleased to meet you," the young woman said, and curtsied.

Franto jumped up and down, up and down.

"But we know her already, Mama. You teach her to sew. You are her maestra."

Everyone, including Dorotea, laughed.

"You are right," she knelt to Franto. "And, because your mother teaches me well, someday I will be able to work for a signora in her palazzo as your mother does here."

"No doubt you will," said her uncle, whom Bronislav motioned to sit on a leather-cushioned bench near the fire. Milaslova had pieced together all the remnants of hide she could to make a patchwork of skins that softened the friar's seat.

"Shall we make garlands?" Dorotea asked Franto and Roch.

Franto took her by the hand.

"What are garlands?"

"Interlocked ribbons that we will string over the tops of the windows as if they are draperies," Dorotea answered.

Earlier in the week, she and Milaslova had removed the simple linen curtains that suited the warmer months. They had soaked them in vinegar and boiling water, then hung them on a rope line that they had strung from the four striped poles that marked the Venier landing. Though the sun had dried them, the cold wind had turned some of the curtains stiff. So Milaslova and Dorotea had stood holding them before the fire, waiting for the linen to warm and relax so that they could be folded and put away. In their stead they'd hung brown velvet shades Milaslova had fashioned from two of Signora Elena's discarded gowns. The garlands would brighten them.

"Yes, let's make garlands," Franto jumped up and down again. "Garlands, garlands."

Roch waited while Dorotea went to the table where Milaslova kept her sewing needles, scissors, and fabric. Franto followed her. When she had retrieved all that she needed, handing the soft material to the boy to carry, she knelt on the floor by the table, sitting back on her calves, and proceeded to cut long strips of fabric from remnants that she and Milaslova had saved.

"Come, join us," she called to Roch.

In a goat-like movement that Michael recognized from his long ago first sighting of Roch on board the galley, the cabin boy capered to Franto and the young seamstress. He fell in a purposefully comic leap onto the floor.

"You are silly," Franto said, and Roch pretended horns on his forehead with his fingers.

It was the first time Michael had seen Roch laugh in many months.

Michael looked down at Dorotea and the two boys. He realized he still held the large carving knife in his hand. He saw Bronislav look at him.

"I think scissors will be sufficient for the garland," Bronislav said, and he and Giubbe laughed uproariously.

Michael made as if to stab the Slav, and Bronislav crossed his arms in front of his face in feigned terror.

"I am to carve the meat," Michael said, and returned to the table where the pork had cooled sufficiently for him to slice it.

He took his time, basking in the warmth from the fire, the kitchen conversation between Milaslova and Clara, the good-natured ribbing about who was the stronger fellow, Giubbe or Bronislav, and Dorotea's simple, clear instructions to Franto and Roch. Everyone here, it seemed, had a place in the little kitchen. It wasn't home. It wasn't the galley. But it was good.

"Now then," Milaslova announced. "We are ready to eat."

"The pork has been carved," Michael called out. Wiping his hands on a kitchen rag that Milaslova had dipped into the water barrel for him, he bowed to the assembly. He was showing off for Dorotea and he seemed unable to stop himself.

A flurry of movement ensued.

Clara went to the open cupboard and found ten plates.

"Nico will be joining us, yes?"

Milaslova nodded, "But only for some soup. He cannot yet chew or swallow properly."

Clara returned one of the flat platters and replaced it with a wooden bowl. Giubbe took all the plates from her and arranged them on the table. Four plates close together on each longer side, one plate each at either end.

"I have presents, a napkin for everyone," Dorotea said. And from the wall peg on which her cloak hung, she lifted a woven sack.

"Help me, Franto," she said, and the little boy pulled out ten festive pieces of scarlet cloth, upon which Dorotea had appliquéd with white fabric the initials of everyone present.

"Beautiful!" Milaslova said, looking closely at every stitch on the napkin that bore the "M." "Thank you, Dorotea," she said, and hugged the girl close. "A present for each of us."

The girl blushed.

His carving job done, Michael now had the leisure to stare at her. Dorotea was of goodly height, the top of her head reaching, he could see, almost to his shoulders. Her hair, lighter than Milaslova's, was braided and wound around her head so that it looked an intricate halo. She wore no headband to hold her simple blue veil in place, but rather had affixed two hair pins on either side just above each ear. Her robe was deep green and fell gracefully, skimming her slim body. Its bell sleeves stopped at her slender wrists. Her hands showed no scars yet from years of cooking by the fire, nor did she have any blemishes on her cheeks. Her nose was her uncle's, Michael realized, upturned at its point. A tiny scar made an "L" at the corner of her left eye. When she smiled, which she did now, she did so with her mouth closed.

"Another 'M,'" she said, when Franto looked to her with a napkin raised. "This must be yours."

And she handed the napkin to Michael.

"Thank you," he said, and again he bowed.

Dorotea laughed. "I am not a great lady," she said. "You needn't keep bowing to me."

Her voice was gentle, but her almost instantaneous distress showed she had realized her mistake as soon as her words were out. She looked down at the floor.

"I did not mean to offend," she whispered to Michael. "I am sorry."

"I took no offense," he replied. "No offense at all."

He bowed so that his head hung lower than Dorothea's chin. Then he turned his face up at her and smiled.

Everyone else was watching, but he didn't care.

Dorotea, though near tears, smiled back, this time showing her teeth. One, just below the curve of her top lip, was chipped. Michael decided it did her face no harm.

"Perhaps Michael has decided you are, or one day will become, a great lady," said her uncle, no trace of irony in his voice.

Michael raised himself up and looked to the friar. As he had on the dock in Corfu, on the galley while hearing confession, and in the Contarini loggia during the deposition, he was helping Michael. Once again, here in a humble kitchen, Friar Martino was leading him somewhere important, though the young Greek did not know where.

Michael heard the word "lady" repeat in his mind: "Lady, lady, lady."

He loved his mother and his sister, had let himself be hoodwinked by a whore, envied Bronislav for having Milaslova, appreciated Clara's unschooled kindness, tired of Signora Elena's dim wits, respected and admired Signora Contarini. Now here was another female nature to ponder.

"Look!" Franto called, "I have made a garland."

"Bravo!" his father said to the boy.

All of a sudden, as if his own twinkling realization coincided with the announcement of Franto's bright decoration, the young Greek realized what he should do. Draping his monogrammed napkin over his left arm, he went to Dorotea and offered her his right.

Looking into her uncle's approving eyes, Dorotea slipped her arm into the young Greek's. Michael walked her to the table. He drew out a bench. She sat. No one laughed. Bronislav took his place at the head of the table, Milaslova at the other end. The friar sat on the fireside, between Clara and Giubbe, while Roch and Franto were canal-side to Dorotea's left and right, respectively. Nico's place, near Franto, was still empty. "The poor fellow is no doubt standing behind the captain's chair upstairs," Friar Martino said. Michael seated himself last, next to Clara, who whispered none too softly in his ear, "Do you like her, Michael? Do you?"

Embarrassed though he was, Michael imagined what Signora Contarini would expect of him if she were there. He wanted to be a man she regarded noble, a man whose homely birthright did not prohibit or limit courteous demeanor and upright actions. He inhaled a long breath and held his back straight.

"She is lovely, Clara," he said, but he did not whisper. Neither did he turn to his jovial, goodhearted friend. Instead, he looked directly at Dorotea, whose own gaze, at first tentative, then firm, met his. "As I believe your name tells us, Dorotea, you are a gift from God."

"Thank you," Dorotea answered, and she did not lower her eyes, but took in the measure of the young man across from her.

As Michael had, she too drew herself erect and tall on the simple wood bench. Were it not for her modest clothing and unadorned person, she might have been mistaken for a dogaressa seated on her throne in the Basilica of San Marco to celebrate Christmas Day.

"Well done, my boy," Bronislav raised his glass. "Well done."

"You are my sister's own dear child," Friar Martino blessed his niece from across the table.

"Will we ever say grace? For I am very hungry," Franto said, and the glowing assembly, still minus Nico, laughed, then joined hands to pray.

Chapter 26

A NEAR MISS

"I have kept Nico far too long from his friends," Captain Loredan said.

It was so, Michael admitted, though he did not concur aloud with the captain.

It was already dark when Signor Loredan and Nico at last appeared in the Slavs' kitchen. Bronislav sat snoring close to the fire, while Friar Martino, Milaslova, Clara, Giubbe, and Dorotea played a game of strings, one person passing a labyrinth of threaded design to the next, while trying not to collapse it between their fingers. Giubbe and Dorotea were proving to be quite adept, while Clara was not so. No matter the person or the arrangement of strings, she began giggling even before the labyrinth was placed upon her outstretched hands. But at the appearance of the captain and Nico, she let her strings drop altogether and rose to search for a small metal pail for Nico's dinner.

"Take it with you, shouldn't he, Milaslova? Take it home. It will cool in the snowy air and not be burning on your tongue when you eat."

Clara did not wait for her hostess's response, but began ladling the soup from the large cauldron over the fire into the pail. If

Milaslova resented the bossy woman's intrusions, she kept silent, merely exchanging a fleeting glance with her husband.

"Thank you," Nico said.

Not long after, they departed. Nico held the pail in his lap, covering it with Dorotea's gift-napkin, as Michael rowed the Loredan gondola to his captain's palazzo.

"Buona notte," Captain Loredan called out when he and Nico approached the door nearest the canal.

Loredan scanned the lane of water and the buildings around him as he spoke. Though Nico held the door open for his master, as was customary and expected, this evening Loredan had insisted Nico precede him.

After Nico had disappeared inside, Signor Loredan turned back to the boat and said to Michael, "Be wary. Take care you have at hand the torch and your knife."

"Why, Uncle? What is wrong?" whispered Dorotea. She sat in the boat next to Martino.

"Shh, now," the friar said, and, pulling Dorotea close to him, encased her within the folds of his ponderous cloak. "Sometimes a man of the sea imagines the sea's terrors even when he is at home."

"I see," the girl said, but Michael knew she could not possibly.

As he pushed the gondola towards la Carità, where Dorotea boarded with the nuns, Michael did not try to assuage her fears. In fact, he could not. He was having enough trouble trying to set aside his own. As far as he knew, Zen and Jacopo still roamed Venice. Neither of them brooked even slight opposition. That Michael had already experienced and understood. And here, in the city of their birth, a foreigner and stranger such as himself suffered a clear disadvantage. Alley, campo, church, bridge, court, canal, boats, dialect, and custom—all were to them familiar. They had learned as boys and practiced as brazen bravi how to navigate both the Republic's geography and the social waters. He, on the other hand, was finding it difficult to differentiate between the actual and the reflected, the said and the meant, the threat and the boast. The myth of Venice—la Dominante, la Serenissima—and the

Venice in which he rowed right now—a cottage mouse pursued by galley rats—were not, of that he was certain, one and the same.

Michael, Friar Martino and Dorotea were silent. The gondola became a black swan gliding over water murky with darkness. While the fresh snow dabbed both boat and canal, it did not make a permanent cover. Instead it fell white, then soon melted to clear droplets on all that moved—boats, wavelets, figures. Not even the sound of sea birds punctuated the night. Every shutter save one, from which a woman shook a long covering of some sort, was closed and locked tight. Venice had gone to bed and drawn the bedding over itself.

"Alora," Michael called out, as the boat met the dock of the convent.

And though they slipped and slid, he and the friar held Dorotea's hands between them and shuffled their way to the convent door. All three were crusted with snow and wet droplets on top of their hoods and robes.

"Thank you," Dorotea said to Michael, and, forcing foreboding from his consciousness, he bowed to her yet again.

She laughed and curtsied, easily now.

"Perhaps I shall see you at Christmas Mass," she said. "And you, Uncle, sooner."

"Good-bye, then," Michael waved at her as he turned. "Good-bye." He hoped his farewell was a temporary one.

The friar waited until an ancient sister opened the door.

"Blessings upon you, Sister," he called and signed the flaky air with a cross.

The nun bowed her silent answer, motioned Dorotea past her, then waved an unspoken farewell. The door creaked as it closed and the friar waited until its heavy lock sounded.

"Thank you, Michael," he said. "Thank you for not scaring her."

"No use in that, I suppose," Michael said.

"True," the friar agreed. "She has already experienced fear enough."

Michael waited. He knew the friar would tell him his niece's story. He began even as Michael helped him lumber back into the gondola.

"As have so many, like your own brother Petros, my sister and her husband died in the same night, when The Death came near to Assisi five years gone now. In fact, all who lived on their lane, not one day's travel from our founder's own birthplace, suffered and went to their justice or reward in fewer than three days."

Michael almost forgot he was rowing. He saw a candle flicker in a window above.

"Then, on the fourth day—I was told this by another of Francis's own friars, Michael—when the watch was going through the lane, masked, of course, to curb the stench of death, he heard a cry from within the cottage he was about to torch. He followed the cry and found Dorotea. She was but nine years old. She stood before him, surrounded by death, wrapped in an altar cloth. My sister laundered the parish altar cloths, you see."

"'She told me you were coming,' Dorotea said to the watch. 'All I had to do was pray and wait.'"

"'Who told you?' he asked. The watchman was not sure a live girl actually spoke with him. He thought it was a spirit or, worse, a demon in disguise. Who would not, who had to look on death in the faces of his neighbors so many times?"

Michael saw another candle flicker, this time from a roof top.

"My niece approached him and held out her arms. 'In imitation,' he said, 'of the very statue of the Virgin in our monastery.'"

"'The lady, the Virgin. She told me to keep close the cloth and you would come to save me.'"

Michael wondered if the story could be true. He pulled on the oar and pushed the boat away from the broader canal, turning into the narrower one that lapped against the friar's dwelling.

"Since then, Michael, since then, I tell you true, Dorotea has possessed a healing touch. Whatever cloths or linens she works, they, all of them, I tell you, soothe and heal. I have no doubt that what the watch encountered was a miracle."

The friar lumbered up and rocked the gondola with his movements.

"I doubt you not, Father," Michael said. "May her cloth keep me safe and soothed on my journey back to my captain.

"Yes, Michael," the friar said as he blessed the young Greek. May the grace beyond our understanding keep you safe."

"Good night," Michael called, and he felt for the napkin tucked under his cloak. He loosened his scarf around his face so he could grab Bronislav's knife quickly, and made sure the torch in its holder was well within his reach.

Again, as he guided the boat back to his captain's palazzo, almost half way there, he was certain two candles, or perhaps one torch and one candle, signaled one another, this time one from a rooftop, the other from an alley way.

The snow continued to fall. An infant's cry echoed, and he felt watched. Watched and stalked. Evil's own prey.

A whizzing sound, another, and two more.

He ducked and fell flat, face down in the boat. Four arrows fell around him, though none punctured his cloak or pierced his head. There was gruff laughter and a scurrying of hasty feet. He waited, prone with dread, until only the snow fell and the gondola rocked in time to the wavelets.

"I must get up," he told himself. "I must stand up and row."

And he turned, though he did not want to, and sat up. As he did, a fifth arrow whizzed from above to fall at his feet. He started as he grabbed it. A cloth was nailed to it. He held it near to the torch. Words were painted on it.

"Blood! It is blood!" he cried, then he read: "You may be the captain's favorite, Michele, but you will never hold the rope."

He pushed the cloth under his rowing stand. He must show the message to the captain. He must get back quickly. He took up the oar again.

"No, not yet," he said to himself. All of him was shaking.

He reached under his tunic and found Dorotea's napkin. He took it in hand and stuffed it under his black woolen scarf so that it covered his mouth. He bit it with his teeth to keep it in place and prayed that the Virgin's miracle to Dorotea would, unworthy and doubtful as he was, nonetheless extend to him.

Chapter 27

MONDAY MORNING

Though he slept not at all and kept on the floor near to his bed the five arrows and the blood-lettered cloth that had been shot into the boat during his solitary return the previous night, Michael could not help but notice how soundly Nico slumbered. His mate had not stirred at Michael's clattering arrival, nor did he now, even though a brilliant sunshine flooded and suffused the valets' chamber when Michael unlatched and threw open the shutters. He was about to wake him, to tell his recent ally of his disturbing nocturnal misadventure, when he beheld Dorotea's blood-red napkin folded neatly over Nico's mouth, the valet's palm resting upon it as he slept. The white appliquéd "N" showed pristine against Nico's tawny complexion. A pleasing disconcertedness came upon Michael, warming and brightening his otherwise gloomy thoughts. What if the friar's story were true? What if Dorotea really were a gift from God? What if...?

The captain's apartment door opened.

"Nico," Loredan called, "Where are you? I am waiting for my toilette."

"Captain," Michael answered instead, opening the door to their room as he spoke, "Nico sleeps deeply and I have something to show you. Please, if you do not mind, Captain, come."

Signor Loredan came into his valets' room.

He did not speak while Michael relayed the events of the night after he had left the friar. How candles and torches punctuated the dark flurries, how the arrows whizzed and fell, dropping into the gondola. "I admit, Captain, it was fear and horror I felt. I just hoped to get back here unwounded and alive."

"It is good you are here," the captain said. "They wanted to scare you, to put you off the chase."

Now the captain sat upon Michael's narrow, long bed, devoid of the fringed and silky pillows that softened his own massive island of rest. Nico exhaled a contented sigh, moved his legs under his own coverlet, and, seemingly unaware, patted the napkin that stayed upon his lips.

"But I have other news for you, and for Nico, should he decide to wake." The captain spoke loudly, but to no avail. He laughed, his earlier annoyance gone.

"Perhaps Milaslova's soup contained a potion," he said, and laughed again.

"News, Captain?" Michael asked, eager to hear.

The captain, as he did whenever he launched into explanation, began to pace the room, to the window, to the door, to the bed again, and so on. Michael leaned against the far, windowless wall, out of Loredan's path.

"Signor Dandolo of The Ten, it has become clear, prefers to inflict the more strenuous methods of interrogation upon others rather than to have them inflicted upon his own, mutilated as it already is, person." The captain tightened and knotted the black silk belt that matched his ornate robe.

"I am told by Signor Aiano that Dandolo had only to hear another prisoner's cries at the strappado and he banged on the bars of his cell, begging to relate the plan of escape that Zen and Jacopo have devised."

For a moment, Michael said nothing. "Praise, thanks, plea, pardon," echoed in his head.

"What then? Tell me, Captain, that we may thwart them."

Then, walking to his friend, he said gently, "Wake up, Nico, you must wake up."

He took the napkin from his ally's lips and, as he did, the valet's eyes opened.

"Hello, Michael. Is it already morning?" Nico's words, as they would for the rest of his life, sounded thick and ungainly. "I have not slept so still since before..." Then he saw the captain and leapt from his bed.

"Signor Loredan, I apolo—"

"No need," Loredan said. "I have news, and a plan to relate."

In less than an hour, the three stood before Signora Contarini, and Loredan told her what Dandolo had confessed.

"Zen and Jacopo have fled to the island of San Lazzaro. Disguised as holy monks, they wait in one of the small huts where visitors, rightly averse to physical contact with the island's lepers, go to leave packages of comfort for those doomed by the disease."

La signora, a heavy woven shawl covering her own morning clothes and slippers, listened intently. Her lopsided frame, without benefit of her doctored shoes, shivered. But she did not complain.

"Go on," she said.

"Today, Monday," the captain continued, "just before dusk, they are to board the weekly supply boat that goes from market here and circles the lagoon, dropping necessities to the various islands and across the Lido. The boat, whose owner has accepted a hefty bribe from Zen, will escort them to the galley that tomorrow morning sets out for Libya."

Loredan paused to draw breath.

"And?" La signora prodded. "Why to Libya? I believe I have heard of that place. Does the Republic's arm extend even so far as Libya?" She touched each of her fingers together as she spoke.

"Yes, it does," the captain said. "According to the arrested Signor Dandolo, signora, they go to Libya to purchase boys of darker skin, boys who are, I am sorry to be so uncouth, signora, particularly valued by some of their band, for their diabolical purposes."

La signora's fingers stopped moving. The captain put his hands behind his back and paced the loggia.

"We, that is, two of the Republic's executioners, Michele here, Bronislav, though I must see him yet, and I, will come upon them. In preparation, the executioners have already arrested and detained the supply boat's owner."

"Good," la signora said. "Good."

The captain stopped his pacing and now stood before the lady.

"I come to ask you, signora, will you allow your man Donato and his son Ezio, to masquerade as the supply boat's owner and son? I am assured that the two are unknown to Zen and Jacopo. I believe they may well assist us in a capture."

"Certainly," la signora replied.

"And we will meet here with Bronislav."

"Yes," la signora said.

Nico did not speak, but Michael saw that he was crestfallen. He had not heard the captain speak his name.

"Nico," la signora spoke now. "I see there will be no one here to assist me this afternoon and evening, when I expect a guest."

She looked to the captain.

"With your gracious generosity, my friend, might you spare Nico? He will be most helpful. And I would rather not be in the presence of the gentleman alone. It would be most unseemly."

"Of course," the captain replied.

At his words, Nico nodded to the lady. He was disappointed, of that Michael was certain. But Nico kept silent and obeyed.

"Oh, so that you are aware, Nico, it will be Michele Steno, our doge, who comes."

Michael, Nico, even Captain Loredan, stared at la signora with wide and equally astonished eyes.

"Of course, he will be discreet and disguised," the lady continued.

"Of course, signora," Nico answered thickly, already acting as her man.

"And you all will remain ignorant of what I have told you."

The three of them, as if one, bowed long and low to the lady.

Chapter 28

LEPERS

"There they are," Ezio pointed so his father could see.

A violet dusk was descending over the lagoon, a winter dusk, night folding over a luminous silver day.

"Ready?" Captain Loredan whispered, and the group, each man nodding his assent, took their places.

The supply boat, of rectangular shape but for its curved prow, was covered and draped in an awning meant to keep its occupants and provisions protected from wet winter winds. A counter constructed of wood snaked along the outer walls of the boat, with four open spots for a quartet of rowers, two on each side of the vessel, and three rows of similar planks comprised its middle portion. Only by the prow did there stand a resting bench.

The two executioners, along with Bronislav and Michael, had rowed, and each wore the simple black uniforms of their function. Ezio had been designated the laborer, Donato the boat owner and captain; with these roles they answered to the names Ettore and Luigi respectively, as the boy and man they were replacing. Both likewise were attired for their duties as suppliers of wine, flour, cheeses, bread, and—for the island of San Lazzaro that housed the lepers until they died, their very flesh diminishing and falling away to the ash all become—funerary shrouds.

"Good fathers," Luigi's hoarse voice called out from the boat to the shore where the pretend monks, Zen and Jacopo, stood.

The two miscreants were hooded in black, the top of their hoods pointed, their arms folded under roomy bell sleeves.

"Watch out," Bronislav whispered. "They are sure to hold weapons."

"The taller one is Zen," Michael said to Ettore. "Beware. He is as strong as the other is fast."

"Take your places," the captain said, and Bronislav and Michael crouched beneath bags of flour on the port side.

Across from them, the two executioners did the same.

All four of them held matching knives at the ready. Signor Aiani had brought along three, for himself, Bronislav, and the captain. They were, Michael realized, the same knives he had seen the executioners on board the galley use to put out Vincenzo's eyes.

"You act in the name of Venice," Aiani had said, seeing the group off from la signora's dock earlier. "May God and Saint Mark accompany you on your task."

Again, as the supply boat approached the dock on which no sane person would willingly walk, Luigi called out, "Good fathers, we await your company as soon as we unload our cargo."

And Ettore lashed the boat to the dock. He wasted no time getting four sacks of flour, two lengths of tied shrouds, and a barrel of wine off the vessel. He left them, as he had been instructed to do, on the stone path where, once the boat had set off, an unfortunate leper or two, still able to function, albeit imperfectly, would collect the supplies for those in the island colony plagued with suffering and certain death.

"Finito," he said, panting some and brushing his hands against each other. "You may board."

The two, their hands folded under their sleeves, walked along the dock, Zen first, Jacopo following. Ettore stood behind Jacopo while Luigi put out his hand for Zen.

The moment Zen's shod foot met the floor of the boat, one of the executioners kicked him in the groin so that a butcher's knife dropped from inside his sleeves.

"The Devil!" he cried, crumpling and trying to cover his genitals from further attack. As he did, the second executioner dealt him a blow on his back with a truncheon, so that he fell face down. His legs squirmed and he writhed in pain. Bronislav stepped on his back and kept his foot in place while the executioner cuffed him.

Hearing the commotion, Jacopo ran. As he did, Michael and Captain Loredan leapt off the boat and made after him.

"Either side," the captain shouted, and the two, with Ettore following straight behind Jacopo, came at him from left and right.

As they did, two lepers, each carrying a torch, approached.

Seeing them, Jacopo stopped short.

They hailed the Venetian and, eagerly it seemed, went toward him, dressed as he was in a holy man's attire.

"Father, father," they called. The taller of the two cried out, "You have not abandoned us! You have come to comfort us. Come!"

And he held out, Michael could see it in the torchlight, his stump, a fingerless hand.

"Stop," Jacopo ordered. "Stop where you are."

Jacopo himself now did not move.

Ignoring him, the two lepers came closer. While they did, Michael, who had taken with him from the captain's dock a length of rope they used for the boats, tied a snare. The captain saw what he was doing and spoke to distract Jacopo.

"Here, Jacopo," Loredan cried. "Come with me or go to a leperous death. Your choice."

"No!" Jacopo hollered. He turned to face Loredan and pulled his knife from beneath his sleeves. "I will kill you all."

He made for the captain, and, as if omnipotent and immortal both, Captain Loredan walked toward him even as Jacopo's long knife flickered. In fact, the captain let drop his own weapon and strolled, as if in pleasant greeting, toward the wiry Venetian.

As he did, Michael lifted and spun his rope so that it circled above Jacopo like a gull over garbage.

"Come," the captain spoke in the voice of his sure command. "I am your own captain. Better you should be with me. At least with me we can talk, we can perhaps mitigate your circumstances. You saved my nephew Lucca from drowning. I remember."

Loredan continued walking toward Jacopo. He was not twenty feet away from him. The lepers stood still. From the other side, facing the back of Jacopo's robe, Michael flung the snare.

As it fell over Jacopo, he howled and tried to cut it, but Michael was too quickly upon him. And though Jacopo slashed the young Greek's arms as he worked, Michael roped him round and round from ankle to shoulder so that soon he was no more than a struggling length of flesh tackled to the ground by Captain Loredan and Ettore.

The two lepers still watched.

"What is his crime?" the taller one asked. "What has he done?"

"Be damned, you," Jacopo cursed. "Be damned," he said, though to whom his words were directed was not clear.

The shorter leper answered him.

"We already are," he said.

Chapter 29

CONFLAGRATION

"Swift," Bronislav reminded Michael. "Venetian justice is swift."

Though Christmas would be celebrated on Friday and the bakers were hard at work night and day to supply Venice's citizens with the cross-marked breads and dried fruit and jellied nut rolls they enjoyed on the day of Christ's own Birth, a conflagration greater than any bakery's was about to flame up in the piazza.

It was twenty minutes before noon. The Arsenale's furnaces were cooling. They spewed no hot soot into a pale blue sky. Aside from the bakers, whom even—or perhaps, especially—The Great Council understood needed to continue their work lest the populace grow unruly for lack of holiday custom, the shops were closed and the business of the various confraternities and guilds were suspended. Unless a soon-to-be mother labored to give birth, or an aged citizen taken ill waited to die, Venice had gone still with anticipation. Even the San Marco choir boys did not sing.

Instead, citizens and visitors, out of curiosity, righteousness, or boredom, waited in orderly formation before three equidistant pyres. They stood, noble and not, all male but for a few brazen women of the streets, with their backs to the lagoon and their faces to the indisputable locus of the Republic's justice. The ducal palace stood on the right, the basilica just behind, and across from it, the looming bell tower.

The drums sounded, and the congregation turned to look right, their movement a singularly unified one.

The procession, the first Michael had witnessed, was as scripted and coherent as any official text. The drummers, the gaolers, the court valets, members of the Avogadori, The Great Council, The Council of Ten, and finally the doge himself, all dressed in attire announcing his particular service to the Republic, walked in sober, measured paces to the seats and areas of the piazza that had been cordoned off with iron stanchions between which were draped swags of red velvet.

The crowd made no noise, neither jeers nor cheers.

When the official party was in place, another set of drums sounded. These, their beats those of a dirge, preceded the prisoners, each shackled at his ankles, cuffed at his wrists, and garbed in the meanest woven cloth tunic of grey. Barefoot all, they trod across the cold stones from the prison to the pyre.

Zen stared straight ahead, unbowed, his ponytail gone, his head, like the heads of the other two condemned, shaved close.

Jacopo, who followed him, babbled incoherent words and twitched, as if lice covered his entire body.

Finally, Signor Dandolo, his hands without mitts now, and cuffed higher on his arms than the other two, wept openly and mumbled without ceasing, "Dio, Dio."

A woman ("Whore!" a few young roughs called out at her) ran to him and tried to throw her arms around him. But two of the guards, swords drawn, pushed her to the ground and kicked at her, forcing her back into the crowd. She covered her face with a scarlet scarf.

Each man was tied to a stake. Zen on the left, Jacopo in the middle, and Signor Dandolo closest to palace of justice where, until his own reckoning, he had determined the reckonings of others.

Friar Martino went from one condemned man to the next, hearing whatever confession or final words he had to say before the searing commenced. "It is one of my most arduous duties, Michael," he had said on the way to the proceedings. At each pyre, the friar drew the Lord's own sign, not on the man's forehead, but over his entire body, each one's use of his body, Michael shuddered with shamed recollection, having brought him to this dreadful end.

When he was done and had made his way back to his seat beside Signor Aiani and the rest of The Ten, a replacement for Signor Dandolo, one Signor Clementino Tiepolo, having been named, the doge signaled the three executioners by raising his right forefinger.

The executioners' timing, as deliberate and synchronized as it had been when Michael witnessed it months earlier on board the galley, again manifested itself as both distressing and impressive.

"Ah," the crowd breathed heavily as the first flames leapt.

Michael watched, his curiosity at first trumping revulsion as the flames neared each man's feet.

Zen was the first to scream and, though he did not want to, Michael for a moment relished his nemesis's torture. Then, as one scream became a cacophony of screams, the young Greek wished he were deaf.

Flames engulfed the trio. Bits of cloth flew from their bodies. Roasted human flesh, though it would not be the last time Michael smelled it during the rest of his days on sea and on land, now sullied forever the pleasure he had heretofore enjoyed of pork or lamb or chicken or fish over his mother's homely fire.

"All of us suffer every other's sins," his uncle used to tell him.

"Not so," he remembered saying.

"Now so," he whispered.

The flames and the voice of the crowd were roaring around him. The sounds of his fellows, loud and indistinguishable, told neither joy nor sorrow, satisfaction nor rage. They seemed to Michael instead to be the voice of all who lived. Of all who knew that living was hard.

He walked away and kept walking. He would wind his way through the alleys he was coming to know, adopting as his own. He would wind his way to beauty.

"I understand now," he said to himself, as he left the flaming piazza toward the Venier palazzo. "I must notice beauty. I must find and not lose sight of beauty."

He walked, fast, then faster still. Ironic and implausible as it seemed to him as he tried to forget the screams of human suffering, beauty, like its opposite, the very brutality that plagues us all, is itself unspeakable. Unspeakable and real.

He needed to see Milaslova and her pupil.

Chapter 30

CHRIST IS BORN, A SON IS RISEN

The basilica's glittering candles lit the priests' vestments, the sumptuous gowns of the noblewomen, and the wriggling forms of the congregation's visiting children as they sat on the benches that had been arranged before the main altar.

Michael and Nico sat either side of Signora Contarini, as she had insisted, despite their inferior status. They might have been two lions of Saint Mark, each one protecting one of the Republic's most revered women from harm of any kind.

"It is because of you that the Republic is a bit safer for little mischievous angels like these," she had told them.

To their left, in four rows of benches reserved for them, sat the families of the young singers. If any of the nobles disputed Bronislav's and Milaslova's places near them, they did not say so aloud. Perhaps, Michael concluded, they dared not, seeing that Signora Contarini had deigned to sit with him and Captain Loredan's valet.

At the insistent jingle of a hand bell signaling the start of the Mass, the congregation stood. The congregants turned, half to the left and half to the right to face the center aisle. Michael offered to switch places with Signora Contarini so she might have a better view, but she refused. Organ music swelled solemn and triumphant, filling the basilica with exultation at the Lord's Birth.

La signora had told Michael that as far back as 1316 the basilica had supported fourteen organists. Now, matching their steps to the present organist's measures, four acolytes--boys younger than Michael but older than the choir boys--carried thick, tall candles, the flames of which flickered and leapt, forming a path of moving light toward the altar. Behind the acolytes processed four clerics, each in gold-edged ivory vestments. They walked in pairs, two shorter men preceding two taller ones. After them, sure of step, walked the primary celebrant, the archpriest of San Marco. Vested in thick gold fabric, he held his folded hands close to his chest. As he passed Michael's row, he slowed his stately pace and nodded to Signora Contarini, blessing her with the Sign of the Cross. She bowed her head, the tip of her veil brushing against Michael's right hand. The organ went silent as the archpriest kissed the high altar over the relics of Saint Mark. The holy men assumed their proper places in the sanctuary while the acolytes lowered the candles into gilded holders. In the choir loft of the left transept with his boys, Maestro Romano turned from the archpriest and signaled the putti, raising his left hand in a wide sweep upward. Until now not visible, the boys stood in unison, and those in the congregation whose sons they were instantly forgot themselves. Ignoring the quiet mien expected at liturgical functions, they called out and pointed. But the boys kept their eyes trained on Maestro Romano.

No longer did they appear the undisciplined rascals they had been at the start of their musical enterprise. Each boy, even the prankster Giorgio Zanchi, stood as he had been instructed, hands at his sides, straight as a pole. Gowned in red velvet robes, the boys waited, as did Michael and Signora Contarini, who leaned forward when Maestro Romano lifted his hands.

His right hand gripping his baton, his left palm poised upward, the conductor awaited the archpriest's cue for the Kyrie. When it came, the celebrant's voice concluding the introductory rites of the Mass, Maestro Romano pointed his baton at his choir, and the voices of the putti pierced the basilica's magnificent expanse.

If Michael had been glass, he would have shattered. The clarity of the putti's voices proved painful in its sharp and pristine beauty. Signora Contarini clasped the glass rosary beads in her hands, then clenched them to her mouth as if to stifle a cry. Michael looked across the aisle to see Bronislav weeping silently and Milaslova smiling upward. All in the congregation who had just moments ago neglected prayerful composure now sat transfixed, drawn to voices of little boys who had become instruments of God.

Only after the Credo, when Maestro Romano again looked down to the altar and awaited his cue for the Sanctus, did Lucca Loredan Venier waver. Three times in quick succession he rubbed his recently doctored ear, flinching the third time. Maestro Romano wagged his finger at him and shook his head vigorously enough so that his mane of hair flapped. The boy lowered his head, but touched his ear no more as the Mass continued.

Just after the archpriest had held aloft in his hands the Body and Blood of Christ and even the choir had gone silent, the massive vestry door opened. Its echoing groan, though some distance from the altar, distracted Maestro Romano, who looked toward the noise. Michael's eyes followed Romano's, but he saw no one. The heavy door closed with a slow creaking.

Returning to his task, the conductor led his choir in the Communion hymn. As the communicants processed to the boys' delicate yet sure harmony, Maestro Romano left his station and walked to the far right of the choir loft, though he still kept time with his baton. Whatever he saw brought a brilliant smile to his face as he returned to his former position. Signora Contarini nudged Michael's arm. He looked to her, his eyes questioning. "I do not like this," she whispered. "I suspect some mischief." But before Michael could ask what she meant, she shushed him and fingered her beads. She shivered, and Michael felt her bodily agitation against his arm.

After all had received the Body of Christ, the celebrant raised his right hand toward Maestro Romano, who turned to face the congregation.

"Esteemed members of the congregation and all the rest who today have joined us to celebrate the Birth of our Lord as told to us in the Scriptures, I thank you all."

He bowed, his baton by his side, his mane of hair shining in the candlelight.

Then he continued.

"But I would be remiss if I did not single out one whose generosity and guidance has allowed for the creation and formalization of the San Marco Boys' Choir. One whose continued largesse and wisdom assures that the choir will be ready to receive a wider audience in this exquisite basilica by the Lord's year 1403."

Here the maestro looked down at Signora Contarini, then swept his arm, baton firmly in hand, across the spacious expanse of the basilica.

"Signora," he spoke directly to the lady. "I have for you a surprise, a surprise which I am quite sure you will receive as your most precious Christmas gift."

He pointed his baton over the heads of his young singers. The celebrants, the boys, and, following their lead, all in the congregation, strained to see at what, or whom, he directed his attention.

Michael's dark epiphany struck even before la signora's.

"Your own son, signora. Returned safe to you from Cyprus, the Reverend Clario Contarini."

Clario Contarini bowed to the maestro and stood in front of the choir.

La signora rose and Michael and Nico each held an arm. She was trembling. The rest of the congregation rose after her and, with the maestro leading them, began to applaud. The cleric was dressed not in the white robes Michael remembered him wearing on Corfu, but instead in a thin column of black. He did not smile or in any other way acknowledge the growing ovation from below and beyond the altar. He merely twisted around and around the substantial monogrammed ring on the middle finger of his right hand. When the applause at last subsided, the chief celebrant intoned his final "Amen," and the maestro, bowing again to la signora, turned back to his singers, lifted his baton, and counted.

> "Christ is born and we give thanks,
> Christ is born to save us."

When the putti concluded their recessional song, Clario Contarini, led by Maestro Romano, met each boy, learned his name, and imposed a gentle blessing on his head. The congregation, meanwhile, milled about the basilica's main portal.

Michael looked to his left at Bronislav, who nodded a message to him.

Excusing himself from Signora Contarini, who took to her seat again, having not said a word throughout the entire surprise, Michael met Bronislav to make their way to the choir stalls. And, as had been their custom during Advent, they took their places among the boys, Bronislav leading them, Michael following behind, and escorted them to the vestry.

"Mother," Michael heard Clario Contarini call from the altar. "You appear not a bit glad to see me."

Chapter 31

A DE-BRIEFING

"According to the report filed by our authorities in Cyprus," Signor Aiani explained to Captain Loredan, Bronislav, and Michael, "Clario Contarini was wrongly accused."

The group had gathered in Captain Loredan's loggia the Monday after Christmas. Michael and Bronislav stood either side of the fire while the captain sat in the chair he favored, near the windows that faced the lagoon. Signor Aiani gave his report from under the curved entryway to the main corridor of the palazzo. In his hands he held a metal box with all the missives regarding the proceedings, from arrest to trial to exculpation.

"It seems a boy, in years barely an adolescens, but in experience and temperament a veritable man, pushed the six-year-old twin boys out a second-floor window of the rectory where Contarini lived, after beating and raping them."

Michael took in a shamed breath. He knew them all and had been too ignorant to save them.

"What was the boy's name?" Michael asked. He approached Aiani. "Was his name Cleanth?"

Signor Aiani came into the room and put the box full of parchment down on a table next to a leather divan. He opened it and rifled through the stacked documents.

"Let me see."

Michael stood over his shoulder as he searched. He found and pointed to a name.

"Yes, Cleanth."

"I met him," Michael said. "I met the three of them. Cleanth and the two dead."

Loredan watched Michael, who paced now from the entryway of the loggia to the windows and back again.

Signor Aiani continued.

"The thing is," he said, "and this confuses me: both the twins who were pushed and the boy who pushed them, I am told, bore the same kinds of welts over their legs and arms. Welts caused by scourging, by flagellation."

The sketch that Cleanth had drawn, that sketch had shown a flagellation.

Michael groaned.

"He was doing it to them. Clario Contarini was whipping them, or making them whip themselves and each other."

The young Greek paced some more. A dreadful scenario unfolded in his mind as he walked. Contarini was the teacher, Cleanth his star pupil, the twins the pitiable objects of their combined sadism.

Signor Loredan did not comment, but only rubbed his face with both his hands.

"And when the boy, who was hanged by the neck until he died," Signor Aiani continued, "when he was asked if he had been coerced into admitting guilt by Contarini or anyone else, he would not say."

Michael, who now stopped pacing, asked, "Did he say anything? Anything at all?"

Signor Aiani sat down on the divan, looked up at Michael and said, "Yes, according to three officials who witnessed the proceedings, he did. He said, 'Father Clario makes us repeat every morning before we sketch, we are all guilty.'"

"Contarini controlled them," Michael said. "They were terrified of him."

Unwilling and unable to restrain himself, though he knew the truth would shame Signora Contarini, Michael told what he had seen. He told how the crying twin had cowered beneath the cleric's raised arm. How both twins had held each other close, shaking. How Cleanth must have been both abused and abuser.

"My God," Bronislav said. "My God."

"Was Contarini present when the boy was questioned?" Captain Loredan asked.

Michael read the agitation in the captain's rubbing of his face.

"Yes," Signor Aiani said. "So I was told."

He was forced then, Michael understood. Contarini had forced Cleanth to plead guilty to his keeper's crimes.

"Was there any interchange between the boy and the cleric?" the captain continued.

"Yes," Signor Aiani said. "And this is as disturbing as it is puzzling."

"What?" asked Michael.

"When the boy's guilt had been determined and his death sentence was subsequently pronounced, the cleric approached the fellow and slapped his face."

"Then what?" Bronislav asked.

His eyes were daggers, Michael saw.

"Then, even the witnesses were disturbed," Signor Aiani continued. "Then, they told me, the boy thanked him and kissed his cheek."

Michael resisted the urge to vomit.

"He will never be near Franto!" Bronislav bellowed. "Never!"

"I too am to blame," Michael said. He slumped and lowered himself to the floor.

"I was there," he said. "I saw." He sat holding his knees to his chest. "I was present and I walked away."

Chapter 32

BETROTHED TO VENICE

It was Signora Contarini who had suggested the gathering to Michael.

"My son has taken his own apartment at my request," she said to Captain Loredan, who had asked Michael to row him to la signora's palazzo the morning of her invitation. "It is better that way, as his comings and goings at hours of the evening best devoted to sleep and domestic solitude, disturb me."

"I understand," the captain said.

"You will all come here, then."

And so it was decided.

Exactly one week after Christmas, then, at four o'clock in the afternoon, Michael of Rhodes was officially betrothed to Dorotea, formerly of Umbria, the province of the sainted founder of her Uncle Martino's order.

Those who had come to comprise his adopted Venetian family were present to mark the occasion:

La Signora Francesca Alighieri Contarini, who would continue to educate Michael in the dictates and details of courtesy and inspire him to prove himself a man of virtue and knowledge;

Captain Pietro Loredan, who recognized in his Michele the potential for leadership the young Greek yearned to acquire. The captain was the first to reward the oarsman's talents, diligence, and loyalty to the fleet that had admitted him to its ranks;

Friar Martino, late of Assisi and presently residing at the Frari, who every day demonstrated to Michael through his own example how to infuse earth with heaven and heaven with earth, and introduced him to both realms in the person of his niece, Dorotea;

Bronislav of Ragusa, who saved Michael from his lesser self and dwelt in a domesticity that felt as important and as deep as the sea;

Milaslova of Ragusa, who for Michael contradicted both the texts and the accepted tenets that insisted a woman was either and only a virgin or a whore;

Franto, the boy whose angelic voice alone made Michael believe in God;

Giubbe and Clara, who adopted Roch as their own without a moment's hesitation;

Roch, the captain's cabin boy, whose need and plea taught Michael to be compassionate and to defend the innocent with the ferocity of a warrior;

Nico, who welcomed Michael as his fellow and did not blame him for the high cost of their friendship;

Dorotea, God's own gift to Michael. So diligently would he try to be worthy of her, and sustain her, so long as they both lived.

Then there were the others, those not with him in la signora's loggia: his Uncle Elios, who had instructed him well; Petros and the orphaned boys on Corfu, whom Michael did not save. Never, he swore, would he forget or dishonor them. His mother who, though it had pained her to do so, smiled and waved good-bye forever when Michael could not yet have imagined what forever was; his father, Theodore the Humble, the simple man who had begotten him, who had carved him a little lamb from wood, who had taken him first to the boats, who had taught him how to fish, and who had raged at his leaving. Not until this very moment did Michael understand that his father simply knew he would miss him. He was missing him now, and would continue to miss him without respite until his final breath.

EPILOGUE

Everyone was preparing to leave when la signora called out, "Wait. Please wait a moment."

The assembled group stopped fussing with their cloaks and listened.

"How would you like to work for me, Roch?" Signora Contarini asked. She put a finger to her lips and she waited for the cabin boy to answer.

Roch looked to Giubbe and Clara, then to Captain Loredan and Michael, then to Friar Martino. They all five smiled and waited.

"Yes," Roch said.

He clasped his hands together and blushed. His webbed feet tapped the floor. "Thank you," he added. "Thank you, signora."

"Good," la signora said, clapping her own hands as if she were young again. "You will live here, then, with me. And Donato, who is getting too old to be working alone every day, will teach you what you need to know about keeping the rooms in order and a difficult mistress content."

Clara could not contain herself. "Such a chance, Roch, such a wonderful chance!"

Then, gaining a modicum of composure, she looked to la signora and curtsied in the manner of one not used to curtsying. And la signora bowed back to the bustling woman in a gesture so gracious that Michael could not help but commit it to memory.

"And," Captain Loredan bellowed now, as if he were addressing his crew and not to be outdone, "after Friar Martino has made him a married man, Michele will once more set sail with the fleet."

Bronislav raised his hands, as if in victory, while Milaslova wrapped her knowing arms around Dorotea.

The captain continued. "After the New Year in March, Michele will be wed to Dorotea and to Venice. He has proven, as we are all here agreed, that he is worthy of both alliances."

"To Michael," Nico, said, as clearly as he could.

"To Michael," the assembled echoed.

And though his heart swelled and he felt prouder than he ever had before, Michael remembered himself and all that he had discovered since leaving home and Rhodes.

"Thank you, Captain," he said, and bowed to his superior. "I will strive to be worthy of your command.

The End

GLOSSARY

Adolescens—Young man not yet of legal age

Alboro—Mast, 14 paces tall

Alboro de meza—Midship mast, half the height of the foremast

Alora—Now, then

Andiamo—We go

Armiraio—Man in charge of crew discipline

Attenzione—Attention

Avogadori—Venice's communal attorneys

Bancho—Bench

Basta—Enough

Bene—Good

Benvenuto (s.), benvenuti (pl.)—Welcome

Beviamo—We drink

Buona notte—Good night

Bravi—Young toughs

Bravo (m.) brava (f.)—Well done

Buon giornata—Have a good day

Buon giorno—Good morning

Buona sera—Good evening

Campo—Small public square

Cittadini—Venetian middle class

Dieci—Ten

Dio—God

Dogaressa—Wife of the doge

Doge—Elected leader of the Venetian Republic

Dona nobis pacem (Latin)—Grant us peace.

Ducats—Venetian monetary designation

Due—Two

È vero?—Is it true?

Finalmente—Finally

Finis (Latin)—The end

Finito—Done

Forcola—Oar holder on a gondola

Gesu—Jesus

Gondola (s.), gondole(pl.)—Boat or skiff with upturned bow and stern, normally propelled with one oar, traditional to Venetian canals

Grazie—Thank you

Guardiamo—We observe

Homo da remo—Oarsman

Loggia—Great room

Maestro (m.), maestra (f.)—Master, mistress, mentor

Mangiamo—We eat

Nobili—Patricians

Palazzo (s.), palazzi (pl.)—Home(s) of the patricians

Pellagra—A vitamin deficiency disease caused by chronic lack of niacin; symptoms include delusions, diarrhea, inflamed mucus membranes, mental confusion, scaly skin sores

Piacere—Pleased to meet you

Piazza—A public square

Piombi–Lead-ceilinged prisons in the Doge's Palace

Popolani–Venetian commoners

Porta–Door

Proder–Senior oarsman

Pronto–Ready

Putto (s.), putti(pl.)–Mischievous angels

Ragazza (s.), ragazze (pl.)–Maiden(s)

Ricotta–A creamy cheese

Riposa–Afternoon rest

Sandolo–Traditional flat-bottomed Venetian rowing boat suited to the shallow waters of the Venetian Lagoon

Scuola–A confraternity or guild

Sedie piccole–Little chairs

Sensile–A system of rowing in which each rower pulled on his own oar

Signora (f.), signor (m.)–Mrs., Mr.

Silenzio–Silence

Sotto voce–In a whisper

Strappado–Torture by rope in which shoulders are dislocated

Strega–Witch

Stupido–Stupid

Torta–A tart

Traghetto–A gondola ferry

Trireme–A galley with three banks of oars on each side

Tutto (s.), tutti (pl.)–All

Vieni (2nd person s.)–Come

Vino–Wine

Zia–Aunt

About the Author

Mary Donnarumma Sharnick

Mary Donnarumma Sharnick has been writing ever since the day she printed her long name on her first library card. Fascinated by la Serenissima and the islands of the Venetian lagoon since her initial visit in 1969, Mary has returned to Venice numerous times. With the generous support of The Beatrice Fox Auerbach Solo Writer's Fellowship, Mary was afforded the opportunity to conduct research in Venice during the summer of 2010. Her historical novel, THIRST (Fireship Press, 2012), was the result of that sojourn. The novel is presently being adapted for the operatic stage by composer Gerard Chiusano and librettists Mary Chiusano and Robert Cutrofello.

Two Nigel Taplin Innovative Teaching Grants from Chase Collegiate School, Waterbury, CT, where Mary chairs the English Department, have assisted Mary's research for PLAGUED, the first novel in a series based on the historical Michael of Rhodes.

In 2008, Mary was awarded a scholarship to Wesleyan Writers' Conference. Both at Wesleyan and later in private workshops, Mary studied with novelist Rachel Basch. Mary has taught at Auburn (AL) University Writers' Conference (2012) and Mark Twain House Writer's Weekend (2013, 2014). She has read at the 41st annual convention of the American Italian Historical Association (New Haven) as well as at numerous libraries and schools. With her husband Wayne Sharnick, Mary leads her writing students on "slow travel" tours of Italy, the country she considers her second home.

THIRST

BY

MARY SHARNICK

There are passions which can never be slaked.

A tale of murder and betrayal in 17th century Venice: a drowning and a deadly assault on a bridge shatter the dreams of Captain Lorenzo Contarini and his fiancée, la Signorina Caterina Zanchi, members of two noble Venetian families. When Caterina's disfigurement banishes her from society, her parents remove their other daughter, Leonora, from the convent to become Lorenzo's hasty wife.
But Lorenzo's investigations implicate the Abbess of San Zaccaria of murder. The ruthless Abbess deflects attention from herself by exposing two nuns to scandal, ably assisted by the feared and implacable Office of the Inquisition.
The subsequent public trial tests familial, religious, sexual, and political alliances. Old secrets are revealed to an avid crowd seeking cruel entertainment. Is it even possible to discover the entire truth? In Venice, nothing is quite what it seems.

The famous city glitters darkly in Mary Sharnick's polished prose and evocative imagery.

Praise for Mary Sharnick's THIRST: A NOVEL

"*... an outstanding historical novel ... a meticulously researched period mystery, a thriller, a romance, and above all, a psychologically complex novel of ideas and a work of considerable literary merit.*"

— Gary Inbinder, author of *The Flower to the Painter*

Fireship Press
www.FireshipPress.com
www. Fireshippress.com
Found in all leading Booksellers and on line eBook distributers

MARY ELLEN BARNES
PEREGRINE

A THING DONE

by

Tinney Sue Heath

In 1216 the noble families of Florence hold great power, but they do not share it easily. When a prank played by Corrado, the jester-for-hire, goes wrong, a brawl erupts between two rival factions. Florence reels on the brink of civil war. One side makes the traditional offer of a marriage to restore peace, but that fragile alliance crumbles under the pressure of a woman's interference, a scorned bride, and an outraged cry for revenge.

Pressed into unwilling service as a messenger by both sides, Corrado is sworn to secrecy, and watches in horror as the headstrong knight Buondelmonte violates every code of honor to possess the woman he wants, while the ferocious Selvaggia degli Amidei, his rejected betrothed, schemes to destroy him.

Corrado knows too much for his own safety. Will Buondelmonte's reckless act set off a full-scale vendetta? If it does, can Corrado prevent a murder that could start a war between the alliances of noble houses? Or will he and his friends be crushed by the enmity between the Donati and Amidei families? For, as the jester discovers, the consequences of *a thing done* threaten everyone.

Tinney Sue Heath's debut novel A THING DONE vividly captures the intrigues of 13th century Florence, fueled by lust and ambition, and reveals the perils for the common man, trapped in the violence of feuding noble families.

HAWKWOOD'S SWORD

BY

FRANK PAYTON

Hawkwood's Sword vividly portrays the life of a mercenary on the battle fields in 14th century Italy and France. A tough and resilient hero, Captain John Hawkwood commands like-minded fighting men gathered from England and all over Europe. Alongside the German and European mercenaries lead by Albrecht Sterz, they make war for whomever pays them the most. Hawkwood is one of the best at his trade: courageous, a practiced fighter, but also chivalrous. The various lords of Lombardy and the Papal states pay him to sack cities and ambush their enemies, but who of these counts and nobles can themselves be trusted? Hawkwood must rely on his sword and finely tuned instincts to protect his life and those of his men from treachery on all sides. Despite his hard and ruthless profession, Hawkwood is not immune to romance, but finds that here too he must compete before he can win the lady of his dreams.

Frank Payton writes with a sharp eye for historical detail that, combined with well-executed battle scenes, brings to life the mercenaries of Europe's 14th century in this romantic tale of the actual campaign waged by the White Company in the 14th century Italy.

CPSIA information can be obtained at www.ICGtesting.com
Printed in the USA
BVOW11s1330110614

356018BV00002B/2/P